Amanda struggled to keep her eyes off Lord North's flawless features and captivating eyes, and to keep her mind on his shocking proposal.

Since she had been found with him in what society considered a compromising position, she would have to publicly accept his offer of marriage and go with him as his fiancée to his estate.

Once there, she could use the art of letter writing to persuade the man she truly wished to wed, the Right Honorable Sir Giles Boothe, to rescue her from this unthinkable alliance by marrying her himself.

Of course, Lord North assured her, she would be absolutely safe from his well-known seductive skills while she carried out this ingenious plan. But how could she possibly trust this libertine lord whose conquests in love were both legion and legendary? And even worse, could she trust herself. . . ?

LORD OF DISHONOR

LORD OF DISHONOR

by Edith Layton

A SIGNET BOOK

NEW AMERICAN LIBRARY

A DIVISION OF PENGUIN BOOKS USA INC.

SIGNET TRADEMARK REG. U.S. PAT. OFF. AND FOREIGN COUNTRIES
REGISTERED TRADEMARK—MARCA REGISTRADA
HECHO EN DRESDEN, TN, U.S.A.

SIGNET, SIGNET CLASSIC, MENTOR, ONYX, PLUME, MERIDIAN
and NAL BOOKS are published by New American Library, a division of
Penguin Books USA Inc., 1633 Broadway, New York, New York 10019

First Printing, November, 1984

    4   5   6   7   8   9   10   11

PRINTED IN THE UNITED STATES OF AMERICA

Indisputably, for Michael . . .

I

It was a cold, still night. No breath of wind stirred the bare tree branches that stood upturned like freezing beggar's hands beside the quiet road. The sky had a milky cast, the air a metallic tang, and the night lay heavy with the promise of snow. But the traveler sat folded deep within his greatcoat and rode at a leisurely amble. There were no onlookers to shake their heads at his folly, for cautious men stayed by their fires on such a night, and even incautious ones did not venture forth unless there were some urgent reason.

He had felt urgency, he thought, as he pulled his collar closer about his neck, when he had left the docks this dawn. He had felt such vaulting, surging impatience that he had abandoned his carriage and most of his belongings to the hands of others and given them directions to his destination, for he had felt a carriage ride too slow a pace to set for himself. He had packed a few items in his bags and set out at once, alone and on horseback, so that he could arrive ahead of them, so that he could gallop as his ambitions had. But now the urgency had faded, now that he was, at last, within a few leagues of home, he found himself tarrying.

It was amazing, he thought, permitting himself a smile that almost hurt in the frigid air, how he always forgot. For two years he had dreamed of home, and now that he was so close, the old memories came crowding back. Curious how those memories became dull and blunted when he was so far away that there was no possibility of a swift

7

return, but when he was actually so near as to make desire
a reality, reality blunted desire.

He felt his mount's great body heave a great shudder
that almost matched his own. The thought of the beast's
discomfort goaded him as his own had not. He nudged the
animal into a grateful trot. The stallion had made his mind
up for him. He would seek some other shelter tonight.
And perhaps tomorrow night. There was no great hurry,
after all. Two years or twenty, when one came right down
to the point, it made no difference at all when he returned
home.

The inn was small and snug. The warmth that greeted
him was such a contrast to the bitter night that it caused
pain as he stepped through the door. An experienced
traveler, he did not whip off his iced and leaden coat and
rush to the fireside to thaw his constricted hands. That
would only cause more discomfort. He stayed, instead, a
moment to chat with the landlord and agree that it was,
indeed, a very cold night. Then he walked slowly to a
table in the common room. Only when he had ordered
some hot repast, and only after he had warmed his gloved
hands against his mug of hot grog, did he begin to divest
himself of his gloves and scarf.

Only then, when he had absorbed some of the heat of
the room and freed himself of bodily distress, was he able
to fully take note of his surroundings. It was a simple,
pleasant place, he decided. A typical English inn, built by
the side of the road to accommodate travelers. The floors
were scrubbed wood, the tables and chairs simple hand-
hewn things, the fireplace ample, the serving girl casual
and cheeky. Nothing elaborate, nothing for the Quality, it
was merely one of a hundred such places strewn about the
countryside. He had discovered himself longing for the
sight of just such a place in the last months.

There were not many patrons this night. Those with
homes clearly were in them. Nevertheless, there was custom.
An elderly couple seated near him seemed to be a farmer
and his wife. Forced to attend the unexpected birth of
their grandchild, he thought, as he sipped his drink and
listened absently as they consoled themselves about being

so far from home this night with the expectations of a gay family reunion once they reached their destination. A fellow who looked to be an unsuccessful peddler counted and recounted his small store of coins at a far table, while three young local lads laughed and traded heavy-handed innuendos with the serving girl.

When he drew off his coat at last and draped it over the back of an empty chair, he became aware of a sudden silence falling over the room. The quiet lasted only a second and then the various talk picked up again. But the landlord appeared at his table as if by magic, even as he settled back in his chair once again.

"Why sir," the landlord said unhappily, his round face all concern, "you ought to have asked me for a private room. We have such, you know. And as Nan's not brought you your food as yet, it wouldn't take a minute to set you up there."

Clothes do make the man, he thought, leaning back and smiling at his host. For his garb had marked him as a member of the Quality, and the landlord was clearly worrying about the insult of having placed him in the common room. He had not bothered to change for travel; indeed, he had not even thought of it. But now he thought of what the landlord could see. In his high polished boots, with his dark gray pantaloons, gleaming white shirt, and well fitting black jacket, he was as exotic as a parrot among pigeons. Looking down at his green and gold embroidered waistcoat and carefully arranged neckcloth, he amended, no, he was as exotic as a peacock among geese.

"No, no," he said in his soft voice, "I am well content to be here. I've been abroad, you see, for a very long while and am glad to be among Englishmen again."

His host still seemed uneasy, although he backed away. When the serving girl brought dinner, beef and dumplings and ale, fare as simple and warm and ample as herself, the landlord bustled forth once again to line up his guest's tableware, fuss over his napery, and dart censorious glances at the wench for lingering over the table. The gentleman ate in silence, noting that a small pool of quiet seemed to have settled over his corner of the room, as though the others were aware of him but determined not to allow him to know it. He was, in that warm and simple place, as apart as if he had been in his own parlor. But as it was a circumstance he was accustomed to, he finished his meal in charity with his world.

When he had done and the sense of a well-being that the warmth and the food had brought had evaporated, as all comforts do when one becomes accustomed to them, he pondered his next move. He could stay where he was, he thought, looking about him. The landlord surely had several rooms vacant this night. The serving girl had made such a symphony of movement over the clearing of his table that he knew he could have company to while away the small hours of the bitter night with, and a warm bed even if his host had no thought of using a hot brick to take the chill off his sheets. And as he was not expected, it did not matter how long it took him to complete his journey home.

But, he thought perversely, for all its pleasures, the inn was not a home. And a home was what he had promised himself. This was only one of a succession of clean, comfortable places where he had sojourned recently. Though the serving girl was willing and familiar, she was too familiar. In fact, he wondered if he had not already sometime, somewhere passed a night with her. And even if he were expected, it still would make no difference when he arrived at home. He made his mind up quickly, as he so often did.

He beckoned the landlord to his side and asked, "I've ridden most of the day and at the last was too frozen to take note of the signposts. What town is this?"

"Why, Oakham, sir," the landlord replied, with as much amazement as if he had asked if it were night.

"So far?" the gentleman said, as if to himself, for he had not realized how far he had gotten before his will had begun to flag.

"Oakham," he murmured, "Oakham. Tell me, is that not close by Leicester?"

"Very near, sir," the landlord replied, with some worry now apparent, as it seemed, incredibly, as though his elegant guest were preparing to depart. "But it's a bitter night, sir, bitter."

"And is not Kettering Manor in Leicester?" his guest asked, taking some coin from his pocket.

"Kettering Manor?" the landlord gasped, as if he had been asked if the seventh circle of hell lay across the road. "Aye, sir, it is," he finally admitted, as he saw amusement register in the gentleman's eye.

"And would you happen to know if the countess is in residence now?" his guest asked imperturbably.

"Aye, she is," the landlord mumbled, now avoiding his patron's eye. But that was commonplace, too.

"Then for all your hospitality, thank you," the gentleman said smoothly. "And further thanks if you can give me a swift route there. For I am expected, I think."

As the landlord gave directions, his guest noted that all attempt at conversation in the room had ceased and that he was being watched with an admixture of shock and envy. It was as if he had announced that he was about to dine with the devil. He shrugged into his now warm greatcoat once again and left a larger amount of coin upon the table than was strictly necessary. It was to compensate the serving girl, who looked after him reproachfully as he left. He tipped her a sweet smile as he paused at the door, which only seemed to sink her spirits further.

Even as he closed the door behind him, he could hear the babble of voices rise in his wake. He strode to the stables and apologized silently to his mount as he prepared to travel again. "Only a little farther tonight," he thought, for himself and his horse.

"Ah Nan," cried one of the three young fellows as soon as the gentleman had left, "seems you've got to pick one of us after all. The fine gent's off to the countess, the more fool he, for he'll not find a prettier wench in all the land than you."

The compliment did not seem to content the young woman, as she savagely swept the gentleman's largesse into her pocket.

"Maybe not, Jem," another of the fellows chortled. "But

maybe he's after quantity, not quality. He'll have at least three ladies to share his bed at the countess's."

"Three?" roared the third fellow, who had taken on so much to ward off the chill he could now feel neither heat nor cold. "Why, I hear tell it's no fewer than six that share a likely lad there. Aye, and the countess herself, as well. 'He's expected,' he thinks. Why such a pretty fellow would always be welcome there."

"Oh, stop nattering," the girl said angrily. "Especially about your betters."

"Betters?" cried one of the fellows in such comical amazement that the entire room joined in the girl's abashed laughter.

The gentleman outside heard the burst of laughter even through the tightly closed doors and windows. He gazed back at the inn, seeing the light glowing from out the fogged windows and scenting the wood smoke that poured from the chimney. For a moment, he regretted his hasty decision. Then, realizing that he would have been discontent with whatever his course of action might have been this night, he sighed and spurred his horse forward toward the road again.

He was not expected, but he would be admitted. And if the countess was notorious, if even her name caused shock and her whole set caused scandalized comment in the simplest of country inns, why then, he would most assuredly be welcomed. As the cold took hold again and he hurried the last weary miles, he thought that he was making haste to a home, at least, where his presence would be greeted by its mistress with glad welcome. Which was, he thought as he spurred his horse to a bracing gallop, a good deal more than what could have been said for his original destination.

"North!" the lady cried, clapping two little hands together as a child might when her butler brought the news. "Here? It's the very thing! Just what was needed. Show him in, Gilby, at once. Only think," she said to the room at large, "North has come to visit us."

While a murmur went up among her company at her

words, the lady turned to a tall, heavy-set elderly man at her side.

"Robert, it is North who's arrived. I haven't thought of him in ages. And now, he comes in the dead of night, in the most inclement of weathers. Never let it be said that there isn't a divine providence, Robert, never," she said fervently.

"Don't know why you're making such a to-do," the elderly gentleman said crossly. "He's a good enough chap. But I thought you were enjoying our little party just as it was. Don't see why you're carrying on like he was your savior. You could have told me if you were bored. We could have taken ourselves off somewhere or the other."

"No, no, dearest," the lady said, calming herself. "Do not misunderstand me. I was enjoying myself enormously. It is only that . . ." but here she hesitated and then went on swiftly, peeking up at the gentleman winsomely, "He will make the party complete. For now we have fourteen, such a pleasant number."

"Fifteen," the gentleman corrected her, "for I wouldn't have been easy with thirteen present in all. I take note of such things. Not that I'm superstitious, Fanny, but a chap notes things like that."

"Oh fie, Bobby, you know how wretched I am with numbers," the lady said peevishly, fanning herself in her agitation. "It's only that now all will go perfectly."

" 'Course it will," the gentleman said in a placating manner. He forgot the matter immediately as he turned to speak with one of his guests, just as he forgot all matters that were even slightly troublesome. His lady took herself apart from the others, however, and stood expectantly waiting for her new guest to be ushered into the salon.

She was an exceedingly diminutive female to bear such a great load of names as Fanny Juliana Octavia Amberly, Countess of Clovelly. And if words bore physical weight, and one added to her title the measures of notoriety which had been heaped upon that name, she would have been unable to move at all. But as it was, she moved with as light a tread as a child, though she had left that estate behind decades ago.

The Countess of Clovelly was one of the few middle-aged females whose admirers did not exaggerate wildly when they swore she resembled a girl. She was wise enough to enhance the imposture where she could and clever enough to deny it where she could not. Thus, if she allowed gray to creep into her golden curls, it was only because it enhanced her fairness. If she permitted a few extra pounds to round out her once well defined curves, why then, they also helped to smooth out wrinkles upon her merry countenance. She denied herself heavy powder and paint not to make a point of her youthfulness, but because she knew that accentuating her features *too* clearly would only point out the passages of time. She wore colors fit for an ingenue when she realized dark tones made her look hagged, and she smiled constantly because she discovered that when laugh lines cannot be hidden, they might as well be called into constant play. At fifty years and counting forward quite slowly, the Countess of Clovelly was a charming, cuddly miniature temptress, still capable of causing stableboys to sigh as she passed.

Now she stood atip with delight, like a cherub on a Christmas morning, in her grand salon awaiting her new guest. When he appeared in the doorway, she did not hesitate. She flew to his side and impetuously brushed her cheek against his before he could properly take her hand. When he did lift that little white hand, she blushed prettily and then said only one word, breathlessly and dramatically.

"North!"

"Countess!" he breathed, twinning her utterance with just a faint undernote of mockery.

"Here at last?" she asked in more normal tones.

"You have asked me to visit for years, and I have been churlish enough to deny you. But tonight, I chanced to be passing through, I confess on my way to some other port of call. But when I saw your house ablaze with light, it looked to me on that lonely heath like some great bright ship sailing through the seas of night. So I chanced to stop and hail it. Am I welcome aboard, countess?"

"Always!" she said fervently, as his speech had been just

the sort of poetical nonsense she adored. "You need no special invitation."

"Look everyone," she cried, taking his cold hand and leading him into the room, "it is North at last!"

Her words were unnecessary, for the others in the room had ceased to speak the moment he stepped into their midst. As he greeted them, he was smiling widely at the interior thought that he need only to step over a doorsill this night to effectively cut off all conversation. All those present were known to him, although he had not seen them in several years. There was a middle-aged baron and his temporary lady, a light female known to consort only with the wealthiest protectors; a beaming, aged French count and his ancient dame, with a handsome young couple one might take for their children if one did not note to which bedrooms they repaired each night; a tulip of the *ton* and his flushed, bibulous wife; a minor poet with a major appetite for fame; and two slender young scions of the nobility with a famous divorcée in tow for show purposes only, as the pair well knew the penalty for their mode of friendship if it should ever be discovered and attempted discretion even in a circle such as this.

It was their host who took it upon himself to ask his new guest all the questions the others might have cared to inquire about. Robert, Duke of Laxey, fired query after query at the new arrival. And so Lord Christian Jarrow, Viscount North, a practiced guest, stood in the center of the room, cradling a snifter of brandy that had been pressed upon him, and told them of his past two years' adventuring. He spoke of the present conditions in Vienna, in Italy, in France, and even upon the tiny island of Elba.

Lord North stood at his ease and chatted amiably, parrying questions and asking some of his own as though he had just risen from his armchair to greet unexpected visitors. There was no way either from his speech or manner that one could guess he had spent the better part of three days in arduous travel, or that he had breakfasted at sea, had luncheon upon the road, and had only just arrived hoping for no more than a few words and a suitable bed. He stood in the center of the bright, warm room as though he were host himself, and no eye strayed from him.

The countess stood at the edge of the company grouped around him and said not a word. Usually she would have been in full spate by now, for she dearly loved attention and would normally have made the most of presenting such a glittering guest. But she only watched him. If there had been any in the room who would have taken the trouble to observe her similarly, they would have seen her small white teeth worrying at a corner of her delightfully rosy lips.

She could not blame any of them for neglecting her, not even her dead Bobby, who hovered at the viscount's shoulder and would not have noticed if she had sunk to the floor in a dead faint at this moment. North was a gentleman worth noticing. Even if he were not, the rarity and brevity of most of his appearances would have made him so. For he never stayed too long in one place, or within one set. He was the quintessential traveler, a bright, wandering comet that briefly lit each corner of his world and then left all his acquaintance in comparative darkness by his absence. He was witty, he was clever, he was reputed to be heartless, and he was undeniably beautiful.

It was not only the two young noblemen whose eyes covertly studied his graceful, well-made form, and neither was it only the baron's expensive playmate who watched the play of expression on his face with the soft, rapt breathing of a predator. His was the sort of physical beauty that attracted even as any great work of art ensnared the eye. One did not have to wish to own such a creation, often it was enough just to study and appreciate it.

Only a little above average height, his form was well proportioned and well muscled, with not an extra jot of flesh. He had a fencer's easy play of movement. But it was his face that first and last attached the eye. It was a lean countenance, the ivory white skin so taut across the fine bone structure as to appear to have been stretched to fit. Feature by feature, it was not a classic visage, but the sum more than compensated for the parts. His cheekbones were high and perhaps too pronounced. The nose was straight, a trifle too long and thin, the mouth not at all the full, plump standard of Greek statuary, for while well cut it was thin as well, and bore at times a half-quirked, sensuous smile. The eyes were long and almond-shaped and pulled down slightly at the corners, rather than tilting upward in classical fashion. But despite the astonishing thick, bright-silver-tipped gilt hair and slightly darker brows, it was the eyes that one's gaze returned to again and again.

From afar, or even in shadow, Lord North's eyes were unexceptional save for their keen expression. But in clear light and up close it could be seen that they were extraordinary. For to speak with the nobleman from his right side, one would look for answer in his grave gray eye. Yet to approach him from the left, one would seek response from his cool blue orb. His eyes were not so dissimilar as to shock, but seeing him once, the viewer would be troubled by some nagging discrepancy and turn to search his face until his varicolored eyes were at last discovered, and the viewer amazed and enchanted.

To see him once was to remember him forever, to hear his name was to recall him instantly. His reputation was as varied and colorful as his strange countenance. He was said to be a libertine, he was whispered to be beyond mere libertine. If the ladies were enthralled by him, it was said that he reciprocated their interest, often and variously. He was wealthy, attractive, and titled, and shared only his fortune and person freely, but never his title, as he was rumored to have foresworn the idea of wedlock. As he entered his third decade, he had given himself, but never his heart, to whomever he fancied, and it was well known that he entertained some unusual fancies.

The countess watched him closely, but with more of deep calculation than of desire in her expression. This was not surprising, for though she bore an infamous name, her constancy was never questioned. She had been with Robert, Duke of Laxey, for over a decade, and it was hardly likely that she would sunder such a settled relationship merely for the excitement of dallying with an exotic young gentleman, no matter how compelling he might be. Still, she remained silent as her guests thronged about Lord North, and only broke from her reverie when she noted the merest hint of fatigue upon him as he closed his remarkable eyes for a moment, and seemed to have just a second's difficulty in reopening them.

"But Christian," she said pouting, pushing through the others and coming to his side at once, "what brutes we all are. For if you have only just arrived today, you must have been traveling leagues. And in such inclement weathers! Why Bobby, we have treated poor North's horse better than we have himself. I'm sure the animal must have been fed, well rubbed down, and put to bed already, and here is poor North forced to hold forth on the state of the world for us."

"My dear countess," Lord North smiled, "I've already dined, but I would have foregone even that if I knew what further treats you had in store for me. Surely I deserve no less than a mere animal?" he went on as the company roared with laughter and the countess called him a "wicked boy" for misconstruing her remarks. But the laughter did not reach either Lord North's weary eyes or the countess's mock-shocked ones, as they both were well aware of the sort of sallies they were expected to trade with each other for civility's sake.

"Enough of this," the countess cried, all abustle, ringing for her butler with a great show of concern. "North, we must get you to your room, and you must promise to sleep half the day away tomorrow."

"You do not leave us at once, do you?" she asked after he had made his good nights to the assembled company and followed her and the butler out of the room to the wide staircase.

"Not at once, no," he replied, "not if you do not wish me to do so. I only return home, and there is no great hurry."

"Oh wonderful," she answered, with the happy enthusiasm of a child. She spoke to the butler absently as she gazed up into her guest's eyes.

"Gilby, give Lord North the gray room—no, no, not

the gray, it is not at all what it should be. Give him the blue, yes, the blue."

"But my lady . . ." the butler began.

She cut across his hesitation quickly. "No, Gilby, the blue it is. It is the only suitable one."

As the servitor stood in confused fashion, she abandoned her air of charming infant and spoke in a voice of command,

"The blue, Gilby. Oh bother," she said angrily, "to tell the thing takes longer than the doing of it. Come along, Christian, I've got to have my maid repair my hair, for if you are only bound for bed, we have a full night ahead of us. That is all, Gilby, only see that his lordship is not disturbed further tonight."

"Only think, Christian," she prattled softly as they went up the long, circular staircase, "I was just dreading the possibility of snow, for the company's becoming rather flat—don't breathe a word that I've said so, my love, but there it is. And then you chance to come along. It's providence, I vow it is," she said as she led Lord North and the footman with his portmanteau past the head of the stairs. Her guest listened with half an ear, for now that he was arrived at his destination, he was in truth, almost drugged with weariness in the way that one is when one at last admits to it.

"Do have a good night's rest," she whispered as they came to a halt before a doorway. "And pray be quiet as a wee mouse, Christian, for Lady Alcott is down the hall and she was up half last night with a dreadful toothache and the poor old dear is resting at last."

"I shall restrain my tendency to drunken revelry," he said softly.

He took her hand for a good night, and watched with a half-smile as she prodded the hesitant footman and hurried off with him down the dim hallway.

Lord North sighed and cracked the door open. He took up his bag and went quietly within. The room was in darkness, the only available light a dull red gleam from the embers of a dying fire in an ornate central fireplace. He paused for a moment, for in her haste his hostess had neglected to ask the butler to have a new fire lit, and the room was striking chill. But he was so exhausted now that he merely placed his portmanteau upon the floor and walked to the pitcher and basin he could discern on a washstand to his right. It was obvious that the room had recently been in use but had not been refurbished due to his sudden arrival. That was not unusual; the countess's guests often treated her accommodations as a superior sort of hotel, arriving and departing at their whim. He hoped the sheets at least were clean, but was too tired in any case to quibble. It would be enough that they were there, and upon a soft bed.

He stripped off his jacket and shirt and hastily washed, grimacing as the cool water struck his skin, realizing that his frivolous hostess had also forgotten to ask that hot water be brought for him. But he thought, as he clenched his teeth and soaped himself, he was fortunate to have found a warm welcome at least. For while shocking, the countess was no fool and did not consort with just any rag-tag that chose to land himself upon her. For all her notoriety, she had birth and title and, even yet, some social sway because of them. In London, she had access to many in the *ton*, and if at home she chose to disport herself with rather more raffish company, she never lowered herself completely from society's view.

Like the Duchess of Oxford, who also flaunted society's conventions but remained within its orbit, Fanny Juliana Octavia Amberly, Countess of Clovelly, was in many ways circumspect. And if, also like that infamous lady, the countess's six children reputedly came from so many various fathers that wits named them "the Amberly Assortment," why then, she lived after all with only one of those purported gentleman at a time. Her legal husband, the earl, might drink in morose solitude in the countryside, but she and the Duke of Laxey had lived in open, comfortable domesticity for ages now and were one of society's most devoted couples.

Lord North toweled himself dry but found the room grown so chill that he snatched up his shirt and wore it unbuttoned as he made his way toward the great four-postered bed. He was about to abandon all thoughts of his flighty hostess and her hospitality and give himself complete and utter rest. He pulled off the shirt and tossed it upon the counterpane before he swept back the high-piled comforters with a huge yawn. And then he stood still and instantly wide awake as he stared down at the bed. For it was, he discovered, already occupied.

With sudden stealth and neatness of motion the viscount drew back. He studied the sleeping form for a moment. The scratch of the tinder box was the loudest sound in the room. By the vague light of the one candle he had lit, he stared down at what lay before him.

She was young, he had almost mistaken her for a child. The close-cropped tangle of shadowy curls upon the pillow certainly bespoke the schoolboy. But by the candle's light he could now see the outline of full breasts beneath the modest white gown and one outflung leg had eluded the material enough for him to judge it very shapely indeed. The face was beguiling, with delicate features and soft parted young lips.

Lord North relaxed and chuckled softly to himself. There could only be three reasons for her presence in his bed, and all were amusing. His hostess could, in her fashion, have considered the chit a gift, and left her as an elegant host might leave a book or a mint upon a valued guest's pillow. Or she could have been a female who had become enamored of him and had slipped into his bed to surprise and delight him. Or, more ominously, she might be of good birth and be party to a time-worn trap for matrimony.

He stood and considered. For all her reputation, the countess was not such a care-for-nothing as to leave such a scandalous souvenir. No one had known he was coming, and in any case, he had never seen the girl, so it was doubtful she had been impelled by reckless desire. And certainly, there was no one so proper of good birth within this house who would seek such a crude solution to a daughter's spinsterhood. In any event, he thought regretfully, watching the slow rise and fall of her sleeping breast, he was tired.

And, he thought, with a touch of fastidiousness, he did not choose to lie with a female he had not chosen. Whatever her reason for occupying his bed, he would leave quietly and whisper the predicament into his hostess's ear.

He sighed again and reached across the still form to pluck up his shirt, and had his hand upon it when a cool, low voice said unexpectedly in the silent room,

"One more move, sir, and I shall be forced to put a ball through your heart."

He drew back slowly and looked first into a pair of wide dark eyes, and then into the bore of a small but serviceable pistol. The girl sat upright now, having raised herself in one quick motion. She gripped the pistol tightly and, he noted peripherally, her hand was steady though she propped it with her other for insurance.

He smiled at her words and looked at her with growing attention, but he did not move at all, and only stood arrested, half bent, before her.

"Leave at once or I shall be forced to fire," she said adamantly.

"I was only just reaching for my shirt," he explained reasonably, not moving at all, so close to her that the barrel of the weapon almost touched his chest.

"I cannot miss from this close," she said, her voice now becoming quite anxious.

"But I do not know you!" he said with interest, lowering himself to sit upon the bed in front of her.

"I cannot think," she said a little wildly, "that the chance for a few moments of carnal pleasure is worth your life."

"And clearly," he said, with much delight, "you cannot know me."

II

Lady Amanda had known none of the guests at Kettering Manor when she had come to visit. Now, three days after her arrival, she devoutly wished that were still the case. For if some of the guests frankly startled her by their bold interest, some of the others distressed her with their constant spite.

The aged Comte de Florac had seemed a dear, grandfatherly sort of fellow until she understood the general gist of some of his suggestions for future friendship. Amy Farrow had appeared to be a charming young female even though she traveled with the sensational Baron Hyde. But then Amy had begun to make sly comments about her new friend's hair, form, and upbringing whenever the baron had taken an interest in their conversation. The only two whose company Lady Amanda rather enjoyed were the young lords, Jeffrey and Skyler. But there again, it was distressing to be chatting with them in jesting fashion and to suddenly interrupt some of the warm, long, meaningful glances that so often passed between them.

She had set aside a week for her visit, and now it seemed as if even one day more was too much. She was not homesick, that was never the case, but again, never had she so longed for home and the security of familiar surroundings. It was one thing to go to bed each night secure in the knowledge that she had been right, that this trip ought never to have been embarked upon. It was quite another to wake and remember with a sinking heart that there was yet another dreadful day to somehow be gotten through. Being right was cold comfort when one was constantly being wronged.

She had been craven this night. She had decided to escape the revels that passed for pleasant society and pleaded a headache for an early bedtime. The thought of even one more evening spent ignoring innuendos, smiling in brittle fashion at things that were not amusing, and playing ignorant gooseberry while the two young gentlemen sighed over the top of her head at each other was unendurable. The thought of having another pleasant coze with her hostess was positively unthinkable. So she had crept to a sickbed when she felt as fit as a fiddle, and heartily detested herself for it. She soon found, as she lay awake in the dark (for if she read a book, there was always the chance that her solicitous hostess would discover the sham), that self-disgust was even worse than self-sacrifice.

She had been lying there counting sheep and stiles and stars in an effort to court sleep when her door had opened and, incredibly, a gentleman had stolen into the room. Her first reaction had been horrified shock, her second had been grim awareness. Her hand had stolen immediately beneath her pillow to feel the reassuring shape there. It had been a mad start to include a pistol in her baggage, and she recalled that even as she had secreted it there she had laughed at herself for doing so. But she had known in what sort of a house she was to be a guest, and had sworn to be prepared this time. What had seemed to her then to have been a bad example of old-maidenly fluttering, now appeared to have been sound common sense.

She could have challenged him immediately, in the first instant that his shadow had appeared in the doorway. But she had given him the benefit of doubt. It was, she reasoned, gripping the pistol tightly, entirely possible that he had imbibed too much and had mistaken the room. In fact, when he had headed straightaway for the washbasin she had been sure of it. When he had stripped off his shirt she had drawn in her breath, to be sure, but when she had heard the water pouring she had felt easier. She could not imagine so fastidious a rapist.

So she had lain absolutely still. It would be far better,

she reasoned, if he were to think she was sleeping. Then they both could be spared embarrassment and he could leave, sure that no one had witnessed his foolish mistake. It had been difficult to keep her eyes half-shuttered and her breathing even when he had approached the bed, and almost impossible when he had lit the candle. But she felt that in his cast-away state he had needed the clear light of verification before he departed. But then, once he had decidedly seen that he was not alone and yet he had begun to reach toward her, she had acted immediately.

Now she sat up before him, her pistol primed and ready and almost touching his heart, and still he did not stir. In fact, he sat beside her and smiled easily at her. She did not really want to kill a fellow being, and her finger froze over the triggering mechanism. Maddeningly, in that moment, the only thing she could think of was of the amount of noise and subsequent gore that would fill the room if he pushed her too far.

"Please leave at once," she managed to say, hoping that it would not sound too much like pleading.

"A charming request," he said softly. "Where do you propose that I go?"

Certainly, he must have drunk too much, she thought. They were so close she could hear his every exhalation, and yet she could scent only the faintest breath of brandy upon his lips. She considered herself an expert on the matters of degrees of intoxication; it was, after all, how she had learned when and where her father was capable of having coherent speech with her. If the gentleman was half sprung, he must indeed be very susceptible.

"To your room," she replied tightly.

"Why then," he said sweetly, "there is no problem. For I have already arrived there."

"This," she said very patiently, deciding that he must be, however he had achieved it, very drunk indeed, "is my room. You are mistaken."

"I do not think so," he said thoughtfully, cocking his head to one side, "for my hostess specifically assigned me to this one. In fact, she led me to the very door."

She drew in her breath in a gasp. This was far worse

than she had first thought. Seeing her consternation, he looked at her keenly.

"We have two choices," he said after a moment's thought. "Our hostess clearly was remiss, though I think it more than likely the excitement of the evening scattered her brains, for she is, no matter how she attempts to conceal it, a most singularly acute female. We can either share this comfortable bed . . ."

At her wide-eyed alarm and the sudden raising of the pistol, he smiled and went on, "Or I can simply nip downstairs and demand another room, explaining that I found this one already taken."

"No," she said at once, thinking of the reaction of the company when they discovered he had come upon her in her bed. Their minds would leap to so many conclusions that she was sure her reputation would be in tatters, no matter how they construed it.

"I could say that I find it too cold, and I do, I do," he said, looking at her with such mock sorrow that to her surprise she had to restrain the impulse to giggle.

"But then," he added blithely, "no doubt our hostess would wish to come up and see for herself. Or at the very least, send someone to light the fire. Of course," he said triumphantly, "you could just as easily trot downstairs and lodge a complaint."

Her teeth worried at her lip as he spoke, for she began to see that even if the gentleman were blameless in this, it would not be an easy situation to extricate herself from.

He began to reach toward her once again, and she left off her ruminations and raised the pistol till the barrel actually lay against his skin.

"My shirt," he said softly. "My dear, I only reached for my shirt. It is deucedly cold in here and it may have escaped your notice, but I am half naked."

Incredibly, in all her distress, that had not occurred to her. But now, looking at him, she became slowly aware of the breadth and shape of the undraped form before her. She did not lower her weapon, but only stared at him, finally taking careful note of the actual man she had surprised.

He was, she thought, so spectacularly handsome that it might yet be that she had actually drifted off to sleep and was now only dreaming his presence. For surely she had never seen such a radiantly attractive male in a waking state. She did not take the time to minutely inspect every detail of his brilliant aspect, it was enough that she noted the imperfect, yet striking face, the glow from his flaxen hair, and the strong, almost sculpted torso. It was when she noted the very human golden down upon that torso that she momentarily dropped her gaze in confusion. It was, she thought with embarrassment, hardly likely that such a specimen needed to creep into unsuspecting females' bedchambers to have his way with them.

As though echoing her thoughts, he said then, with deep amusement apparent in his low voice, causing her to open her eyes wide and look upward hastily, "You see? I make no effort to wrest your very fine pistol away as you weigh your options. Really my dear, I find rapine a very tiresome business. There's all that thrashing about, and caterwauling, not to mention the distinct possibility of getting oneself bitten, or worse, in the process. No, love-making should be a slow process; one should at the very least be able to relax when one attempts it. Should you like to see?" he asked suddenly, charmingly, shattering her momentary calm.

"No?" he said softly. "Ah, well, I thought I might at least try, for you will grant the circumstances are most unusual and I thought that perhaps the difficulty lay in the fact that I had not asked."

She glowered at him because, in truth, his earlier words had been so seductive that she had indeed dropped her guard and no doubt had been gaping at him like a smitten ninny.

"Do you think it possible," he asked calmly then, "that you could put the pistol down? Not only am I cold, but I am now beginning to entertain the unpleasant notion that the force of your emotions might force your finger. It's a very fine weapon, with no doubt a hair-trigger mechanism. I should hate to think that I've ended my days simply because you had to sneeze. I promise you, for what it's worth, that I shall not attempt you. But I hesitate to say a thing that might make you laugh, or even shudder, for a lively fear of what those reactions might do for my remaining span upon the planet. And if we are to find a solution for our present difficulties, we must be able to communicate."

She looked hard at him once again, and then sighed and lowered the pistol. If he had been a less comely gentleman, she would not have. But it was undeniable that if he had been ill looking, she would have immediately shouted the rafters down. If he had even been only well enough looking, she might have not even bothered to hold rational discourse with him.

But seeing him was to believe him. It was not possible to assume he was a lurking deviate. She could not imagine that such a gentleman would even desire her, or note her at all, if he had not found her in what he thought was his bed. Such an exotic fellow, she decided, would only consort with females who could match his splendor. Although she had often been told that she was well enough looking, and even had a little vanity about herself, she could not think that she fell into such an exquisite class.

It seemed that he matched her sigh. Then he took up the pistol from where she had placed it on the bed and examined it.

"A breech loader. A very nice weapon," he concluded, and handed it back to her. "I suggest you put it away now, so you are not tempted to do mayhem for anything I might say. Only *say*," he said emphatically, and then laughed as she slipped it back beneath her pillow.

"Now," he said decisively, "I am going to reach for my shirt. I am going to pick it up. Then I shall first put one arm into it, then another. You understand? There will be nothing alarming in that, will there?"

She nodded, faintly smiling. He reached across her, almost touching her in the action. As his lean, nude torso blocked her vision for a moment, she did not see the door open. But he did, and stopped in mid-motion again. She could, however, hear the voices.

"Oh! Oh my heavens!" cried the Countess of Clovelly as

she paused in the doorway, a branch of candles held high enough to illuminate both the room and the avidly interested collection of persons behind her.

"Oh lud!" cried the countess in failing accents. "Amanda! North! I never imagined . . ."

Everything was in motion now, Lady Amanda thought, squeezing her eyes shut for the moment as if that would make it all go away. The countess hurried into the room, five or six other persons popped their heads through the entrance, and the gentleman upon her bed merely sat down again with an oddly forced smile upon his lips.

"I only came to see if your headache was better, Amanda," the countess said in agitation. "I never suspected. But I am not too late, for North, you are only half undressed. Or am I, and are you only half dressed? Oh lud, that is never what I meant to say."

Amanda could say nothing. All the reasons and excuses died in her throat. The gentleman that had been called North similarly sat still, but with a look of wry expectation upon his face. Then the countess took a deep breath. She turned to the rest of the company who stood on the threshold with looks of unholy appreciation readily apparent.

"If you please, friends, find your way back to your rooms without me. I have some business here."

With much tittering and whispering, the guests evaporated into the dark hall, for the countess had used an imperially imperative tone. Then she turned to the couple upon the bed.

"North, I must ask you to leave. Your room, as I said, is the gray room, just down the hall. But in light of the circumstances, I think, if you don't mind, I should rather you took the bishop's chamber for the remainder of your stay with us. It is very commodious and is at the end, then around the corner of the hall. A footman will show you there. And then, I think, you and I and Robert should have a little talk in the morning. And Amanda, as for your behavior . . ." The countess seemed to find herself speechless, and only let out a loud exasperated exhalation.

"But Mama . . ." Lady Amanda began, and then stopped

as the gentleman, who had been slowly buttoning his shirt, paused and wheeled about to stare at her.

"Ah, 'Mama,' " he breathed. "That tells all."

"Amanda," the countess cut in brusquely, "I shall speak with you in the morning as well. I am just too distraught at the moment. But I am staggered, I am confused, Amanda. For with all your high morals and principles, I am . . . There is no way I can speak tonight," she finished, and turned toward the door, gesturing with the candles dramatically as though she were the angel sent to drive Adam and Eve from the garden.

"Are you coming, North?" she demanded.

"At once," the viscount said through tight lips.

But he paused a moment to look down at the girl in the bed. And then said in a whisper so low, she could not be sure she heard it, "Perfect sense, my dear. The pistol, I take it, was not insurance for you against my advances. Rather it was to ensure that I did not get away."

Then he straightened, strode to his portmanteau and, taking it, followed the countess and her candles out of the room. The door shut, leaving Amanda in relative darkness, in all respects.

The clock in the hall tolled three strokes when Lady Amanda Amberly at last decided to desert her bed entirely. Lying down, she discovered, only made her feel more vulnerable; thinking was a thing that ought to be done on one's feet. Still, after pacing the carpet for a space, she took up a position upon the window seat in her room and discovered it to be the best choice of all. For there, she could stare out into the night and watch it become lighter as the snow slowly turned the dark shadows to milk.

Sleep was, in any event, out of the question, as was any attempt at rational converse with her mother. Even if she did dare seek out that lady in her rooms, and risked the embarrassment of finding her there with her Robert, she could not think she could as yet make coherent comment on the happenings this night.

She would have to have been born under a cabbage leaf not to know what the penalty for an unwed female's being discovered with a half-dressed gentleman in her bedroom was. As she had been born, in fact, as one of the detestedly named Amberly Assortment, she knew full well what the consequences were. If the gentleman were unmarried, then one would have to marry him straightaway or be shunned by polite society from thenceforth. If he were married, one might as well pack for the continent immediately.

Even in her mother's wild set, which could be called "polite society" in only the loosest construction of the term, there were certain limits beyond which one did not go. If certain of her own brothers and sisters were known to be only her half-brothers and half-sisters, still her mother was, after all, married. Marriage was a license, in many cases, for free license. Once a lady had presented a legitimate heir or two for her husband, she could live her own life according to her own whims and society would politely look the other way. Perhaps, Amanda thought with a grimace, that was why it was called "polite" society.

But that was precisely the sort of life that Amanda had been trying so desperately to evade since she had come to the age of reason. She was not the sort of person to go about feeling sorry for herself, but it was undeniably true that it had been difficult growing up as one of the Assortment. Jerome and Amanda had been born to the earl and his countess while they still lived together. Mama had left her husband's home before Amanda could even properly enunciate her name. And although she was herself legitimate, as her subsequent siblings came into the world the fact of her own legitimacy mattered less and less. Mama had come home each time to bear forth Mary, Alicia, and James. But by the time Cecil was brought into the world, Mama had removed herself forever from Caldwell Hall.

All of the children were sent to school as soon as they were able to be packed off; perhaps even Mama had thought it hard to have them about to constantly remind the earl of his wife's inconstancy. Not that that seemed to matter greatly to her husband; he seemed happy or unhappy enough with his port, his hounds, and his hunting. In fact, the only spark of interest he ever showed in fatherhood was in his eldest, his legitimate heir, Jerome. There were times when Amanda thought that her father himself scarcely remembered that she was, indeed, his own child.

But the whispers had begun in boarding school. The sly asides, the little jibes had increased until she scarcely heard them any longer. It was only unfortunate, she often thought, that if another girl wished to win an argument and had clearly lost the battle, she could be counted on to bring up Amanda's history to her as a final coup de grace. She had learned to live with that, which made the shock of her first Season difficult to explain.

Amanda shivered as she sat and watched the snow, but it was not from the cold. She had been eighteen, Mama had prevailed, and she had allowed herself to be talked into making a debut in London when she left school. Her title was, after all, valid. Her fortune was an absolute reality, though her beauty and grace were things that Mama nattered on about but Amanda had tended to doubt. Yet it seemed from the moment that she made her bows that she was enormously popular. It had been delightful, those first few weeks, those assemblies, balls, and routs. She had received flowers and compliments and invitations and compliments and gowns, and she had the hope for proposals. It had been nothing short of wonderful to have been so very much wanted at last.

It was young Charles Dearborne, a baron's son, who had at last opened her eyes to the truth. For he was her first taste of calf-love. He had been tall, very dark, slender, and clever. Socially adroit, with impeccable breeding, he had completely overwhelmed her with his constant attentions. She had begun to dream of a future with him. Then one night, he had smilingly lured her out onto the terrace at a great ball. It had been a perfect lover's night, with a great chalk moon staring above them, and she had dared to hope that it was the night he had chosen to make his offer.

For all his wit and habit of light jest, he had spoken not one word, but only gathered her up in his arms and kissed her. She remembered it still; she had only been able to sigh with gratification at how lovely it was. Then he had pressed another kiss upon her willing lips, and again she was speechless with sheer happiness at the perfection of it. He had drawn back a moment and she waited for his utterance, but he had only captured her once more and kissed her again. And then yet again, with more fervor. As his hands strayed to her bodice, she began to wonder when he would declare himself; as his hands began to reach within her white debutante's frock, she began to grow confused.

She had pulled back and whispered hurriedly, fearing for her own boldness, "Charles, haven't you anything to say?"

"What else is there to say?" he had grinned, pulling her toward him again.

"But what are your intentions?" she had said witlessly.

"Aren't they apparent?" he laughed.

"No," she had cried, wresting herself from him. "No, they are not."

"Then I will make them so," he had chortled, and kissed her once again, this time quite savagely.

She pushed him away and stood staring at him aghast.

"Charles," she had finally gotten the courage to gasp, "aren't you going to declare yourself?"

He had gotten some of his composure back and stood facing her, his face grown suddenly very cold in the moonlight.

"Declare myself?" he had mumbled, and then he laughed again. "I declare myself very much entranced with you. Very much in lust for you, puss, but that is all. Did you think me ready to declare anything else?"

"Yes," she had said quietly, "yes, I did."

"Are you serious?" he asked incredulously. She could only nod. "My Lady Amberly," he said finally, after a moment's thought, "I declare that I should very much like to make love to you, but only that. Your kisses led me to believe you would very much like to do that as well. But if you think I am willing to offer for you, you are wrong. And do not cry that I have led you on. For you have led me on just as much."

Then he seemed ill at ease and said defensively, "And if you think to trap me by having me compromise you here,

I tell you it won't wash. I expected no more from you than your mama is so famous for giving. And there's no one who'll believe otherwise. Do you think me such a flat that I want to have you mother "The Dearborne Collection" or some such lot for me? Now come, puss, let's drop this nonsense. It was a good try. Now come to me and we'll continue."

She had left him where he was standing. She had gone back to the ball and danced until her toes were numb, for she would not give him the satisfaction of knowing what he had done to her. But she had never spoken to him again.

After her encounter with Charles, she had looked carefully at all her suitors and listened closely to all that they were saying. What she had taken for gentle raillery, she discovered, was always a good deal warmer in content than that which she heard addressed to other girls. The looks she received were always more speculative and leering than were directed at other girls. Most damning of all, she suddenly realized that no other young females making their debuts had offered her friendship. To prove her worst suspicions, the Season ended, and for all her popularity she had received no offers.

She went to her father's home after that, and never returned for another Season in London.

Life went relatively placidly for her, then. Though she was in her father's constant sight, she was never on his mind. He had his bottles, his hunting cronies, and his housekeeper-mistress, in that order, to keep him amused. From time to time, some errant whim would remind Mama of her yet unwed eldest daughter and she would be summoned and quizzed about her matrimonial prospects. She would stay at Kettering Manor and spend her time with various of her other visiting half-brothers and -sisters. They liked each other well enough, for all that there could be no bond between them. Sometimes they would laugh at their appearance when they were all assembled, and it was fitting, for they were the only ones who had a right to do so. But it *was* amusing for them to see dark-eyed, dark-

complected James, freckled and fair Mary, tall and hearty
Alicia, delicate Cecil and Jerome and herself together.

Mama had offered her a home, but she had swiftly
refused. On her infrequent visits, Mama always offered
her prospective husbands too, but she was quick to discourage them as well. For although she was old enough to
know better, she again had hopes. They were all embodied
in one man, her near neighbor Sir Giles Boothe. He reminded her a little of the perfidious Charles, but only in
appearance. He too was tall and, though his hair was as
brown as her own, he was slender and as irreproachable in
appearance as he was in birth. But if he was not so
dramatic and dashing as Charles, he was also not such a
rattle, nor near so flippant and ardent.

Giles was a prudent man. He had come to know her
when she had returned from London. It had taken a year
for him to stop and chat with her when they encountered
each other in the village or when they were out riding. It
was another year before he came to pay her formal calls.
Only of late had he begun to make those calls with
frequency, only recently had he started to invite her to all
the assemblies and fetes in the district as his guest. She
could not blame him for being such a hesitant suitor.
Perhaps he, too, thought her capable of eventually presenting her husband with "The Boothe Bevy" or some such
burden, she thought.

Obviously, Giles was wary of her even as he was attracted to her. As she was above the age of consent, he had
kissed her, though never as thoroughly as Charles had
done. But when she reciprocated, or even seemed to lean
toward him in encouragement, he would back away from
her. She did not suffer from conceit, but she did not
believe the problem lay in her looking glass.

She was not a large person, as so many of the stately
fashionable beauties were, but neither was she quite so
tiny as her mama. Her form, she knew, was pleasing,
Charles had often told her so. Her hair was not just a
common brown, rather Charles had often said it resembled,
as well as bore the scent of, cinnamon. When she had had
a raging fever at seventeen, her nurse had shorn off all her

hair so that it would not sap her remaining strength.
Looking into the glass when she had recovered, she had
been delighted to see the mass of tumbled curls the crop
had given her, and kept her hair that way when Mama had
said admiringly that it was just the mode that Caro Lamb
had adopted and looked delightfully. At any rate, Amanda
thought, it needed little care and spared her the tortures
of curl papers, so it would do. Her eyes were large and
gray, though she thought them too long, and while well
formed, she considered her mouth too generous. She had
no complaints about her nose, which was straight and
unexceptional. If she were not the stuff of ballads, she
reasoned, at least she would not give a viewer a disgust of
her.

But likely, she thought on a sigh, as she sat and kept
watch in the night, it was the blood beneath her pale
complexion which distressed Giles the most. When she
met his advances with enthusiasm, he must wonder if she
were not signaling that she shared the same tastes as her
mother. As always, Amanda felt her stomach knot up
when she herself wondered at the truth in that.

Now, she thought in despair, what would Giles think
when he heard of what had transpired here? There was no
hope in heaven that such a collection of reckless people
could keep the secret. It was the sort of gossip that they
would gladly dine out upon. She would not blame Giles if
he did not believe a word of her innocence. She was an
Amberly, and blood would tell.

She had come to Kettering Manor this time much against
her wishes. Mama had made it clear that as her daughter
was about to turn three and twenty she wished to felicitate
her. None of Amanda's siblings were in residence, and
when Amanda arrived she received not only congratulations but a lengthy lecture on the evils of remaining
unwed at her great age. When she had, at last, mentioned
the possibility of an offer from Giles, her mother had only
sniffed. "Is he going to tarry until you are thirty to be
sure?" she had demanded. Amanda had remained silent,
for it was true, and she had often mused upon it, that
Giles's father had wed only when he reached forty. If his

son emulated him in that, she would be in fact thirty and past it, if and when he offered. Her mama had finally left off and given her a golden locket for the occasion. And for the crime of coming to collect that golden trifle, she had lost all hope for her future, and all the respectability that Giles embodied.

Where had she erred? Amanda almost cried in vexation. She had done all she could to prevent such a crisis. Once before when she had visited, the stout Sir Crosly had tracked her to her room filled with whiskey-brave amours. She had repulsed him with a candelabra and sent him groaning to his room. This time she had taken a pistol with her, but it had only earned her disgrace.

Her past might be muddled, but at least her way forward was clear. If all her ambitions were thwarted, she yet could have serenity. Even if the gentleman who had entered her room were married, she could still return home and live there as quietly as possible to the end of her days. Father wouldn't mind, even if he noticed. If the gentleman were unwed, it made little difference. She would not have him. If he were beautiful as an archangel and clever as satan, it would not matter. To wed a gentleman from her mother's wild set would be to be absolutely sure to follow her footsteps. She could not lead such a life. She would not have him, she resolved, though her name be blackened to pitch for refusing him. It hardly mattered, she laughed bitterly at last, for had not her art mistress at school once taught her that black cannot be made blacker?

The gentleman that Amanda so resolutely denied lay fully clothed in his room upon a great canopied bed and slept the sleep of the thoroughly exhausted. While Amanda paced and prowled and flailed herself and then sat sadly to weigh her options, he slept dreamlessly. This might have made her very angry had she known it, but she would undoubtedly have been cheered if she could have been privy to his last waking thought before sleep overtook him. For he had muttered aloud to the empty room before he lay his weary golden head upon his pillow,

"I shall not have her."

III

Lord North arose early and much refreshed after his deep and deserved sleep. He went to the window to assess the amount of the snow that had fallen. No great amount had accumulated, and the sun glinted brilliantly on the few inches that had. He nodded to himself and then went about his morning ablutions with the swift, sure motions of a gentleman who had often awakened in strange surroundings and who had done for himself many times before. As he washed, shaved himself, and dressed, there was an expression of smooth unconcern upon his face. When he went to check his appearance once in the glass before he went belowstairs, there was a cold and placid set to his expression. No one would guess that this was a gentleman about to be at the very least lectured, at the very most condemned, by his hosts.

The viscount seemed to be self-assured and calm as he took the great stairs lightly and made his way to the center of the vast house. It was no imposture, for he was totally resolved. He had decided upon his course of action before he had closed his eyes the night before. Though he remembered no dreams or decisions coming to him in the night, it was as though some ever-wakeful portion of his mind had worked upon the dilemma as he lay sleeping. For now that morning had come, he was sure of his course of action. There were no conflicting emotions to forestall him. The thing was simplicity itself.

It was a shoddy trick for his hostess to have played, but he could not blame her overmuch. It could be no easy feat to bring one of her Assortment to the altar. It was merely that she had miscalculated, for he was not green enough to sacrifice himself on that altar for respectability's sake. A gentleman should, of course, offer his hand to a young lady of quality whose reputation he had deliberately or mistakenly jeopardized. That, Lord North mused, permitting himself a little smile as he halted in the great hall, seeking the direction of his breakfast, was decidedly what a gentleman should do for a lady. But, he thought, scenting the unmistakable odor of ham and coffee coming from a long way off, he was not precisely a gentleman and the Amberly female was certainly not a lady.

His hosts were in for a crushing disappointment. He would not do the acceptable thing; he was not, after all, an acceptable gentleman. No one would be surprised to hear of his refusal even if the lady had been a lady. As she was one of this household, no one would even turn a hair at hearing the tale. It had been a foolish, desperate attempt, the viscount decided, and it would only make the mating of the young woman a harder thing to achieve in future. The circumstances of the young lady might even become in time, he thought with real amusement, a tale to be savored at London clubs; the stuff of epic tales, a legendary pitfall for unwary male travelers, like the sirens, or in this case and more aptly, like the Procrustean bed.

The viscount made his way to the breakfast room. Pausing for a moment in the doorway, he spied his hostess seated bolt erect at a laden table with an untouched plate before her, her consort at her side, sleepily perusing a paper as he sipped at his coffee.

The countess saw the viscount first, and rose to her feet.

"North," she said sternly, trying to place the same expression of censoriousness upon her face as she had in that syllable. The duke looked up, then down, then at his paper, as though profoundly embarrassed and discomfitted by the entire scene.

"Good morning, my lady," her guest said sweetly, making his bow and then coming up to his hostess to take her hand. "What a comfortable room. I passed the most restful night, thank you so much. I had not hoped to see you quite so early, for I often rise with the birds and am surprised to see you do the same. What a happy coincidence! Now I shall not have to breakfast alone."

"I could not close my eyes all the night," the countess said in dire accents. She looked rested enough, her guest thought, although it was obvious that she had put on a great deal of powder in order to accentuate or simulate pallor.

"Ah, too bad," the viscount sympathized, looking over to his host.

That gentleman squirmed beneath the viscount's benign, inquiring gaze and then mumbled, "Slept like a dead man myself."

Then encountering his lady's baleful stare, he added unconvincingly, "But that's m'way. Not like the dear lady. I'm not sensitive in the least. She prowled all night, like a damned tabby." Then unsure of whether he ought to be commenting on the lady's nocturnal habits with a gentleman who was supposed to be doing the right thing by her daughter, he subsided into a sort of anguished silence by biting off far more than he could chew of a fruit scone and rendered himself incapable of further speech.

"We must talk," the countess said in accents of high emotion, holding her clasped hands before her in a noble posture. Unfortunately for her intent, the viscount thought her size, form, and face made her resemble more of a field mouse at bay than a valiant tiger defending her cub.

"Certainly," her guest replied smoothly, raising a brow and directing one brief glance at the butler's impassive face, "but before breakfast?"

"Why no, of course not," the countess faltered, seating herself again.

The duke shot her as much of a look of caution as he could, as his cheeks bulged with half-chewed scone. She waved her guest to the buffet table and bade him select his breakfast. As he did so with alacrity, the duke managed to swallow enough of his mouthful to whisper somewhat thickly to her, "Told you so. The fellow knows the right thing to do. Man of the world. A bother about nothing, m'dear."

The viscount chose his repast with concentration and then sat down with his hosts. While he ate, he put them further at their ease by holding light converse about the weather, the state of the nation, and the excellence of fresh eggs. Not one of the attentive footmen, nor the butler, nor after a space, his hosts themselves could quite believe that this collected gentleman had anything on his mind except the business of breakfast. For one horrible moment, the countess herself had the insane notion that the previous night had happened only in her imagination.

But then the young lords Jeffrey and Skyler wandered in, in search of sustenance, and were visibly startled to see the viscount engaged in such equitable discourse with his host and hostess. They then made such a failure at trying to conceal the looks of shock, awe, and disappointment that they constantly darted toward the golden-haired guest that the countess felt herself upon firm ground again. So it was that she was able to say, in the most casual of tones, "Oh, North, now you've finished your breakfast, do you think you might have time to have a private coze with Robert and me?"

Lord North only rose and bowed slightly, and with the most charming smile, said affably, "Of course, I am at your service, my lady."

It was when they were out in the hall again, safely out of earshot of any retainers or guests, that the viscount spoke again. The unhappy duke, lagging behind his guest and the countess, his gaze riveted upon the floor as though he had lost a valuable coin and was searching for it, picked up his head at the utterance.

"I should like to speak with you and the duke my lady, at any time, but do you not think it best if I speak with the young lady—your daughter, I take it—first? After all, she, you will admit, has the most to either gain or lose by this morning's business."

"But you have it wrong way around, Christian, I'm sure, for first you are supposed to address her——" the countess began catching herself just before she uttered the word *father*, as she realized that the word was singularly inappropriate in this instance. Instead, she made a feeble recovery by saying, "mother."

At the polite but disbelieving look upon her guest's cool countenance, she fell silent. The duke at once leaped in to say bluffly,

"Of course, dear fellow. Just the thing. You two ought to have a get-acquainted chat. That is," he said, beginning to see the deep waters he had plunged into, "if you have not already, last night, I mean. Devil take it," he foundered.

"I do believe," the countess said winsomely, discreetly putting her tiny foot down upon the duke's boot tip, "that is a most excellent suggestion, Christian. Amanda has been fretting all morning. She hasn't even had breakfast. She's in the small salon awaiting our discretion. A conference alone, between the two of you, would certainly be in order now. I shall not even insist on staying with you to play chaperon, in light of the circumstances," the countess added with stress underlying every syllable.

"Robert and I will be in the study, when you have done," she said pointedly, as she led the viscount to the small salon. "And will be waiting your announcement."

She could do no more, the countess thought in exasperation, without writing the thing out in bold letters and picking them out with a pointer for him. North had been so adroit at setting a mood of civilized commonplace that there was no way she could state the thing more firmly without seeming to be an underbred boor.

"Don't fret," the duke said happily as they watched the viscount enter the salon after tapping lightly upon the door and being bade to enter. "The thing will go off swimmingly. North's got a head on his shoulders. Not a nodcock, after all. Trust him to know the right thing."

But the countess paused to stare at the closed door for a moment and sighed. She did not bother to dispute dear Robert, but the thing was that even if the viscount knew the right thing, one did not trust him to do it at all, if one were at all wise.

"Good morning," Lord North said pleasantly as he entered the room. He saw the young woman start to her feet as he approached.

He wore an easy, amiable smile, and as he took the young woman's icy hand, he gazed into her fearful eyes and said, without changing his expression at all, "You look very well, even with your clothes on, my dear."

She stepped back as though he had struck out at her. But it was true, he thought with detachment, she had no need of candlelight to flatter her. For even here, where the tall glass windows of the french doors admitted the harsh light of the sun's reflection upon snow, she looked very well. Delicately made, perhaps, he thought, but not so diminutive as her mama, and nothing like her mama in aspect or attitude. She was, rather than openly seductive, almost a gamine. He thought her curls charming, her form delicious, her face enchanting. He would have been delighted to become her protector, but he was determined she should not become his bride.

He had decided to put the matter to her openly, before he ever broached it to her parent and her noble consort. Then, of course, he would have to pack and leave. But he thought it only fair that he should inform the young woman of his decision first, as he would doubtless not have had the opportunity to do if he stated his case straightaway to his host and hostess. She deserved to know of the failure of the plot from his own lips at least; some honor must be dredged from this sorry incident. The viscount, as his hostess had suspected, knew the right thing to do.

"Your mama," he went on to say, noting that she was gazing at him with something like horror manifest in her expression, "agreed that I should have a word with you before I spoke with her. I could talk the thing up and down for hours, but that would be hardly kind to her, as I'm sure she's on pins and needles to hear my decision. I'm convinced it would be equally distasteful for you."

As she made no reply, but only stood gazing up at him with her features so immobile now that he could not read them, he said a bit more abruptly, "I'm sorry, my lady, but it won't do. I'm sorry to have kept you up so late last night on such a fruitless mission, and to have kept you from your breakfast this morning as well. By the by," he smiled, trying to elicit some response from her as it began to seem that he was addressing empty air, "the eggs were excellent. Very well," he sighed as the pleasantry died upon his lips unnoticed, "no more attempts at dressing the thing up. I won't have you, my dear, I won't offer for you, and wouldn't have even if you had accommodated me immediately last night, rather than waiting for your mama's fortuitous entry."

He braced himself for a slap, prepared himself for an outburst of fury, and waited for her to storm or weep or fling herself upon his chest to beat at him with her fists. He was taken aback, then, by the one thing she did do.

She sank to sit upon a divan and let out all her pent-up breath in a gusty sigh. "Thank heavens," she breathed. Then she turned a radiant face up to him and said happily, as though they had come to some most agreeable terms, "I am so glad. I sat here wondering just what sort of scene there would be when Mama and the duke called me in to hear your offer. I didn't know how you would take it, but I was dreading their response. I'm so very glad that you flew in the face of custom."

"You are glad?" he repeated slowly, playing for time, trying to fathom what new gambit she had come up with to snare him.

"Of course," she answered promptly, "for I had no notion of accepting your offer, my lord. The whole thing is bizarre. Someone played a trick on us. I don't care to think of whom it might have been," she said frowning for a moment, "but it makes no matter. I would not live out the rest of my life with a stranger who had wandered into my rooms one night unless I was wandering in my wits. The entire idea is ludicrous. I don't blame you in the least for thinking me partner to such a scheme, but I assure you I was as appalled as you were when Mama came marching in. The pistol, you see, was not to hold you there, it was to discourage any gentleman who might have had similar ideas. But it doesn't matter what you believe actually," she said, as if to herself. "Good day, my lord."

The viscount, a gentleman famous for his quick wit and decision, stood quite still. If he could believe the lady, the situation tickled him enormously. If he could not, whatever further scheme she was hatching challenged him.

"But what will your mama say?" he asked softly, playing devil's advocate to get to the crux of the matter.

"Just what you would think," the young woman answered, shaking her head. "But I shall not let that change my mind. I'll be leaving for home almost immediately, so it won't sink me entirely."

"You do not reside here?" he asked in surprise.

"Oh no," she replied, half attending to him. "I make my home in Doncaster with my papa."

"And it will not matter what society says of you?" the viscount said very softly.

Her shoulders went up at that, a little defensive shrug as though to ward off a blow, which touched him as no words could have done. But her words were mundane enough.

"Oh that. But I do not travel in society, you see."

"Miss Amberly, or Lady . . . I do not even know your proper name," he said on a laugh as he came closer to her. "I really do think we stand in need of an introduction. I am Christian Jarrow, Viscount North. And you are . . ."

"Amanda, Lady Amanda Amberly," she said, gazing up at him as though for the first time.

"May I sit?" he asked carefully.

At her nod, he sat in a chair near to her.

"My lady," he began, "in truth, when I first came in here I had you painted as some sort of villainess. If I can believe you, then I become some sort of villain. Since so much rests upon the outcome of this, our only chance at private speech, can you not be plain with me? If this is all some sort of machination to force me to declare myself through guilt or pity, I repeat, it won't do. I shall not marry you. It has not so much to do with the method of our meeting, although that certainly makes it impossible for me to offer, since I am remarkably resistant to blackmail, but a great deal to do with the fact that I do not care to be wed. Not now. To anyone. And most probably, not in future. I am a determined bachelor. So please, with that idea firmly fixed in mind, speak plainly to me."

Amanda looked up at the cold, exquisite countenance before her and laughed, although the sound had more anger than merriment in it.

"And I tell you, my lord," she said through clenched teeth, "and have told you, that I do not want you. Not now. Not any time. So, if you will be so good as to stop telling me in every sort of way not to angle for your person, I will tell you to leave, please. Immediately."

The viscount relaxed. He sat back and beamed at her.

"Is that all you ever say?" he asked pleasantly. "I seem to recall that phrase from when we first met. Accept my apologies," he laughed. "But you will admit I had little cause to believe you then. For what it is worth, I do now. Come, tell me what you know of the matter and we will see what we can make of it. You see, I was very weary when I arrived last night, and extremely surprised to find I had a bedmate assigned to me. The rest you know. Now tell me what part of it do I not know? I deserve at least that," he added as she turned her head away. "It will be not only your reputation that will be extinguished when I give your mama the sad tidings; whatever little is left of mine will be swept away as well."

Amanda considered the viscount openly now. She had had no speech with her mother in the morning, she had only been told curtly to go and sit in the salon till she was called. When he had come walking in, she had been prepared to make her speech of denial and had been startled by his own rejection coming first. Worse than that, the moment she had seen him in the cold light of day, she had taken a long look at that remarkably beautiful face. When at last she had discovered the secret of those astonishing eyes as they fixed a chill stare upon her, she had known his identity at once. There could not be two such noblemen in the kingdom.

He was fully as infamous as her own mama. Even if one took exaggeration into account, his reputation was as stunning as his physical presence. If she had feared association with the rakish set that revolved about Kettering Manor, she had found herself confronted by perhaps the most prime example of a rake in that or any other set. The thought of being manipulated into wedlock with exactly the sort of gentleman she most reviled had struck her speechless, and the enormity of the idea took even the sting and sense of his first words from her.

But now, perceiving that he was at least as eager as she to elude the consequences of their accidental meeting, she subsided into relief. She still could not believe such a dazzling creature could have any designs upon her. Such an exotic's interest could only be for curiosity's sake. Thus, there could be nothing lost by putting their heads together to seek a way out of this coil.

Briefly, then, she told him of her situation. Very briefly, in fact, for there was a great deal she did not mention. So it was that she gaped at him like a kitchen maid at a fortune teller at the county fair when he said slowly, when she had done,

"So it is not only that you don't wish to marry a stray who happened into your bedroom at your mama's instigation, but you also have hopes for another match."

Since she had said nothing of Giles, or any other possible suitor, and did not want to think of Mama's possible culpability, Amanda was at a loss for a reply. Before she could think of one, he smiled and said gently,

"Come, my lady, circumstances lead to an obvious conclusion. You are past the age of a come-out and are still unwed. It's enough to terrify any mama."

"Past my last prayers, you mean to say then," she shot back, stung at his cavalier assessment of her years and unmarried state.

"I mean precisely what I say," he said, a bored look coming into his eyes. "I did not seek you out this morning to pay you pretty compliments and engage in light flirtation. You know full well you are an enticing baggage, and as you have title, wit, and dowry, it becomes obvious that your single state is more a matter of choice than chance."

Amanda did not know whether to be complimented or infuriated by his calm appraisal, but before she could decide what reaction to present him with, he went on obliviously,

"So it only follows that you have been biding your time,

and no female ever bides her time without some object in view. I take it, then, that this object does not meet with your family's full approval? Is he so unacceptable then? A smithy, or is he only that cliché, an impecunious dancing master?"

She was very gratified to see his surprise when her only reply was a peal of laughter. Before he could ask why she was so amused, her laughter stopped and she said with a coolness to match his own, "Oh yes, biding my time. Of course. There are so many gentlemen falling over themselves to declare for me. And why not? After all, I am an Amberly, and one of the famous Assortment, as well. What fellow would not wish for the thrill of wedlock with me? Which of them could bear to pass up the chance to spend a lifetime with me, and wait with baited breath each time I present him with an heir? What fun he would have scrutinizing every infant I produce, looking at eyes and hair color and bone structure, wondering which of his acquaintance sired which of his offspring. Their mamas and noble relatives as well, earnestly long for such a union. And as for smithys and dancing masters, why, they are no less eager to vie for my hand. What sort of fellows could deny themselves such a treat?"

"I see," Lord North said reflectively, ignoring her outburst. "But then, who is the fellow? For you took such great care not to mention him, I am quite sure he exists. You seem too realistic a young woman to have plucked him from between the pages of a book. Come, my lady," he said with the merest trace of sympathy, "it may matter. It may help to tell me all."

It was that vague hint of fellow feeling that undid Amanda. She capitulated.

"He is a near neighbor at home. But we are not lovers, nor is there any understanding between us as yet. But I have known him for several years and, I confess, I had . . ." She bit off her next words and then said, head held high, "And there is no question of his being unacceptable. He is only, I imagine, somewhat slow to offer, at least in Mama's view."

"But not in yours," he replied with a smile. "Since any

young woman dreams of a suitor who makes up his mind with the speed of a glacier. In any event," he said with a lightening of his countenance, "you can scrape by well enough, I see. You have only to return home, tell him of your narrow escape from disgrace, and he will speedily restore you to respectability."

The viscount rose and straightened himself, pleased with the outcome of the conversation. He would doubtless, he thought, remain in the countess's bad graces, and his reputation, such as it was, would bear yet another blot. But at least the young woman who, he could see now, was only victim to her mama's impatience, would be well out of the situation. Her next words, spoken as quietly and thoughtfully as if he had already left the room, caused him to sit again.

"Oh yes, I'll scrape by," Amanda said sadly. "I shall go home and live with Father. But as for Giles, I doubt I shall see him ever again."

"What a delightful suitor," the viscount said enthusiastically. "Slow to make up his mind, quick to change it at the faintest breath of scandal. No wonder you yearn for him."

"I could not blame him," Amanda cried, stung from her mood of sad reflection. "How would you feel if you heard that the lady you were considering marriage with was found in her bed with the most disreputable libertine in the land, he half-clad and she an Amberly?"

After her outburst had cleared her head as well as her vision of the murky fog of self-pity, Amanda noted that the viscount sat silently looking at her with a quizzical expression.

"Oh," she gasped, "I am so sorry."

"Not at all," Lord North said calmly. "I was half clad."

Amanda began to make hurried excuse, but the viscount waved his hand dismissively.

"There's no one who will dispute your reading of my character," he said. "I think, however, that you undervalue your own attractions. You are, if we are to speak perfectly frankly, one of the legitimate ones, I take it?"

"Yes," she said quietly, still very sorry for having touched his feelings, although he gave no sign of having any.

"But," she added, "I am my mama's daughter, and people set great store by such things."

"Well I know it," the viscount murmured, showing some genuine emotion for the first time, though it was too fleeting to be readable to Amanda.

Lord North rose again, but this time he only paced to the long windows and stood, his back to her, gazing out at the brilliant day. Then he turned and spoke again. The sunlight behind him was so bright that it seemed to Amanda that he spoke as a disembodied voice, for all she could see was a dark shape of his form and a nimbus of fair hair.

"I feel somewhat responsible, though lord knows why. Frankly, it makes no matter if I were discovered, half, fully, or totally unclad in a bed with a dozen fair ladies, and their pug dogs as well, for that matter. I am, as you so rightly put it, a libertine, after all. But you, my child, seem to me to be in for a hard time if I just waltz forth from here with another naughty anecdote attached to my biography. And, I haven't even earned that particular tale of conquest," he mused. "Perhaps that's what nags at me. No matter," he went on briskly.

"There is a way out of this, Lady Amanda. It is very devious, very underhanded, and totally delightful. It serves both my purposes and yours as well. It will make your mama ecstatic and nudge your laggard suitor to his destiny, if we play it in tune."

Amanda cocked her head to one side as she listened to him. Her look of total confusion was so pronounced, as were all the expressions that flickered over her winsome face, that he laughed. He came to her then, and sat beside her. He took her hand in his and said,

"My lady, you will have to lend me your hand for this, as well as your ears. We will become engaged. Oh, don't startle like that, you'll do yourself an injury. 'Engaged' I said. Note, I did not say 'married.' The announcement will be put in the papers, your mama will be triumphant, and your name will be cleared. It is one of society's nice-ties that an engagement wipes the slate clean. It would not matter what precisely I had been found in last night, so long as it was followed up by an engagement."

Seeing her look of incomprehension, he laughed to himself and went on, "you will come with me to my own home, and meet my own dear mama and family. But," he said with emphasis, "you will commence to write a series of letters home to dear . . . whatever is that hesitant fellow's name?"

"Giles," whispered Amanda, gazing at her would-be fiancé as though he had run mad.

"Giles, then. Your first letters will be filled with girlish glee at having found such romance, such a princely fellow. But even that first letter will be touched with a slight note of hesitation. Giles will understand that emotion right enough. You will wonder, only in an aside, if you are doing the right thing to throw yourself into such a hasty marriage. Each subsequent letter will contain more self-doubt. By the time he has received six of them, he will, if he has any wit at all, be wondering whether he ought to come to advise you. By the time he has received a dozen, he will, if he has any spine at all, post away instantly to rescue you from my toils. We will say, for I will help you if you wish in the composition, that I am fickle, that I am lewd and licentious, and that I am unprincipled. We will not need to strain for invention, we will only write the truth. Then, he will come to free you from your unholy pact with me, and you will have all that you originally desired."

"But I don't wish to deceive him," Amanda said in hesitation.

"Yet, what choice have you? You've said he will not believe the truth," he answered reasonably.

"But if he does not come?" Amanda asked, awestruck at the possibility of his proposal.

"Then you are well quit of him, for if he fails to be moved by your distress, he would make a most disastrous match. But still, you will be free again. Breaking off from an engagement with me would be certain to win you approval in the most austere reaches of society. What say you, Lady Amanda? Shall we give it a try? It seems your only course."

"But won't your family be disturbed by my masquerade?" she asked in a wavering voice, unsure that this master stroke of strategy could be the godsend she saw it.

"They will know no more of it than your enchanting mama," he said calmly.

"But won't they be disappointed at its outcome?" she asked.

"Not in the least," he answered smoothly. "They will applaud your good sense."

"But why should you do this for me?" she asked at last.

"Why, I have nothing better to do at the moment," he explained as though surprised by the question. "And it promises to be quite entertaining."

It was only a short while later, when the Countess of Clovelly had trod around the edges of her Turkish carpet so many times that the duke feared for the rose design at its edges, that a knock came upon the door of the study. The countess stopped and shot a look of high tension toward the duke.

When the door opened, she had her hand posed dramatically against her heart. The viscount came into the room and poised himself at the entrance. Then he opened his arms wide and said, smiling hugely,

"Mama!"

The countess dropped her hand and flew to embrace him.

As the couple met, the duke had a few seconds of hesitation as he hurriedly did mathematics in his head and frowned. But when the countess cried, "I am so happy for you both," the duke at last understood and, chuckling to himself at the constant rightness of the world, went to congratulate his lady's new prospective son-in-law.

IV

There would have to be a party. It was in vain that
Amanda tried to explain that she had no liking for parties
and hadn't prepared herself for one. Vainly too, her new
fiancé hinted and then flatly stated that as he had been
from home for all of two years, he was all haste to return.
There simply must be a party, the countess exclaimed. It
was inevitable, the duke chuckled fondly as his lady had
her secretary scribble a growing sheaf of invitations. The
only concession to the guests of honor's requests was that
the party would be held sooner than the countess would
wish, and that some of her plans would have to go by the
board for reasons of expediency.

A great many hostesses would have been handicapped
by the suddenness of the event, a great many more would
have been defeated by the pressing lack of time. But the
countess was undaunted. Kettering Manor, after all, was
made for festivity. She and the duke lived for gaiety, and
the entire establishment was in a perpetual state of readiness for guests and entertainment. Even more happily for
her, those of her set were equally always available for
celebration. If galas had been known to have been arranged for such occasions as dogs' birthdays and winning
derby horses, a genuine engagement party was certainly
enough cause for a major fete.

No sooner had the viscount extricated himself from his
prospective mama-in-law's gleeful embrace than she announced her intentions. After hearing all the objections to
her scheme, she conceded only that the ball she planned

would have to be held two weeks rather than three hence.
And immediately after she had looked in on her daughter
and bestowed an ecstatic smile upon her, she wiped away
a happy tear and rushed off to compile her guest list. The
duke, of course, was called into conference with her, and
as they arose one by one, her present guests were invited
to come and offer up suggestions as to the make-up of the
great celebration. By late afternoon, the only persons aside
from the household staff who were not merrily planning
the forthcoming ball were the two for whom it was to be
given.

Now that his name had been offered and promptly
accepted, the viscount decided that a conference with his
newly coined fiancé might be in order. At least, he
thought, he might get to know her a little better. But when
he presented himself in the same salon where he had made
his offer, she only sat and blinked at him. It seemed as if
she had not stirred from the moment when he had left.
When he came in to pass the time of day with her, she
shook herself as one coming out of a dream might do, and
then rose.

"I think," she said dazedly, "that I must think this thing
out, my lord. This has all been so sudden." Then, realizing from his twisted smile that the cliché she had uttered
was unfortunate in this instance, she flushed and begged
his pardon, and then begged his leave to return to her
room. At his slight nod, she fled. Not having any desire to
be pressed into service for compiling the guest list for his
engagement ball, as there was no one whose presence he
wanted, the viscount found that he and his horse required
exercise and spent the better part of the afternoon riding
and thinking alone. He was not, as so many newly promised men were, occupied with second thoughts, for, he
thought as he rode over the snowy landscape, he had never
had any but second thoughts from the first.

As the days wore on, he had a great deal of time to
entertain those thoughts as his hostess and her household
prepared to entertain his nominal guests. Now that he was
netted, the announcement sent to the papers, and cards of
invitation sent throughout the land, he was left to his own

devices. His blushing bride-to-be stayed as far from him as from a contagion. The only conversation he had with her was the polite sort, at meal times. But he did not pass all his time in solitary pursuits, for it could be noted that as well as riding the viscount spent a great deal of time roaming through Kettering Manor, conversing idly with stablemen and even, on occasion, with the housekeeper.

He did see a great deal of his future bride, though. Each evening he sat with her, and each evening he found that he conversed a good deal if not with, then about her. For he discovered the chit was singularly unable to defend herself against her mama's guests and their unique methods of communicating their good wishes. He found himself in the position of being a sort of verbal Lancelot, as he nightly slew social dragons for his fair lady.

The very first evening, after their engagement had been declared and a dozen toasts drunk to it, he had come in from the dining room where the gentlemen had offered him another half dozen ribald toasts with their port. He had scarcely noted nor taken offense at the growing sexual innuendos of their comments. He was, after all, as his hostess had claimed, a man of the world. But when he had joined the ladies he had seen his fiancée white-faced and dumbstruck as the ancient Lady Alcott and the tipsy young Mrs. Small cackled together over Amanda's head. He caught only the tail end of their comments, but enough to know that they were quizzing her about what other idiosyncrasies she had discovered about her fiancé aside from the disparate hue of his eyes. The other unusual attributes they suppositioned were physical as well, but rather of a more intimate nature.

He was well used to such banter, but the look he surprised on his future bride's face was one of sick shame. He made his bows to the other females and, with the most winning smile, asked if he could not have just one private word with Lady Amanda. With knowing chuckles they agreed, and he was able to lead the ashen girl to one side of the room.

"You mustn't take too much note of what they say," he said off-handedly. "Lady Alcott's giddy with the height of her years, you know, and the Small woman's cast away most of the time."

Amanda ignored his words. Her lips, he saw, were trembling. He thought that she might weep and was about to suggest she retire to her rooms with that time-worn excuse of a headache, when she spoke. Her voice was not trembling, rather it was one of shaken wonder.

"I almost struck her! Just think, I was about to do physical injury to a female old enough to be my grand-mother! And I looked about for an escape and saw a vase of flowers and was tempted to empty it over that other dreadful female. I did not know I could be so angry," she said, her fine gray eyes searching his as if for an answer.

"I shouldn't, you know," he said carefully, his lips twitching, "for they'd adore it. Come, collect yourself. Let me do the honors. I'll quite enjoy it."

For the rest of the evening, he kept close by her side. His seeming devotion spurred even more comment. He parried comments about their unusual meeting with sly references about the speakers' own companions, he met witticisms about Amanda's attractions with amusing gossip about females upon the continent, he avoided discussion of his own history by oblique references to his inquisitors' pasts. He must have done it well, he thought, for they continued to call upon him to perform for the rest of the week as coachload after coachload of new guests arrived. But his new lady, at least, was able to calm herself and sit by his side, mute and observant.

His hostess was so occupied with her upcoming fete that he had at last to insist upon speech with her. He had time only for one rational discussion, and that on the subject closest to his heart. But, she protested when he taxed her with it, he must be mistaken. And if he were right, she finally conceded ruefully, it must have been only because of her own flightiness, her excitement at seeing him, her eagerness to oblige him. It was his unusual eyes, of course, she admitted. Seeing him standing there before her that night, she had meant sincerely to appoint him the gray room, which was a charming chamber, but had said *blue* only because she had been wondering aloud at his delightfully strange eyes. Thinking *blue*, she simpered, she had led him to the blue bedroom in error, such was her haste to see him comfortably settled.

Comfortably settled, indeed, he thought as the two weeks wound to a close; so might a capon be comfortably settled for a feast. His prospective bride had kept so far from him that all his suspicions were reawakened. When he first spoke with her, she had been so reasonable a female that he conceded she might have been as much a sacrificial victim as himself. Her current absence from his presence fed the meanest forebodings. But though he might feel a twinge of disappointment now, it was directed solely at himself. For he was seldom gulled, and was vaguely displeased that she might have actually succeeded in deceiving him with her affect of innocence. Still, it made little difference to him.

As he dressed with care the night of the ball, he amused himself by thinking that this night's festivities had even less valid reasons for being than had the famous soiree for the Pekingese's birthday. Whether the girl were a cheat or sincere, it would not tie him to matrimony. Being possessed of a base reputation, he could basely step from the arrangement any time it suited him to do so. At present he was content to let matters go forth.

The ball promised to be a bore, his hostess had frankly betrayed him, and his future wife appeared to be a conniving slut, still the viscount wore a pleased smile as he stepped from his room. He was, in fact, very glad at all that had transpired. Taking his spurious fiancée home with him was a charming way of taking the curse from his own homecoming. She would bear all the attention, not he. Her name would stagger them. The Amberly female's plot, he thought, as he at last deemed himself ready to enter the spirit of the evening, suited his needs exactly. It was a thoroughly diverting way to divert his thoughts from home and all that awaited him there.

He could hear the music as he stepped to the head of the stairs. The great house had been thrumming with activity all week, and tonight it had reached a crescendo. Guests had arrived with monotonous regularity since the invitations had gone out, and this night even more came crowding in. There were so many that even the capacious house could not hold the lot, and many had had to stay with nearby friends or failing that, at inns. The countess had aimed her missives well; such a festivity could not be missed by those who had been summoned.

When Lord North reached the bottom of the stairs, he found himself thronged with the company. He was offered felicitations, congratulations, and looks of ill-concealed surprise. But even as they took in every detail of his composed face to assure themselves that he was not distressed with the circumstances of the incredible engagement they had heard of, their eyes were searching beyond him for a glimpse of the lady clever enough to snare such an elusive bird of passage.

There were upward of two hundred people pressed into the lower portion of Kettering Manor, and most were known to the viscount either by face, name, or repute. The countess's guests were culled from the ranks of the nobility, the *ton*, the military, the merely wealthy, the acting profession, and professions never spoken of in polite company. Although guests of every rank were present, there were no royals in attendance. Even noblesse oblige could only extend so far. For this was an infamous set, and though some of its members might be of the highest society, their sport took place in the shadows of those lofty realms.

Thus, a gentleman who would make sure he measured each word in the House of Lords, might relax here tonight and trumpet the worst sort of slanders or silliness knowing that whoever quoted him would have to admit to having been in a similar case and condition to have heard him. A lady who would be accustomed to taking tea in atmospheres so strict that she dare not utter any but the most blameless sentiments, might tonight either gather up or contribute to gossip so scurrilous that even her lowliest maid would be shocked to repeat it in a tavern. But there was safety here as well. For the countess did not entertain scramblers or mushrooms, only the *crème de la crème* of the *ton*, who just happened to wish for occasional lapses into the dregs of their cups of privilege.

There were noblemen without their wives or with another's wife. There were mistresses who had to have good memories to remember to whose side they must return after a dance. There were gentlemen whose strange proclivities could not bear the light of day and ladies whose faces had not been seen by light of day for decades. There was great wealth here and breeding, and the wealth changed hands rapidly and a great deal of inbreeding was natural.

Lord North stood and acknowledged the company while his eyes searched, too, for his lady. Since his valet had been traveling at a slower pace, it had been a simple thing to summon him to the countess's to attend him for the duration of his stay. Thus he was immaculately and soberly dressed as usual, in close-fitting black coat, white cravat, and formal black satin pantaloons. His waistcoat was blue and gray and gold, and even from a distance his golden hair made him unmistakable. So it was that Amanda was able to focus upon him alone in that vast crowd of guests, as the duke and her mother led her down the stairs.

It was as grand an entrance as the countess could have wished, and in that hushed moment, even Lord North could forgive his fiancée her weeks' long excuse that she could never tarry while her mama's dressmaker was fuming. The countess wore a lavender frock, the duke was commonplace in black and white. There was no other spot of color to take the advantage from Amanda's spectacular dressing. She wore a deceptively simple gown of light yellow edged with white and sashed around with deeper saffron. As her curls were cropped too close to dress, they had been bound with a ribboned circlet of white and yellow flowers that seemed to glow against her spice-brown hair. The hue of her frock gave a creamy glow to her triangular, elfin face and her long lashed eyes were wide with expectation. She looked young, hesitant, and delectable.

As the voices around him picked up their excited conversations again, Lord North smiled in approval. It had been very clever of the countess not to deck the girl out in white, for she was no debutante, and he had to applaud the restraint in not permitting her to wear jewels. Almost, it might appear that she was as she claimed, springtime innocent of her mother's schemes. As she approached him, he gazed thoughtfully at her, taking in the whole of her appearance, from her flushed cheeks to her white neck to her small high breasts and gently curved waist. He took her hand and breathed, "You look enchanting, my dear," while he thought, "And now the play begins."

He led her into the dance and soon others followed and the ball was officially in session. She did not speak as they waltzed, nor seem to note the way his eyes never left off gazing into her face. In due course, he surrendered her to the duke and then noted as she was taken up by the ancient comte and then again by Lord Skyler. Those few who were part of the original company when he had arrived at Kettering Manor now enjoyed the status of celebrities, and the order in which they claimed Amanda for the dance showed that they were anxious to remind the others of this. When he saw Amanda claimed by a dashing major in His Majesty's horse regiment, Lord North turned to enjoy the ball upon his own terms.

He found that he was in even greater demand tonight than he usually was. He danced with two females who had fleetingly been under his protection, and five would-be candidates for the honor. He listened gravely to gossip of the doings of various of his acquaintance, and at the last, stationed himself quietly by the punchbowl, taking refuge from the rest by pretending to attend with great interest to the never-ending narratives of a totally foxed duke. Napoleon might be on Elba, indeed he had seen the fellow there, and normalcy might be returning to the whole of Europe, but the pleasure-starved swarm that frolicked before him were yet wary of travel upon the continent. That was why they were here in such great numbers. Some of their set were already in Vienna and with the coming of spring, he was sure the majority of these present now would be off again about the world, but for now they were grateful for the local pleasures of one of the Amberly Assortment's engagement ball.

When dinner was announced, Lord North strolled toward

his fiancée and, with quiet authority, disengaged her from the knot of admirers that had enveloped her when she had left off dancing with an elderly rogue. He gave her his arm and conducted her to a small table that had been set somewhat out of the common way behind an arbor of flowers. The theme of the ball had been spring-time in winter, and the countess, knowing her company well, had devised several such bowers for privacy's sake.

"I'll procure you some tidbits and then you can rest for a space," he said. "You're a raging success. In fact, if you'd like to break off our engagement immediately, I'm sure you can net three other fellows within the hour."

He had meant it as a pleasantry and was surprised to hear her say with some loathing, "I cannot eat a thing. And I should like to leave this moment."

He began to make assurances that he had only been speaking in jest when she cut him off abruptly by saying wearily, "Oh I know, I know, you cannot say a thing in earnest. But I cannot abide a moment more of this, or these people. They smile at me and flatter me and wish me well, while I know that they do not think of me for a moment. They're all thinking of what advantage they can make of me or this evening. It's all such a charade. Not only on my part, but on theirs. When can I leave, my lord? But I've asked Mama and she expects me to dance till dawn. For I shall not. You know of such things, when can I respectably quit this company?"

"Respectably?" he asked, arching a brow. "Why never. But after midnight, you can make your good nights to a chosen few who will then filter the word down to the others, if you wish."

"I wish," she agreed fervently.

When he had brought her a plate laden with expensive out-of-season trifles, he said softly,

"You must expect them to be curious. You've come from nowhere to make a catch from their waters."

"They all know the story," she said abruptly, laying her fork down with a tiny prawn still impaled upon it.

"If it comforts you," he said pleasantly, "they would

have most probably made up the same tale if they did not know. Or worse."

"How I wish we were at your home," she said on a gusty sigh.

"I shouldn't," he said quietly, and as she looked up, startled, he went on, ". . . refine upon it too much."

After the dinner they went around the room with her mother, being introduced to the entire company.

"The clock has chimed twelve, sit-by-the-cinders," he whispered amiably when they were done. "And after this measure, I can escort you to your rooms. They've satisfied their curiosity and now they'll be content to let you go."

By the time he had cleared their passage to the stairs, it was almost an hour into the new day. It seemed that the company could not leave off exclaiming over what a glamorous couple the young woman in her buttercup dress and the gentleman with the hair the color of sunshine appeared to make. Though North was known to them, no female present this night could honestly claim to have held his attention above the changing of the moon. No gentleman could even hint that he had held the countess's delightful daughter for more than the space of a dance. The compliments were effusive. "Such a perfect match," they murmured. "So well suited," they cooed. It would have all been quite gratifying, Lord North thought, if he could be oblivious to their underlying meaning and the frankly avid eyes of the gentlemen as they estimated the charms of his bride-to-be, and if she could ignore the less than subtle invitation upon the lips of the ladies as they saluted her new fiancé. But at last he stood before her door with her.

"Thank you," she said sincerely, "Mama would have had me stay in the midst of all that until dawn if you had not gotten me free."

"I have my uses," he conceded.

They stood alone in the dim corridor and she found that, to her surprise, she was at last nervous with him. For he stood watching her with an expectant expression.

"What shall you do now?" she asked, not really caring, but wanting him to at least speak.

"You mean," he queried softly, "if you are not going to ask me in?"

"I am certainly not going to ask you in," she snapped.

"Pity," he murmured in a voice that belied the words. "I expect then that I shall have to go back to the ball, and presently I shall escape to the library where I shall have a rousing time listening to those few gentlemen who consider themselves political pundits. Or I can go to the salon and trade warm stories with a few fellows. Really, my lady, you are condemning me to seeing the party out to its last breaths. This respectability is a heavy thing."

She looked so perplexed that he laughed at last.

"You see, my dear fiancée," he said, reaching out to tuck one wilting flower back into her ribbon and letting his finger test a curl, "if I should just disappear into my own comfortable, innocently empty bed now, all those assembled belowstairs will doubtless believe that I have, instead, repaired to yours."

At her wide-eyed shock, he went on, "No, you didn't think on that, did you? But they would, my dear, they doubtless would. As I doubtless would if only I were asked. But as I have not been," he smiled at her dismay, "I shall go below and make myself most in sight until the last guest has reeled to bed, while you take to your comfortable bed for slumber. Selfish one," he chided gently, drawing nearer.

"I shall not be sleeping," she said with resolve, stepping backward with her hand upon the door. "I shall be packing. We will leave tomorrow, will we not?"

"Oh no," he said, "I'm afraid it will take yet another day."

"Why?" she cried, putting so much mournful disappointment into that one question that she was embarrassed by her own eagerness to be gone from her mother's house.

"It's not that I want to leave Mama, though it is, for I confess I don't believe that faradiddle she told me about blue and gray eyes and blue and gray rooms, though I suppose it *is* possible," she said, her words and her thoughts all jumbled on the subject of her mama's possible perfidy. "But it's all these other people. I have never wanted to associate with them before, and I confess I can scarcely bear it now. Do you know that three gentlemen have hinted at possible liaisons with me this night alone? And at my own engagement party," she said, almost forgetting her counterfeit status in her annoyance.

"Only three?" He smiled. "I'm sure you misunderstood, it must have been far more. But if we leave tomorrow, who do you suggest come with us as chaperon? Just tell me her name and I swear, I'll be prepared to order up the coaches instantly."

Amanda stood stricken. She had never thought of it, and of course, Mama had not. Mama had only assigned a maid to her for her trip. But he was entirely right. She would need the escort of some respectable female on the journey. Even though the viscount was now named her fiancé, there would be no hope of any eventual reunion with Giles if it were known that she had traveled overnight across the countryside alone with such a man as he. And, to save her immortal soul, she could not think of one respectable female among the hundreds of persons presently within the walls of Kettering Manor.

"Exactly," Lord North said, watching her reaction to his words. "But fortunately, since I was left to my own devices for all these days," he glanced at her wryly as he spoke, but she was still too overwrought to notice, "I had the time to think about it. With your permission, my lady, I have sent a message off to an elderly relative of my mother's who resides in the next county. A very respectable female. So respectable, in fact, that she would never recognize one face in the company here this night. She's a bit long in the tooth, but very fond of my mama and doubtless eager to be in her debt. She will arrive, I understand, two days from now. Does that suit you?"

"Oh, yes," Amanda said with relief. "Oh, thank you."

"Then I bid you a good night," he said, and leaned forward slightly to her. But at that, she took in her breath sharply and said hurriedly, "Oh, wait. Just one moment, please." She vanished within the room.

As the time went on and he could hear her moving within the room, Lord North permitted himself a vague hope of what was going to transpire next. Whatever his ruminations, however, he was not expecting her to thrust several closely written sheets of paper into his hands.

"I've written two versions of a letter to Giles," she said nervously, "and was wondering if you'd go over them and see which is the better to send."

He laughed then, took the papers from her, and promised he'd cast an eye over them. Then he half-seriously cautioned her to lock her doors and prime her pistol again. At her look of distress, he smilingly allowed that while he would in future be most cautious as to which chamber he retired to, there was no telling if all the other members of the present gathering would be so circumspect. Then, bidding her a lighthearted good night, he went to rejoin the company.

As the night wore on, Lord North was not bereft of attention. Though he did not dance another step, he was offered partnership in many other diversions, by many other sportive persons. He denied them all. He attempted to visit the gaming room, but after listening to Lady Slade's complaints about how chill her own room undoubtedly was since she was alone, Mary Whitmore fretting about how cool he had grown toward her, and Mrs. Abernathy whispering over an excellent hand about how cold her own husband unfortunately was, he escaped from the room and from further female companionship. He did not join the other gentlemen either. Not the group trading risqué stories, nor the political gentlemen, nor even the lords Skyler and Jeffrey's select invited guests and their various subtle invitations to amusement.

Instead, as the sky slowly turned to the light of true morning, Lord North sat at ease in the deserted library entertaining himself by reading with interest two different, closely written letters to a disbelieving gentleman named Giles.

V

The Honorable Miss Emily Atkinson arrived at Kettering Manor at the unfashionable hour of ten in the morning, two days after the countess's lavish ball. Her time of arrival was not the least fashionable aspect of her person. For when Amanda hastily abandoned her breakfast to make the acquaintance of the lady who would be her nominal chaperon on the journey to her fiancé's home, she was, for a moment, convinced that it was just another jibe on that disreputable gentleman's part.

The Honorable Miss Emily looked, at first stare, exactly like some sort of elderly indigent who had been plucked from her flower stand in the Covent Garden markets of London. At any moment, Amanda expected her to open her mouth to say, "Violets for my lady?" Instead, she said, "Charmed," in a most unexceptional manner, and displayed no further desire for speech until a light breakfast was offered to her, when she said with as much enthusiasm as was possible to place in so few words, "I think I shall, thank you so much."

For such a meager person, Amanda thought, the Honorable Miss Emily consumed as much sustenance as an army trooper might. Miss Emily was very aged, very small, and extremely thin. Her out-of-fashion jet dress hung upon her as slackly as her threadbare purse hung upon her bony arm. Amanda had always somehow associated small spare elderly persons with wit as acute and sharp as their looks. But Miss Emily was as scant with speech as she was with person, and those few words that escaped her were commonplace and complimentary to a fault. Watching Miss Emily consume her "light breakfast" with the rapacity of a wolf, nodding complaisant agreement to every bit of prattle the countess presented in her eagerness to make a good impression on her daughter's prospective relative, Amanda could not shake the ridiculous notion that somehow an enormously fat, indolent person had become trapped in Miss Emily's insubstantial body.

But Mama had been agog when she had been told the identity of her daughter's chaperon. "Miss Emily Atkinson!" she had cried. "Trust North to do the right thing. Irreproachable, my dear, she is totally irreproachable. She was once lady of the chamber to the old queen, and not a breath of scandal has ever been attached to her. The most amiable of souls, the epitome of good *ton*." Perhaps it was all those years at court, Amanda thought, that accounted for Miss Emily's unhesitant, pleased acceptance of every scrap of information that was fed to her, along with every morsel of food.

Amanda's bags were packed and were already loaded into the coach that would bear them and her maid to Windham House, Lord North's home. She sat in agonies of impatience while Miss Emily enjoyed her repast and her mama burbled on about how delightful the unexpected alliance was, and painted pictures of her daughter that would have been extravagant in describing a martyred saint. Lord North toyed with his cutlery with a look of great amusement upon his face. But Amanda kept note only of the time and wished her mama were wise enough to do the same and let their party make an escape before the other guests awoke and joined them.

Most of the guests at the ball had stayed on, for an invitation to a ball at a country home was readily understood to be an invitation for a week or more, since travel was so tedious and such an onerous task. The guests had been occupied with hunting, dancing, playing parlor games, giving musical recitals, and nipping in and out of various bedrooms since the day of their arrival. Amanda had found herself slinking and creeping about the house in futile attempts to avoid their jovial attentions. Despite her care, she had been the recipient of congratulatory pinches on the cheek and less mentionable parts of her person more than a few times from the gentlemen, and had received more candid and shocking advice about the state of wedlock from the ladies than she could bear.

The most embarrassing counsel had come from her own mama. It was inevitable, she thought later, that her scatter-wit parent should suddenly decide that a daughter might need some maternal advice on certain intricacies of the married state before her wedding date. Amanda had tried to forestall the conversation that day when she had been sought out in her own bedroom by saying that it was, after all, not quite her wedding night, but her mama had said, knowingly,

"Precisely. I'll have quite good advice for you then. But for now, all that I want to impress upon you, Amanda, is the importance of not celebrating that night prematurely."

Mama had the uncanny ability every so often to leave off her fluttery affect and speak with such decisiveness that one was compelled to listen. Amanda sank back onto her bed without further protest as the countess went on, "I am not saying that Roger has not been a good papa to you, but I doubt he has ever given you any idea of how a female should go on in such affairs. Indeed, it would be most reprehensible if he had. But no matter. I assume that you and this Giles person have never . . . ah . . ." Her mother faltered, and Amanda had quickly put in "Never," for fear of hearing anything more explicit.

"I thought not," her mother said with satisfaction, "for I believe I should have seen it in your face if he did, or you had."

Amanda very much doubted this claim of prescience, but as she did not want the conversation to dwell on such matters, said nothing, only hoping it would be over quickly.

"North is a compelling man," her mother said, now avoiding her daughter's eye. "And very clever when it comes to our frail sex. I only wanted to stress, Amanda, that I think it would be very unwise if you allowed your-self to be eased into a more intimate relationship before the knot is tied. Knowing North, I am quite sure nothing too advanced transpired before I stepped into your room; he is not the sort of fellow to rush his fences or even enjoy covering ground too quickly . . ." And here her mother lingered for a moment, the expression of wistful musing upon her face more shocking to her daughter than anything she had yet said.

"At any rate," the countess went on, shaking herself from her distraction abruptly, "I only wanted to say, with no further frills upon it, that it would be a bad idea to consummate this marriage before it has taken place. North is a fellow who grows bored quickly, and who has, alas, little faith in your innocence. You do know what I am saying, don't you?" she asked suddenly, suspicious of her daughter's silence.

"Of course," Amanda shot back with heartfelt truth. "And I assure you, I have no intention of allowing any intimacies with my Lord North."

"That is not precisely what I meant," her mama said thoughtfully, "for a few tantalizing hints of what is to come would not go amiss. I only advise against fulfillment of those promises. Do you take my meaning? Oh dear, how complete is your knowledge of the married state, Amanda?" she asked with a look of trepidation.

"Quite extensive, Mama," Amanda said, laughing. "After all, I did go to boarding school, and there is little that we did not discuss among ourselves of the matter."

"Lud," her mama said, aghast, "then we really must have a good long talk before you actually marry."

Although Amanda had agreed, she had privately resolved from the moment she had shown her mama to the door, that if she did manage to retrieve something from this tangle and actually marry Giles, she would not return for that chat until she had presented him with at least two infants.

For all her confused wondering about her mama and that lady's motives in the mix-up of bedchambers that had resulted in her present engagement, she still could not like deceiving her. But truth to tell, she did not know her parent too well, and feared that if any hint of the truth of the odd arrangement with the viscount slipped out, her

mama's hand might be forced to even more disastrous
lengths. Although, she thought, it would be difficult for
her to be compromised more firmly than she had already
been, unless Mama actually drugged her and dragged her
to that gentleman's sheets. Nonetheless, the sooner she
was quit of Kettering Manor, the better. Then she thought,
brightening for a scant moment, the only persons she would
have to keep the truth from would be the Honorable Miss
Emily, the viscount's mama, his other relatives, and his
entire household staff.

It might have been her doleful expression that prompted
Lord North to say idly, cutting into Mama's comments
about how cunning an infant Amanda had been, "But dear
cousin Emily! Just look at the hour. Why, if we tarry here
any longer, it will be past dinner time when we arrive at
the Fox and Grapes. I did book us there, since I recall the
inn has a marvelous reputation for its cuisine."

Miss Emily ingested the last crumb of her toast and
stood up in one rapid motion.

"How delightful it has been," she said.

The countess gave Amanda a tearful and fulsome good-
bye, entreating Lord North again and again "to take good
care of my little girl," while the duke beamed and Lady
Emily said "Delighted" with the regularity of a clock counting hours.

Amanda and Miss Emily climbed into the first coach,
their maids into a following vehicle. Lord North swung up
upon his horse and they were at last away as the sun rose
directly overhead. Amanda waved through the rapidly
fogging window, and noted that a few persons in the house
had pulled back their curtains to see their departure.

As the coaches disappeared down the curving drive, the
countess turned to her dear Robert and said happily, "The
wedding, of course, shall not be such a paltry affair as the
engagement party was. I shall have time to sit and plan,
and with any luck, Robert, it will be the social affair of the
season."

The duke lost his habitual smile and then answered,
somewhat tentatively, knowing he was treading upon very
thin ground, "Did North say it was to be here, then? Not

that I'd mind, be delighted, puss, as you well know. But his mama—ah, his family, that is to say . . ." He let his words trail off unhappily.

His lady gave him one of her rare sharp looks.

"Don't be nonsensical, Robert. They may well not like it, but there's no other rational course. I am her mama."

"Ah well," the duke said, growing expansive once again, "we shall make it memorable then, never fear. When's it to be, puss, May or June?"

But at those innocuous words, the countess paled. Her step faltered and she looked back fearfully at the faint traces the departing carriage wheels had left upon the last trace of snow.

"I don't know!" she cried. And then, squinting her eyes as if to shield them from glare of the snow which was no longer there, she said slowly, thoughtfully, "They did not say."

They had only traveled a little while when Amanda collected herself, gave a final discreet sniffle, and then turned her attention fully to her companion, the estimable Miss Atkinson. That lady sat across from her comfortably peering out the window, although Amanda could not guess what she was seeing there. The hot bricks that had been placed at their feet, combined with the warmth of their breath, had succeeded in making the interior of the carriage cozy, and the resultant steam effectively blurred the windows completely.

Amanda had prepared herself for being quizzed or openly confronted with myriad questions from the viscount's honored relative the moment they were alone, but she soon found that the lady seemed to have no intention of breaking the silence within the swaying carriage. Since any extended silence in the close company of another human discomforted Amanda, and as she read both condemnation and accusation into this absence of conversation, she began to prepare the way for discussion.

But she discovered that comments upon the weather drew only an immediate pleased response of agreement on the fact that winter was generally cold. When that subject

was exhausted, Amanda found as the miles slipped by that
Miss Emily agreed that the carriage was well-sprung but
that travel was indeed tiring, and that she too was anxious
to arrive at their destination. The only information Miss
Emily volunteered, and that hesitantly, as though she did
not wish to give offense by holding such bold opinions,
was that Lord North was a delightful fellow, and Amanda's
own parents were similarly so. As she lapsed into defeated
quiet again, Amanda did not seek to disabuse the lady of
the notion that the duke was her parent, and wondered
sadly if her companion knew any other word but the
omnipresent "delightful."

Presently, Miss Emily dozed with a delighted little smile
upon her lips. Amanda cleared a circle of fog from the
window with her sleeve and when the road turned, gazed
wistfully at the straight figure of Lord North as he rode
ahead of the coach. When they stopped at last for tea,
Amanda felt a relief that had nothing to do with the
prospect of stretching her cramped legs or being able to
use the ladies' convenience.

As Miss Emily disappeared into the inn, Lord North
gave his horse to the stable boy and strolled over to Amanda
with a secret smile.

"She is, as you have doubtless discovered," he said into
Amanda's ear, "little better than an idiot, is she not? But
very high _ton_, my dear. She was in great demand socially
in her youth, for she could be counted on to never see
what was beneath her nose, and thus to never spread a bit
of tattle. But, you will note, she never uses the wrong fork
or says an unpleasant word. And she has a great fortune,
as well. The only reason such a paragon never married, I
suspect," he added in a low voice as he held the door open
for Amanda, "is that she doubtless never realized she was
being proposed to. An excellent chaperon, is she not?"

Amanda refused him answer to that. But as they took
their tea and sat and watched Miss Emily devour every bit
of cake and cream they had not consumed, they chatted
pleasantly upon a multitude of entertaining, nonimportant
subjects. He was, Amanda thought, a charming companion when he desired to be. But, she reminded herself as

she recovered from her mirth over his account of a tea he had suffered through aboard a ship in a storm off the coast of France, he would have to be facile at such things if all she had heard of him were true. It could not have been only his striking good looks that had earned him his infamy.

As he threw on his greatcoat once again and turned to her to offer his arm, Amanda understood all at once why he was considered so dangerously compelling. His bright hair seemed silver-tipped in the sunlight, his ivory face bore a faint gold glow from the cold, and his odd, jeweled eyes held a secret amused recognition of her unwanted, unwittingly sudden reaction to his splendor. She quickly lowered her gaze and made haste to enter the coach again and to gratefully endure the undemanding company of Miss Emily.

Amanda had deliberately avoided her fiancé assiduously since the morning they had struck their strange bargain. It was clear that his offer had been an act of charity. Offered out of boredom, or mischief of some strange sort perhaps, but nevertheless she knew very well that their bargain had been struck largely as a donation to the needy. She *had* been in need, and was very grateful to him. Therefore, she had decided that she would not presume upon him any more than she absolutely had to; it would simply not be fair. After hearing Mama's lame excuses for the incident, she had known that he had been as grievously wronged as she, and if she were to constantly trail after him, he would be sure to suppose her Mama's willing accomplice. If he had been kind enough to suffer her being foisted upon him, even for a short time, it would be poor payment to him for her to hang upon his sleeve.

But as they began their journey again, she saw that she could not avoid him any longer. For the viscount left off riding alone and now it pleased him to stay within the carriage with the two ladies for the last of their ride to the evening stopover at the Fox and Grapes.

As Miss Emily dozed, he sat back and bent himself entirely to the task of entertaining his fiancée. At first, he began to comment upon the engagement party they had just endured, and soon Amanda found that she was laugh-

ing merrily at all that she had felt fear and revulsion for.
When seen in the light of his clever words, the huge
sinister marquess who had offered her strange delights
during their dance became only a baggy-pantalooned
buffoon; the acid-tongued dame who had made her squirm
with pointed questions became an inept witch from a
skewed fairy story. Soon, she was adding her own ridiculous comments as counterpoint and they were laughing so
heartily that Miss Emily opened her eyes to smile and
whisper, "Charming."

As the carriage horses began to tire and plod more
slowly to their destination, he sobered and with her constantly fascinated questions to spur him on, told her tales
of the Vienna woods and streets and society. Then he held
her spellbound with his tale of how he had dined with
Bonaparte himself in that island retreat that the erstwhile
master of Europe clearly regarded as a hell on earth.
Amanda listened and grew strangely sad and subdued as
he described how the former eagle had been transmuted to
kitchen-cock in his exile. He saw her disquiet, and soon
had her gurgling with laughter again with his narrative
about a bungling spy at that dinner who had sought to get
his companions and himself foxed enough to spill state
secrets they did not possess.

He paced her moods with subtle skill so that the journey
of miles seemed to have been accomplished in mere
moments. It was only when Amanda was alone in her
snug room at the Fox and Grapes dressing for dinner that
she realized how well he had gauged her responses, and
how pleased he had been at the result of his efforts. Now
that she was, given the conversational gifts of Miss Emily,
to all intents alone with him while away from Mama's
house, she was amazed both at him and her own reaction
to him. It was as if, she thought, some great cataclysm of
nature had marooned her with Edmund Kean or some
other gifted actor. She knew full well that she was not the
viscount's usual sort of company and that he had, on a
whim, decided to make do with a chance companion. She
felt he was playing to an audience that was not there and

could not help the fact that some of his vast appeal and talent had dazzled her.

But it made no difference to their scheme, she reasoned as her maid tugged a comb through her curls. Because for all that he was scintillating and glamorous, she could honestly say that he had never been natural with her. For all she knew, he could not be so with anyone. She would do well to remember that. In that way she would be spared any foolish fears that might embarrass herself or him. She would have to constantly remind herself that she stood in no danger from his attentions. His easy seductiveness was not aimed particularly toward her, it was only an integral part of his personality, and would only mean that her position would not be quite so difficult a one as she had envisioned.

Amanda dressed in a thin but warm sapphire blue woolen frock. She threw a pale blue paisley shawl over her shoulders since the walls of the old inn admitted as much cold as the several blazing fireplaces sought to dispel. Miss Emily, she perceived when they met downstairs, had either not changed at all, or had an entire wardrobe of tired shapeless black dresses. The viscount was, as ever, an exquisite, even in his simple buckskins and dark gray hacking jacket.

They dined on the justly celebrated viands of the Fox and Grapes in a private paneled room with a comfortable fire roaring in the grate, and thick curtains pulled across the tiny windows shut out the bitter night.

The food was delicious, the wine incomparable, and the conversation even better than the fare. Soon Amanda felt that she was a privileged person on a gay holiday, rather than an exiled and disgraced young female, tolerated only through the good graces of a notorious stranger. She felt a distinct pang of regret when Miss Emily cleared the last bit from her dessert plate and announced that, while it had all been quite delightful, she was off to bed. Amanda rose to accompany the lady upstairs to their rooms, when she was forestalled by a languid comment from the viscount.

"But it is early hours yet, dear cousin. It has only just struck nine. As Lady Amanda and I have some family business to discuss, do you think you could allow her to remain here with me for a while? It is, I will admit, a private parlor, but as the landlord will soon send servants in to clear there can be no disgrace in a young woman and her fiancé lingering over their dessert, can there be?"

"Why certainly not," Miss Emily agreed at once. "There cannot be."

Miss Emily bestowed her usual benign smile upon them both and left, murmuring "Delightful" so often that the landlord, who chanced to be passing by as she mounted the stair, smiled in gratification at her obvious approval of his inn.

As Amanda settled back, the viscount leaned back in his own chair and grinned at her,

"You understand, of course," he said, "that she would have replied the same way if I had said, 'But as it is early hours yet, there can be no harm if Lady Amanda and I throw off all our clothes and make mad passionate love upon the floor until morning, can there be?' "

His words startled her, but the look in his eye had her giggling until he added, in an undertone, "There would be no harm in that either, you know."

But even as she drew in her breath, he changed his manner abruptly and sat upright and said in a businesslike fashion, "Now as to those letters, my lady . . . do you mind if I call you merely Amanda? I think that we have reached the stage in our acquaintance where even such a strict arbiter of fashion as Miss Emily would agree it was proper."

At her consenting nod, he went on, drawing her letters from his jacket, "Now, as I see it, the first letter is far too enthusiastic. The fellow will think you're crowing over your achievement, and the last little hint, let me see . . . 'I wonder at my precipitous judgment of the viscount, as I hardly know him . . .' is far too tame. You seem to be more like a lady who has discovered a diamond in her knitting basket and wonders only if it is entirely flawless. No, the tone is too bright, entirely too self-congratulatory. As for the second effort, it is too morose. Giles will think there's something smoky afoot if he reads it carefully. Too many, 'I wonder' and 'Whatever came over me, I do not know' sort of digressions. You need a letter that is a combination of the two. Come, let us ask the landlord for some clean sheets and we will put our heads together to compose the perfect first shot in our battle with the fine compunctions of Sir Giles Boothe."

After the table was cleared, they bent their heads literally, the sun-struck golden one and the curly brown one, over the sheets of paper the landlord provided. The hours went on unheeded as they labored over the letter they collaborated on. There were many times during its composition when the pen had to be laid down, as the lady who held it was laughing too hard to write a straight line. And many times when the pen was laid aside absently, as she explained pensively what she imagined Giles's thoughts, emotions, and character to really be. Though she thought that she was explaining only Giles, her co-author sat and watched as her expressive face and soft words told him a great deal more of herself than she ever imagined.

Two hours had gone by when she finally laid her pen down with a gratified sigh.

"It's done," she said. And then she looked up into his strange eyes, now less strange through constant association and because in the candlelight their oddity was unnoticeable, and said with wonder, "But look! I've only written two pages. It seems as though we've composed a saga together, and there's only these few pages."

"But there's a great deal in them closely packed," he commented, taking the letter from her. "I'll have the landlord hold it for the mail coach. Unless Giles is made of sheer granite, this little effort of ours will give him much to think upon. He does not even need to read between the lines to understand that you went to your mama's to receive a birthday gift and found yourself receiving instead the thrillingly complete and close attentions of a practiced seducer. Your mama, however, was nervous about such a devious fellow and, indeed, surprised him entering her dear daughter's boudoir. Now, you've committed yourself to the evil fellow, for you're a good girl. But you wonder if you've done the right thing by such a sacrifice to propriety, and hope he can advise you. Since you're so set on being as truthful as possible, you'll agree the only things we've fudged are your dear mama's and my intentions."

Amanda nodded, thinking back on the words she had put down on paper.

"And," the viscount went on, "to cap it all off, you find yourself attracted to the fellow, even though you know full well that he has no constancy, nor any morals at all."

"Yes," she breathed abstractedly, still thinking of the letter.

They sat quietly for a moment as he regarded her closely and she thought of their efforts. Then Amanda reluctantly rose from her seat. The wind was howling outside the windows and the fire, having been fed again while they were busily writing, crackled pleasantly. Again, she was reluctant to leave for the chill hallway.

"Ah, but it is early yet," the viscount said, rising as well, but only so that he could reseat himself in one of a pair of comfortable chairs by the fire.

"Come," he gestured. "Stay a while; don't rush off simply because dull work is done. There can be no harm in lingering over a cordial. You can even rouse dear Cousin Emily from her slumbers, if you want, to ask permission."

Amanda laughed, and feeling more pleased with herself than she had in days because the letter was at last written and about to be sent off to Giles, walked toward the other chair and sank back happily into it.

"A good day's work," she said with satisfaction.

"Yes," the viscount agreed, smiling happily back at her. "And just think," he added, "the day is not even done yet."

VI

Amanda leaned her head back against her chair and closed her eyes for a few moments. It was quiet in the room, save for the singing of the logs in the fireplace and the faint click of glasses and gurgle of liquid as her benefactor, Lord North, poured her the promised cordial. As he had said, the day was not yet done, yet she felt as though she had come a long way further than a mere count of hours could encompass. She was far from her home now, far from her mama, and equally distanced from Lord North's residence. She felt safe in her cocoon of comfort, in that limbo between the onset of her troubles and the resolution of them.

She accepted the fragile glass of clear liquid and drank a measure without thinking. A moment later, she was sitting erect, breathing with difficulty and gasping a plea for water.

"No, no," Lord North laughed from behind her, "water would ruin the effect. Just sit back again and take a small sip, then open your lips and breathe out from your mouth. No, don't look daggers at me," he chided her as she swung her head around to glower at him. "Just try to do as I say. Then you can rail at me."

Amanda sat back again reluctantly, and after she had her respiration under control, did as he suggested. The first shock of the little bit she sampled produced the same burning effect upon her palate, but as she parted her lips and breathed out, she slowly became aware of the over-whelming taste and fragrance of raspberries filling her mouth and nostrils. She stopped in wonder and gazed down at the glass.

"Yes," Lord North said in agreement with her unspoken thought, "it is quite marvelous, isn't it? A distillation of raspberries the good friars invented. A subtle thing, like so many other pleasures. First the fire, then the slow flooding of the senses. As Cousin Emily would say, 'Delightful.' "

Amanda took another sip and another breath, and found herself smiling. The viscount's voice came from directly behind her, as though he bent to speak into her ear.

"A singularly good feeling, is it not, to sip berries brewed in flame, while the cold, hard outside world fades away? There is nothing evil in such pleasure, is there, Amanda?"

This time, Amanda distinctly felt his warm breath upon her ear. She began to grow very wary and her muscles began to tense, until she realized that again, it was probably no more than his usual banter. If friendliness moved him to couch his conversation in such rich, ripe, seductive terms, he could hardly be aware of its effect upon an untried, unripe chit such as herself. But then, she felt his hand gently touch the back of her neck and begin to stroke the vulnerable region her curls did not cover.

He spoke softly, coaxingly now, but she could scarcely hear his words about "pleasures" and "joys," while her anger grew until it seemed to overflood her reason.

"What did you say?" she finally managed to ask, scarcely able to believe that which she thought she had heard through her veil of fury.

"I merely suggested," he said softly, now so close to her ear that she could feel each warm breath, as well as the light caress of his lips upon her earlobe, "that as it is yet early, and as we are unoccupied, and as I know it will bring you pleasure, as well as my poor self, that you accompany me to my room now."

When she did not answer at once, he went on softly, "Dear Cousin Emily will not know, nor care, unless we repair to her own room, if that is what makes you hesitant. Come, 'Manda, we have hours of blank night to spend deliciously."

"How dare you?" Amanda finally exploded, shooting up from her chair and wheeling about to face him.

He straightened, his face as bland as if he had just suggested they go for a stroll, and answered her calmly, "How dare I what, Amanda?"

She thought for a moment that the liquor had disordered her wits. But she could not have imagined his words even after ingesting a quart of alcohol-soaked berries.

"How dare you ask me, just coldly ask me to . . . to . . ." Amanda cried, unable in her disbelieving anger to vocalize his suggestion.

"Make love to me?" he supplied helpfully, much to her relief and appalled disbelief. "Well, I suppose that it might have seemed rather blunt, but really, my lady, I did not think you so wet behind the ears that you required the entire artificial scene: the light touch, the few hesitant kisses, the bolder embraces, and then finally, triumphantly, the finale, with me catching you up in my strong arms and bearing you off, protesting futilely that it is against your better judgment, to my bed. I thought you a female of rare good sense. I paid you the compliment of honesty. I'm sorry if I displeased you, but really my dear, it would have been rather difficult for me to tote you out of the room, off into the corridor, and up the stairs under the eyes of the innkeeper, his servants, and other clientele. And while this is a private parlor, at any moment just as I told Cousin Emily, some sort of servant might wander in. I do not approve of lovemaking as a spectator sport," he said reprovingly.

Amanda was in such a state of anger now, about all he had said and all he had left unsaid, that she found herself in the position of having so many things to declare that they all rushed to her lips and, finding a bottleneck there, struggled fruitlessly to get out.

She was furious at his estimate of her state of grace and curiously also enraged that this aloof and elegant gentleman should bring all the forces of his considerable charm to bear against one small unworldly girl. It was unfair, as though a sorcerer should conjure up a tidal wave to extinguish one little candle. And paradoxically, she was equally insulted at the vague idea that he had not, after all, exerted himself to bring forth quite as much persuasion as he could have done. She struggled for words to express some of this, while he stood waiting patiently for her next utterance.

"How dare you," she cried ringingly, sure that her face was red as a berry, "think that was what I wished, think I was that sort of female, think that I was someone you could while away a boring night with?"

"Is it that you are insulted that I did not painstakingly go down the list of your charms?" he asked curiously.

Since that, Amanda discovered suddenly, had been one of the grievances that she had not admitted even to herself—the thought that he was only making do on a tedious night with a female who was not up to his usual standard—she denied it hotly.

"No," she almost shrilled in her vexation, but he went on as though she had not spoken.

"But of course. I thought you were aware of your fine points. You are a lovely creature. I thought you hardly needed me to state the obvious. I could, of course, go on about your form, which is magnificent, your eyes, which are beguiling, your perfume, which has made my head swim more than the Framboise ever could have, your skin, which is as smooth as——"

But she did not wait for him to tick any further items from his seemingly never-ending list, as the soft cadence of his voice and the astonishingly complimentary things he was saying discomforted her almost as much as his touch had. She instead only cut him short by saying bluntly, "You are being deliberately obtuse." Growing calmer now, as the seduction he had attempted seemed to be dwindling to a discussion, she added, "I meant to say, how could you have thought that I was the sort of female who would just take to a gentleman's bed when asked?"

He made no reply to that and only stood head cocked slightly to one side. She did not give him time to answer, in any case, but went on in cold anger, "It is because my name is Amberly. It is because even though I am legitimate, I am nonetheless one of the Assortment. It is because of where I come from and the reasons why I am here tonight, is it not? You thought me just as base as yourself."

He picked up a bottle and refilled his glass, not meeting her angry stare.

"As you say," he whispered.

"Well, I shall trouble you no longer," she said bitterly. "I shall take the post back immediately in the morning. I will not stay a moment longer."

As she turned from him and gathered up her shawl, he said quietly, "Come, Amanda, do not leave in anger now. There is no further cause for it. I am suitably chastened. No purpose can be served by your flight. We shall go on as planned. You stand in no danger from me now."

She hesitated, for in truth, she feared the repercussions of a precipitate flight from him. She could even now hear the excited, scandalized comments she would receive from all the guests at her mother's house. Giles would be lost to her forever, she would be ruined, and most likely her mother would stop at nothing to achieve her connection with yet another wandering gentleman.

"No, I speak the truth, my lady, this is a safe retreat for you. I only attempted your seduction. As I mentioned at our first meeting, I do not champion rape. There is nothing I can think of at the moment which repels me more. And you may stay and sip your raspberries until dawn, for I do not take advantage of drunken or fuddled females, especially not drunken females," he said feelingly. "For that is a brute activity for swinish men. I may well not be a moral fellow, but I do have standards," he said in wounded tones. "We vile seducers have gotten a very bad name, I can see," he laughed, his swiftly changing mood lightening. "But I can think of few things more antipathetic to pleasure than either coercion or force. You do not wish to lie with me, that's clear. Let's have done with the notion then."

She paused, for his words did not ease her mood, rather they made her feel both childish and rude.

"It is not that I don't wish to . . . stay with you," she said, scarcely believing the sort of conversation she was entering into. "It is that I would not with any man. That is to say . . . why should I have to explain myself," she wondered aloud, "when any properly brought-up young woman in the land would not have to do so? Because I am an Amberly does not mean that I behave as you might have imagined. I am really quite a conventional creature, my lord. Quite as straight-laced as any female of a good family might be. I'm sorry if my name led you to believe otherwise. It has been a stigma to me all my life. I have always attempted to ignore it and thought others might do the same, but I see that I have erred."

"Of course," he said smoothly, offering her another glass of the heady liquor. "You are completely to blame. You should have informed me of your reluctance to bed me the moment you clapped eyes on me. In fact, you might even have held a pistol to my heart as you told me so."

Amanda had been seating herself, but stopped to stare at him at his words.

"No, my innocent, you see the fault does not lie in you, if indeed, fault there is in this. I presumed you were 'up to snuff,' as discreet gentlemen say, precisely for the reasons you so sweetly shouted at me before. I was a doubting Thomas, and was served the same as that unfortunate fellow for my disbelief."

He sat in the chair across from her and raised his glass in a salute.

"To peace, Amanda. I promise I will not make the same mistake twice. But," he added as he noted she did not raise her glass as well, "if I am to be completely honest, I cannot promise I will not make similar suggestions in future. I am, after all, a creature of habit. And you are, as I have said, a very taking little article. You cannot put a doe in a lion's cage and expect the creature not to swipe at her with his paw every now and again," he complained. "Some men play at hunting, some collect rare gems. I have my own methods of diversion. But if it makes you feel any better, I shall not lunge at you and you need only to put me firmly in my place, should I err again. Of course, if you ever feel so inclined at any time until the good Giles comes to claim you, to invite me to such an encounter, pray do not hesitate to mention it," he added on a hopeful note.

At that, she laughed at last and gravely lifted her glass to him. After she had taken a sip, she said earnestly, "But please, my lord——"

"Christian," he said. "At least that much forgiveness, please."

"Christian, I should feel easier in mind if you would not make such a request," she said a little plaintively.

"Don't fret. I shall honestly try." He smiled gently, watching her, his light eyes strangely luminous in the wavering firelight.

"I think," he said carefully after they had sat quietly for a space, "that we ought to talk, Amanda. As you see, I hardly know you at all. And if we are to fly the flag of an engaged couple, it would be helpful if we knew each other better, don't you agree?"

She quickly concurred, but as nothing dries up conversation faster than the all-encompassing request to tell someone about yourself, she sat dumbly, pondering what precisely she should mention first. As though he knew her predicament, he said easily, "The name has always given you trouble then?"

"Yes," she admitted, but again, as she had already told him that in quite emphatic fashion, she subsided and stared down into her glass.

"I have found," he commented idly, "that though a person grows up with a thing, there is always that precise moment when one becomes acutely aware of it. Was it that way with you?"

"Why yes," she said, "it did happen just that way."

Now she looked into the fire and avoided his eyes and let herself think back as she had not in years, for in truth, she realized that no one had ever spoken frankly with her about her infamous name. Charles had only flung it at her. Giles never did or would name the very thing that kept them apart. It was far too sensitive a subject for them both, for him to broach to her. Mama certainly never had. Father scarcely spoke to her at all. Jerome ignored it and the other children somehow avoided actually speaking of the obvious topic after their initial embarrassed laughter whenever they met. But here, sitting in the semi-dark with this libertine gentleman the subject once brought up, would not stay down again. It was now necessary that he understand her. It was now important that she hear her own explanation. The words seemed to spill forth from her, and it seemed quite a natural subject to converse about in this bizarre situation.

"I always knew that there was scandal attached to our family," she said reflectively. "I was four years old when Mama left for the first time, and five when she returned home to have Mary. I was seven when Alicia was born and by the time James came along, I was used to the fact that there was something out of the ordinary going on. But it is curious, you know, rather like growing up with a handicap. In some fashion you believe that there is nothing truly exceptional in your condition and you are constantly surprised at other people's reaction to it."

"But you were aware that it was irregular?" he prodded gently.

She scarcely attended his words as she was attempting to frame her deepest feelings in proper words. It was a novelty and a relief to at last speak freely about her burden.

"What? Oh yes," she said ruefully. "Servants chatter, you know, and all adults seem to believe that children do not grow functional ears till they attain adulthood. I knew, in the words of Cook, that we were all a 'parcel of bastards.' "

She looked up in shock at her words, as though someone else had uttered them, for she had never spoken so about her family, and thought she saw him wince slightly at her utterance. She began to utter shamefaced apologies, but he stopped her at once by saying softly,

"No, no. I can see it was what you must have heard. But there are gentler words you can use if you like. 'Wrong side of the blanket' I can see is a bit cumbersome, but 'natural child' is a kind euphemism. 'Base-born' is a bit harsh, 'illegitimate' too much of a legal phrase. 'By-blow' is altogether too violent, and 'love child' is too sentimental. Perhaps the most poetic term I ever heard was the appellation 'child of the mist.' But I can see that would be a difficult phrase to slip into easy conversation. 'Bastard' is, after all, most definitive, I fear. But go on. I am not easily shocked; in fact, I should very much like to be, just to experience the sensation again, you understand."

Over her laughter, he asked again, "But when did you understand precisely what the problem was?"

"Curiously, it was not at school," she said, slipping back into her vocal reverie. "Although other girls often alluded to my family and though it rankled, it never quite 'hit,' do you understand?" she asked, curious as to the phenomenon herself.

"Oh yes," he sighed.

"It was when I was fifteen and at Mama's for the holidays with my best friend Martha Applegate," Amanda said decisively, seeing it for herself now. "I do believe that was the first time I fully understood the matter, and fully the worst time ever before or since." And so it was, she thought in amazement, even worse than the episode with Charles had been.

She paused, looking up at him, oddly afraid to go into the matter again for her own sake as well as for reasons of propriety. He sat, still as stone, his face, what she could make of it in the shadows and fitful light of the candles and fire, unreadable.

"Oh, don't stop now," he said in a voice as low as her own thoughts, "or I shall think far worse than the truth, I promise you. I am a member of your mama's set, you know."

"It was not so shocking, I suppose," Amanda said at last, "except to me. It was simply that Martha and I were at loose ends one day. Martha's father, you see, was an admiral in His Majesty's service, and as she had no mama, and her father had been at sea a very long time, he had no objection to her staying over vacation at Kettering Manor with me. He had never heard of it, I expect. Jerome was at his friend's home and our own house would have been most inhospitable for us, father being the way he is. And the other children were younger, and we were bored with them, you see."

"I see," the viscount said in a gentle tone, "that you are reluctant to tell me what precisely happened."

"Oh," Amanda replied, surprised to discover that he was right again. "Well," she said in a rush, "we wandered into the library one afternoon in search of some books with bright pictures to copy out. Martha fancied herself an artist then. When we dragged out a huge, dusty volume from a high shelf, we discovered several identical volumes behind it. There were six of them at least, all gilt-edge, slim, green-calf-bound, expensive-looking little books. We picked one up to look at it and were amazed. They were profusely illustrated, with a picture facing each little poem—limerick actually—on every other page. The pictures were staggering to us—that is to say, they were unseemly, they . . . were to do with matters not usually illustrated," Amanda explained lamely.

"Pornographic, in short," the viscount said with laughter in his voice.

"Yes," Amanda said, relieved that she did not have to dredge up any more similes. "And we looked at them. No," she admitted fiercely, "we did not, we simply devoured them. When we saw that all the volumes were the same, Martha slipped one into her skirts and we tore upstairs to my rooms, bolted the door, and occupied ourselves with the book for hours."

Amanda looked up at her inquisitor defiantly then. But he only answered languidly, "If you were to show me a fifteen-year-old who would not do so, I should recommend him or her for canonization instantly."

She giggled at that, as though she were fifteen again, and went on a bit more confidently. "The pictures were amazing. We did not bother to read the book itself for several hours."

Amanda paused as she remembered how it had been. The room so warm (or had that been just from the flush upon her cheeks?), Martha and she stretched out upon her bed studying the illustrations. At first they had been too awed to see them aright, and then when they had done emitting their little shrieks and cries and false laughs and pummeling each other with pillows, they had gotten down to scrutinizing the details. Some were caricatures, some workmanlike, some quite well executed. They had decided at the last, though, that they all were a combination of truth and blatant lie. But now she only said, "We decided, at last, that they were exaggerated."

"Oh?" was all the reply she heard.

"That is to say," Amanda said, feeling her cheeks heating up again, as though the intervening eight years had never passed, "some of the drawings might well have been factual, but the majority of them were grossly exaggerated for effect. The females, you see, though crudely depicted, were within the realm of possibility, but the males . . . and some of the activities they were engaged in were clearly impossible because . . ."

But here Amanda's good sense returned and she left off, very dismayed at what she had almost said, lulled as she had been by the strange conversation, the late hour, and her ready listener. She could not, not even if the viscount sprouted a great pair of gossamer wings and a halo, say what she had been about to disclose. For what Martha had said actually, with all her five months' seniority for credence, was that the gentlemen could never really look so. Why, they would have to have special clothes made up to accommodate such clearly fraudulent appointments as they had been given, for they could never fit into everyday attire as they were depicted. They had then both soberly considered all the males of their acquaintance and had agreed, with much mutual relief, that such details that the artists had shown were patently ridiculous.

"It's a wonder," the viscount said in emotionless tones when she did not speak, "that the two of you didn't take yourselves off to a nunnery at once."

"Ah well, but we had surmised that all the illustrations in the entire book were similarly nonsensical," Amanda said reasonably.

"I see," the viscount replied in a stifled voice. "Do go on."

"After a while," Amanda said thoughtfully, her voice becoming rather low, "we tired of the illustrations and began to read some of the verses. We discovered from the introduction that the poems had been written as part of a contest dreamed up one night at a fashionable gentleman's club in London and had been privately printed as a joke."

"It's a common enough diversion when the brandy palls and there are no good wagers running," her listener commented.

"We took turns reading them, and those we understood were actually amusing. We didn't know half the names mentioned, though. For, you see, the book was written about all of the acquaintances of the gentlemen," Amanda said.

"I begin to understand," the viscount said as if to himself.

"First Martha read one, and then I read another," Amanda continued, surprised to note that her lips were trembling even now. "Then Martha began to read one and suddenly closed the book, looking quite conscious. I rallied her, taunted her in fact for her timidity. But she began to lecture me about what a shameful thing we were doing. When that did not stop me, she cried that she was bored with the entire project and made as if to throw the book into the fire. I flew at her, laughing, and snatched it from her hands. I began to read the poem and then I understood."

"It was, of course, about your mama," the viscount said softly.

"You read it?" Amanda asked, returning from that over-heated bedroom of the past to this cozy parlor.

"No, no," he said, "I only inferred as much."

"Well, it was," she said sadly. "I read it the once and then I did fling the book into the fire. I don't remember the poem now, but the illustration showed a line of remarkable gentlemen tarrying outside a ladies' chamber. No, that's not true," Amanda said brokenly. "They were doing rather more than that. And I do remember the last two lines at least. I have never been able to forget them." Amanda recited them woodenly now, speaking them aloud for the first time since she had read them all those years ago.

". . . But she told the gentleman it wasn't important, she'd just have another one for her assortment."

"At least it scans nicely," the viscount said, handing her

a large white handkerchief as she discovered to her astonishment that she was weeping. When she had left off
dabbing her face, he spoke again.

"Did you ever mention the incident to your mama?" he
asked.

"How could I?" Amanda asked in shock.

"I rather think you ought to have done," he mused. "But
no matter. Did you discuss it ever again with your good
friend Martha?"

"Oh no," she said matter-of-factly, having gotten herself
under control again, "for her father returned from the sea
the following year and married some lady he had been
corresponding with for years. She took Martha out of
school. And as she had been in the country and was, in
fact, quite social, Martha was never permitted to visit me
again. I did hear that she married some few years ago
herself."

"You certainly should discuss the book with her in that
case. Or at least the illustrations," the viscount said
obliquely.

"I always did wonder," Amanda said, suppressing a
yawn as the heat of the room and the effect of the liquor
was making her drowsy, "why Mama had so many copies
at hand."

"I expect that she had the duke buy them up so that
they could do the same thing with them that you did . . .
burn them. And knowing your mama, it's reasonable to
assume that she simply forgot where she had placed the
remaining volumes. I'm not keeping you awake, am I?" he
asked with mock affront.

"Oh no," Amanda said, "but you know, it is odd. It was
such a difficult thing for me to relate, and I had never
done so before. But now I've told the tale, I find it was not
such a dreadful thing after all. I feel much better about the
incident, in fact."

"A shared burden is always lighter," he said, rising.
"Lord, you make me sound, as well as feel, like a gray-
beard, Amanda. But I think it is time for you to sleep. We
must be up early tomorrow if we are to leave time for
Cousin Emily to consume our breakfasts and still reach a

comfortable inn by evening. I think we've achieved our purpose. I do know a great deal more about you now, and for what it is worth, you have presented me with an entirely new experience—embarrassment. For my own behavior, my lady, never yours," he added as she sat up sharply. "Now come along, let us allow our landlord to close up."

"But you have told me nothing of yourself," Amanda argued as she rose and went to the door with him.

"Why, there is little more to tell," he said gaily. "I am noble, I am generous, I am truthful, I am entirely honorable, just as you supposed."

He stood at the door with her and looked down at her. She bore a sleepy, tousled look, like a child newly awakened from dreams.

"Now, to bed," he said adamantly.

"Yes," she agreed, gazing up at him, "let us go to bed."

"Shocking stuff, Lady Amanda," he laughed. "How dare you suggest such a thing? How dare you attempt to sully my honor? It must be all that scandalous literature you read."

As he grumbled on about her attempt to smirch his honor, she giggled. He saw her to her door, and then bowed and left for his own room. She did not waken her maid to attend her, as she scarcely had time to draw off her dress and throw on her nightshift before sleep claimed her. He went slowly into his room and lay down upon his bed. He lay there a long while in unblinking concentration. For he had gotten to know his fiancée very well indeed, and he did not like the result at all.

VII

The morning came too soon to suit Amanda. She had wanted a bit of time to herself so she could sort out her feelings about her confessions to the viscount. But she had awakened late, with only enough time to spare to dress rapidly and join him and her chaperon at breakfast. While Miss Emily plowed steadily and soundlessly through a massive country breakfast, pausing in her consumption of it only to wipe her lips delicately now and again, Lord North chatted on about merry, inconsequential trivialities. His relaxed, amused attitude dispelled any doubts Amanda had harbored about her precipitous unveiling of those dark memories that she had felt would be so damning to her name and reputation. Rather than avoiding his gaze and fearing his judgment, she found herself instead very eager to continue the journey as well as any conversation with him.

In that expectation, however, she was disappointed. When the time came to resume their journey and she and Miss Emily had settled themselves in the lead carriage, the viscount saluted them, closed the carriage door, and mounted his horse alone again. Since it was a lowering day, with thick gray clouds scuttling overhead, propelled by icy blasts of wind, Amanda worried that her narrative had given him such a distaste for her that he preferred to risk pneumonia rather than to continue to abide her company. But after a half hour's travel, in which she was only able to extract such information from Miss Emily as the conditions of her bed and the excellence of the breakfast, Amanda readily understood the viscount's reluctance to sit with them. Indeed, when Miss Emily, in a rare burst of conversational bravery, volunteered unbidden that the repast she had just partaken of was—dared she say it—delightful, Amanda found herself envying the solitude of Lord North, storm-tossed and wind-blown though he was.

That gentleman did not think himself an object of envy, however; neither did he enjoy the cutting wind and cold. But it was not Miss Emily's deadening presence that made him eschew transport within the warm carriage, no matter what his sham fiancée might imagine. She would have been, in fact, devastated to learn that her worst fears were founded on solid truth. For it was her own person that the viscount wished to avoid, and he would at this moment endure the bite of a blizzard's teeth, rather than hear one more syllable dropped from her own soft lips.

He had thought that he would get to know her at their stopover at the Fox and Grapes, and that he had. But he had imagined their method of acquaintance would be achieved in a more physical manner. He had accepted that she might not wish to bed him when he was an unknown thrust upon her by her impatient mama. If he had balked at such a deed, he could certainly understand her doing so. Similarly, he understood very well that she might not wish to marry him, especially if she were aiming for another's declaration as well as feeling coerced. But he had been genuinely staggered to discover that she was an innocent, and fully as circumspect as any properly brought-up young female.

It was not often that he misjudged a woman, and the thought of it gnawed at him. She was obviously no chit straight from the schoolroom, she had seemed up to all the rigs. She was bright and lovely. He had thought she was, inescapably, her mother's daughter. It was clear from her reactions to him that she was well aware of him, and she had seemed to be playing the game just the way she ought, in just the way that most delighted him. She had gazed at him when he wasn't looking, had dropped her lashes over her large gray eyes when he turned to return her interested stare. She had sat close to him while they composed that ridiculous letter, letting her curls brush against his cheek, while appearing to be heedlessly letting other parts of her enchanting person brush against him as well. Her spicy perfume had filled his nostrils, as she laughed appreciatively at sallies that were too warm for conventional misses. And all of this, it transpired, instead of being the coy prelude to the bliss he had imagined, had been unknowing acts of friendship.

Lord North shook his head, as though to throw off the first flakes of snow that had settled upon his cheeks. She had not been provocative, she had merely been candid. There was no doubt of that now in his mind. He had been able to fill in most of the gaps in her narration, and no experienced female could have told her tale the way that she had done. Though the story had begun by titillating him enormously, it had ended with his realization of the fact that she had not planned that effect. Bizarre as it might be, he had come to the incredible but inescapable conclusion that the Countess of Clovelly's eldest daughter was as pure as the snow that was now driving into his face.

He shrugged, dislodging some of the flakes that had covered his shoulders. His mistake was explicable, he supposed, only because it had been so many years since he had any dealings with unworldly misses that they were as exotic a breed to him as unicorns were. And that was why he rode on alone and safely apart from her, pondering what his future course of action should be toward her, rather than taking refuge in the warm carriage.

It was not that he was sulking over her refusal of his intimate attentions, for he was experienced enough to take rejection philosophically, and seldom personally. But then, he seldom encountered refusal. He was not a vain fellow, but he would have had to have been a deaf and dumb one not to have long since realized the effect he had upon persons of Amanda's gender. And unlike most beautiful men, he was a skillful lover, well able to attach a female beyond the stages of first attraction. Too often beautiful specimens of both sexes thought it enough to simply present their splendid selves in a state of readiness to their admirers in order to bring about blissful mutual satisfaction.

The viscount, for all his famous physical attributes, knew better. Amanda herself had reminded him that he had learned the truth in a very hard school.

He had been eighteen and home from school on a vacation, at loose ends just as Amanda and her curious friend Martha had been when they discovered their educational volume, and almost as naive as they were, when he had discovered a good deal more explicit compendium of sexual information. All of it had been encompassed in the one compact shape of Helena Burnham's ripe person. Squire Burnham was a near neighbor and young Christian Jarrow had noted his wife's blond beauty from afar for most of his green years. Yet, for all of a young man's arrogance, he still would never have dared to include Helena in any of his fevered dreams of future conquest, as she was a friend of his parents. Although she was a decade younger than his own mama, he was at an age that considered any beings above the age of consent to be teetering upon the brink of eternity. In fact, he recalled now as he rode forward in the snow, and backward in his musings, he had even called her "Mrs. Burnham" the first time he lay in her arms.

He had arrived in those smooth bonds speedily enough, though through no efforts of his own. He had encountered her while out riding. He had accepted an invitation to tea politely, though privately dreading the idea of a nice long coze with one of his parents' contemporaries as only a lad of his age could have done. But he had instead surprised himself by ending up upon her silken sheets and body before a proper tea had had time to brew. Her husband had been away, the servants were trained to her command, and the seduction was effortlessly accomplished.

Although, he thought now with the accumulated wisdom of over a decade's experience, the only task more difficult than seducing a lad of eighteen might be that of breathing in and out, still she had been adept. She had soothed his fears by expressing her need for him, and quelled his conscience by telling of her husband's inabilities. In the main, she had prevailed through the sheer rapidity and expertise of her assault. He left her home dazzled and more delighted than even Cousin Emily could have expressed. He had known that such encounters might be pleasurable; indeed, at eighteen he had thought of little else. But aside from a few unsatisfactory embraces with serving girls, he had not yet accomplished his goals for further education in that area. Helena Burnham taught him what a truly overwhelming experience such sport could provide. Aside from the genuine joy derived from his encounter, he rode homeward feeling omnipotent, whole, and totally a man at last. He grinned now at the thought of how very young he had been.

Yet, even as his visits to her increased at her demand, he discovered his belief in himself shaken by her demands. At first she required only his cooperation, which was then all that he could give to her. But she soon began to require him to attain more polish. As the summer dragged on, she drilled him in the arts of love as a stern nanny might train a toddler in the art of table manners. The young Christian Jarrow had been by turns abashed at his lack of skill, appalled at some of the lessons, ashamed of his reluctance to apply himself, and finally resolved to do better.

He had been glad of a consuming interest away from home and willingly became her apprentice. Long July twilights were passed tracing her lush curves with the focused intent of a navigator studying complex charts of strange sea lanes, whole drowsy August afternoons elapsed as he labored to cull each last secret from her well memorized body. If he wondered at her husband's convenient absence or at her tutorial skills, the issues were soon forgotten in the narcotic haze of the wonder of her lessons. They spent the summer together, locked every stolen moment in mute and concentrated effort.

It was on a late August afternoon, while preparing for a tryst, that he noted he had retied his cravat six times because of his shaking fingers. He had dropped his hands and gazed into space. He was, he realized, facing an amorous encounter with anxiety and stomach-churning dread. He discovered himself suddenly no more eager to embrace her than he was to have a tooth drawn. Visions of her stretched out upon her bed brought equal parts of arousal and apprehension, and he knew that he could predict her future sighs of contentment as surely as he could foretell her terse, strained orders of command. At once, he saw that, for him at least, desire had coupled with duty. She had become, at last, a chore.

He had been many things in his brief span, but never insensitive to the feelings of others. He was puzzled that this discovery of distaste and an ache to be free of his lover should be a relief untainted by guilt or sentiment. But even at the age of eighteen he had come to the understanding that they had no thing to bind them together beyond the adhesive of physical desire. They had no laughter to bind up lapses, no mutual sympathy to gloss over mistakes, no conversation to fill up resting spaces, no affection to spur on desire past repletion. He strove to acquit himself well, she strove to teach him to please her, and that was the sum of their relationship. It was both not enough and far too much for him.

He completed his toilet speedily that evening, suddenly all haste to keep his appointment with her and, by meeting with her, end their meetings forever.

She evidently had not expected him so soon. She obviously had not expected the malice of her servants. But after the oddly sympathetic butler had shown him into a parlor to await his mistress's pleasure, he could clearly hear the conversation she was having with her husband in the adjacent room through a conveniently carelessly open door. It was a revelation to him to hear his abilities being discussed frankly in dispassionate detail. It was almost as though he had eavesdropped on two of his dons debating whether or not he was to have a passing grade in a difficult course of study. Squire Burnham clearly derived as much pleasure from the telling of his wife's experiences as she did from the having of them.

He was, at least, pleased to hear that he had done well. Better, in fact, than young Graham, their steward's son, had done the previous spring. It was flattering to know that she found his performance matched his appearance. But it was decidedly unpleasant to learn of their byzantine plans for his further enjoyment and enlightenment. When he appeared in the doorway, they broke off at once, and turned to him in guilty amazement, like footpads caught squabbling over the contents of a corpse's purse. He bade them good evening, told them he was afraid that he had pressing engagements that made his visit impossible to extend, bowed, and left them there almost as astonished as he was by his aplomb.

Although he deliberately avoided both Burnhams scrupulously on every subsequent visit home, as the years passed he discovered that he was grateful to them. He was enormously successful with women, for he had learned a great deal from his eighteenth summer. He never pursued a married lady again, no matter how delicious she might appear to be, but that was advantageous only to his fellow man. Most beneficial to his own well-being, he had learned that the arts of love were intricate and important, but useless to employ without some vestige at least of fellow feeling between the participants. Though he did not consider himself remotely moral, he shrank from ever using any individual for his own needs as he had been used. So he could easily understand Amanda's anger at his intentions for their evening's entertainment. If she were not so inclined, it would be unthinkable for him to harass her to join him.

The viscount frowned now, and not because of the steadily falling snow. He had offered the chit his support partially because he found her desirable and had thought they might have an amusing time of it together for so long as their bogus betrothal lasted. Now he found himself in the unpleasant situation of entertaining fully as charming and amiable a companion as he could have wished, but one who was unexpectedly chaste as well. He was like a man who had acquired a thirst for a vintage wine he could not afford. Yet he could not place blame upon her for deceiving him, nor even any upon himself for self-deception. It was a maddening business.

When the snow had powdered his hair enough to make him resemble some exquisite fop from a long vanished court, he shook his head to clear it within and without. Though she was blameless, he could not repress a surge of impatience with her. But as it was growing cold enough to turn his thoughts from his dilemma to his comforts again, he prepared to leave off his solitary introspection and face her again. He would help to write such compelling letters to her damned doubting Giles, he determined, that he would soon have her off his hands. Yet, he reminded himself lightly as he signaled the coachman to halt so that he could effect entry into warmer precincts, it might yet be true that blood would tell. And if by some happy chance, the viscount decided as he greeted his cousin and his fiancée with a broad grin, all that dubious Giles feared were to materialize, and the young Lady Amanda's heritage should manifest itself at last, why then, he would be please to accommodate her and help her to fulfill her destiny.

No matter what his intentions, the viscount did not have a great deal of time to tarry in light conversation within the snug confines of the carriage. It was not long before the coachman staged an unscheduled halt to their journey to have conference as to the advisability of traveling much further onward in the snow. The sloping hills of the lake district were scenic enough in summer, but treacherous when coated with the rimes of winter. The driver of the lead coach swore on his forty years of man and boy that the snowfall would not last, even as the handler of the second coach maintained that his four and fifty years of experience, along with his aching bones, told him that their world would be white wilderness by evening.

The viscount, fearing that they all would freeze to death while the argument raged on, settled matters by declaring they would stop at once at the King's Arms a few miles further along the pike rather than pushing on to their scheduled accommodations. The hostelry, he confided to the ladies, while never so fine as the Fox and Grapes, would at least provide shelter and food for the wayfarers.

It provided little else, Amanda sighed, that evening at dinner. Only Miss Emily seemed to be making any headway with the stringy roast, and not even she could swallow the vinegar that passed for wine.

There was no uncomfortable reminscence before the fire that night. Nor was there any comfortable chat either.

The fireplace in the private parlor gave off foul exhalations of black smoke whenever the wind changed, which it did with frequency. It was small consolation to the travelers that the winds now did little more than toy with the snow that had ceased to fall, for they were committed to stay the night. It was then as much to avoid Miss Emily's constant gentle lamentations over their faulty decision to stop at such an insalubrious place as it was to escape the stifling puffs of wood smoke, that both Amanda and her fiancé resolved to retire early. Despite her icy bed and a breakfast fit only for livestock, however, Amanda had cause to be grateful for the viscount's decision. Because of their unscheduled stop and even earlier departure, when she came at last to Windham House, it was a shining morning.

She would always, she thought, remember the house as it was in that first moment that she saw it. Windham House stood high on a gentle hill and as the trees around it were bare, she could see its entire face with its myriad windows glittering like bits of ice in the dazzling light. The house was old, and as each succeeding generation had indulged its whims upon its form, it now rose high and stretched wide, the only unifying thing about it the soft golden hue of its stone facade. Beyond and behind, the absence of foliage permitted the viewer to see the brilliant blue of the long lake the house's terraced grounds rambled down to meet.

Amanda did not even hear Miss Emily's excited prattle as the viscount assisted her from the coach. She walked bemused as he led her through the doors of his home. She said nothing as she surrendered her wraps to a footman and followed her host to a high-ceilinged salon. While Miss Emily nattered on, the viscount stayed silent as well, watching Amanda as she stood and gazed out the long windows, looking out over the wide lake to the gray and purple mountains in the distance. When she tore her rapt gaze from the scenery and looked around herself with an expression of awe, he thought her enthralled by the spectacular scenery.

But he could never have guessed at her thoughts. For as she stood and took in her surroundings, she thought that

she might have known that such a unique man would have
sprung from such a magical place. The room, she thought,
the entire bright house, was the perfect setting for its
master. This house, his home, was equally as much an
idiosyncratic blend of sunlight and grace as he himself was.
It was as though his heritage had given him his own
unique facade. The hues of the lake were reflected in his
odd eyes, his flaxen hair was like the glint of sunlight
upon its changing waters. As he was a creature com-
pounded of light and air, so was Windham House. Never
had she seen or imagined such a perfect blending, such a
sympathetic aspect of dwelling and resident spirit.

Miss Emily kept reassuring them that their hostess would
be along presently, and Amanda sat on the edge of a
chair to await her entrance. The viscount, however, seemed
restless, and he wandered from table to window to mantel,
like a mote of golden light trapped within the sparkling
room. Amanda was so anxious about how she would be
received that when a person she took to be the housekeeper
entered the room, she stood at once. She was glad she had
done so when Miss Emily cried out, "Oh, Augusta, how
good to see you again."

As Amanda tried to hide her surprise, Miss Emily went
on to congratulate her hostess on how well she looked, and
to inform her of how pleasant a journey it had been.
Amanda was grateful for the steady flow of meaningless
compliments and tedious detail of their travels, for she
never would have guessed that this woman was the Viscountess North and might have only greeted her and asked
which room she should repair to if she had not been told of
her identity.

The Viscountess North stood rooted to the spot as Miss
Emily talked, and though she seemed to attend to what
was being said, her eyes sought her son, who gave a
helpless shrug along with a wry smile of greeting, and then
she looked quickly at Amanda and then quickly away
again. She was a short, solidly made female, of a height with
Amanda's own mama, but lacking that lady's pleasant
configurations. She also possessed some decades' more years
than the countess counted. Her hair might have been black

in youth, but now was mottled with gray. Her face was lined and broad, olive-skinned with thick brows above alert dark black eyes. She made no concession to fashion and wore a simple heavy purple garment, partially covered with a beige fringed shawl. Lord North, Amanda thought, must have taken after his father's side of the family, for there was no feature of the viscountess's that could translate to her son's appearance.

When Miss Emily paused for breath, Lord North took advantage of the lapse in conversation and went to his mother's side.

"Mama," he said softly, raising her hand to bow over it, "behold the prodigal son."

Before she could greet him, he went on smoothly, "It is obvious that you have not received my letter. May I present to you then my fiancée, whom I have brought to visit with us? Yes, it is true. I have been nabbed at last. I do not know if word of mouth travels faster than my poor missive, but I assure you that it is the talk of the town. I returned from the continent, stopped off for a space at my dear friend the Countess of Clovelly's charming abode, and there I met and lost my heart to this dear lady."

Lord North came to Amanda's side, took her hand, and brought her face to face with the viscountess. That lady stood stock-still, expressionless, as her son continued.

"And here is the young woman who captured my heart in one blinding assault upon it. Can you blame me for my precipitous action? Her face, her form, her person are all that one could wish for in a wife. How could I bear to wait upon events? I had to act with haste. May I present my lady, Lady Amanda Amberly."

Amanda was so close to the viscountess that she could perceive her slightest expression. But the change Lord North's words brought upon his mama's controlled countenance was not difficult to ascertain even from afar. Unmistakably, Amanda saw the lady wince.

VIII

There is a suitable time of day for every human purpose. The glare of full sunlight is best reserved for those acts of decency, honor, and valor. Most clandestine meetings are better left to be carried out in the dark of night, and twilight is an excellent time for romance. There is a good cause for this division of activity. It is easier to plan deeds of secrecy or commit acts requiring fantasy when there is some difficulty reading one's companion's face clearly. It is no coincidence then that sermons are best given on Sunday mornings and that actors prefer the inconstant flickering flare of footlights in which to create their illusions. Therefore, it was unfortunate, Amanda was to think many times later, that the viscount chose the sunniest spot in the brilliantly lit room in which to tell his mama of his fiancée's identity.

But her governess had the right of it, Amanda thought sadly, as she stood dumbly and waited for the viscountess to acknowledge her existence, breeding will tell. For if in one moment, her fiancé's mama looked so ill at the announcement of her son's betrothal that her dark face became several shades lighter and her lips compressed to a thin line, within the passage of two heartbeats the lady had erased the fleeting expression of pain. She soon was in control again and even in the unrelenting light her expression was unreadable. It was well that the viscountess had such great powers of recovery, Amanda thought, for she herself cringed at Lord North's next careless words.

"Yes, just so, Mama. The dear countess's own daughter.

How singularly convenient for me, don't you agree? But come, aren't you going to wish us happy?" he asked sweetly.

The viscountess put out a blunt little hand and took Amanda's.

"I am pleased to meet you, Lady Amanda," she said in a low, emotionless voice, "and hope that you find Windham House most comfortable."

While Amanda was glad that she hadn't been subjected to false cries of happiness, the patently artificial smile that the lady now wore made her sick to the heart. She was tempted to cry out, "It's none of it true, he is safe from me," but found that she could only take the older woman's hand and shake it politely.

The viscountess seemed about to speak again, but whatever she might have said was lost when a hearty voice cut through her hesitant beginning words. A stocky young man bustled into the room and headed directly for Lord North.

"Chris!" he shouted, and then tumbled upon the viscount, hugging him and pummeling him upon the back, while saying in a loud and happy voice, "Chris, you devil. How good it is to have you back!"

The young man was a head shorter than the viscount, but almost twice as broad. Although not fat, he was compact and seemed to be of hearty stock, resembling a smith or yeoman farmer rather than the gentleman his neat clothing denoted. When he turned his attention from Lord North to look at Amanda, she could see his resemblance to the viscountess was so singular as to be almost caricatured. His complexion was swarthier as he seemed to have been tanned from the sun, but his broad face, jet hair, and dark eyes marked him as her descendant as surely as if she had decided to manufacture a masculine replica of herself.

"And here's the pretty lady, eh?" the young gentleman cried. "Make me known to her at once, Chris, so I can buss her soundly. I won't have another chance till the wedding, I vow. For I don't want you coming to cuffs with me. When I heard the news—we had it from Boggins, you know, the fellow takes all the London papers, not like us rustics—I thought I would burst with impatience till I saw her. I know she'd have to be a stunner to nobble such a care-for-nothing as you. And so she is, Chris, so she is."

The young man stood, hands linked behind himself, rocking back and forth upon his heels, smiling hugely.

"Amanda, let me make you known to my mannerless bother of a brother, Gilbert, for he won't leave off talking until I do. Gil, my impetuous friend, this is Lady Amanda Amberly, my intended wife."

Amanda found herself engulfed in a bearlike embrace just as Lord North had been, even down to the detail of being thumped soundly upon the back as well, as Gilbert chortled in her ear, "Delightful. Lovely. Chris has found himself a charmer, all right and tight."

"Leave off, Gilbert, do," Lord North said languidly, "or the poor lady will not survive until her wedding day. She's not used to such enthusiasm."

Gilbert released her reluctantly.

"Very well, Chris. She's yours to command, but what sort of welcome is this, Mama?" he demanded. "Break out the champagne, let's have a toast. Chris, you must tell me what you've been doing these last years, aside from winning yourself such a prize. Are you going to take up residence here at last? Or are you going to hop off about the world again with poor Amanda in tow? And did you really meet with Bonaparte? What was Vienna like?"

As all these questions were asked imperatively, with appropriate changes of expression for each, Amanda was relieved that she could giggle under cover of Lord North's genuine laughter.

"Have done, Gilbert. We'll have time enough to talk. For now, aren't you going to feed us? For we've had to make a stopover at the King's Arms, and we're dwindling to skeletons after being treated to their fare."

As Gilbert made an outsize grimace of distaste, his mother spoke quietly, "Of course, Christian. In fact, I was about to ask that you join us for luncheon. Perhaps, Lady Amanda, you will want to go to your room to change? And Emily, I'll have your usual room prepared."

*   *   *

Luncheon was lavish, and Amanda was relieved to discover that between Gilbert's constant questioning of his brother and Miss Emily's rambling discourse on their journey with her hostess, she herself was required to contribute little to the conversation. Things had gone more smoothly than she could have hoped. Her hostess was polite, no pointed questions had been asked, her room was cheerful and pleasantly appointed, nothing could have been more congenial than this family meal. Yet still, she could not shake her feelings of disquiet.

She turned her attention to her plate, telling herself that if she looked for unpleasantness, she would surely find it. Gilbert continued to quiz his brother, and she realized as she listened to them that she was learning a great deal about the viscount that she had never thought to ask, or ever thought she had the right to ask. She had not known the extent to which he had traveled or the many famous persons he had encountered and called friend. When Gilbert saw that his questions had her attention as well, he left off his inquisition of his brother long enough for that gentleman to attend to his soup.

"He thinks he's such a sly boots," Gilbert said with enthusiasm, "but just think of the places he has visited, Amanda. Paris, Venice, Vienna, and Elba itself. He cannot pull the wool over my eyes; he was in His Majesty's service unless I miss my guess. What I wouldn't have given to have been there, but I doubt I could have kept my mission secret, I haven't the knack for deception he's got."

"For your somewhat skewed compliment, I thank you," his brother drawled, laying down his spoon. "But though I dislike puncturing your bubble, old fellow, I beg you to think on how successful a spy a fellow with my rather distinctive phiz could be. Can you not just hear one agent whispering to another, 'Oh yes, North has the plans, he's the fellow with the pied eyes and the yellow hair.' No, Gilbert, I'd make too fine a target for army service and far too noticeable a one for any havey-cavey business with cloaks and daggers."

"As you say," Gilbert replied gaily, laying a finger aside his nose and winking hugely at Amanda.

If the viscount was uncomfortable with the topic, it was not apparent, but as he swiftly and adroitly turned the subject to the party where he had met Amanda, she wondered if his brother had not indeed hit upon a clue to his wanderings about on the face of the continent. She did not refine upon it too much for she was soon too fixed in her embarrassment at the tale he told. As he described her mama's house party to his avid listener, Gilbert, Amanda became aware that as Miss Emily attacked her repast in silent concentration, her hostess was now listening carefully to his discourse as well.

"Oh yes," the viscount carelessly continued to answer to his brother's queries, helping himself to a cut of lamb, "the Marquess of Bessacarr was there as well, but only for the one night of the engagement ball. He's far too slippery a fellow to linger longer. But Baron Hightower was there, as you'd expect, as well as the vicar, the lords Skyler and Jeffrey and their set, Prendergast and his latest female, Melissa Careaux, Julia Johnson and her cronies, a few fillies from the opera, Hartford, Barrymore, Cumberland, the lords Lambert, Hunt, and Lawrence, and Count Voronov. Oh, masses of people. Have I left anyone out, my dear?" he asked Amanda.

As she sat, too mortified to speak, for he had just named some of the most notorious rakes, roués and lightskirts in the land, he went on blithely, "I must have. There were hundreds, Gil, hundreds there to celebrate our betrothal. Suffice it to say, almost everyone that I know was there."

From the grim set of the viscountess's lips, Amanda knew that lady was well aware of the nature of each of the guests her son had named. Surely, Amanda thought, the viscount perceived that fact as well, but he continued to speak in just as easy a fashion.

"Oh, the Dowager Duchess of Crewe was not there. Pity, for she and her companions do liven a party. But I hear that she's planning to go to Paris, and doubtless her preparations for the journey accounted for her missing out on such a gala. But almost all of them are to be off for a jaunt on the continent soon. I question their judgment. From what I saw of Bonaparte, I should think there's a dance left in the old boy yet. But luckily, most of my other acquaintances were still in town and able to come to us for the festivities. How delightful it was," he mused, while his brother sat red-faced. It was not from embarrassment upon his part, but Amanda could not know that. It was only that there were several other questions he yearned to ask, but knew were improper to broach among the ladies. In fact, he wondered if some of the mere names his brother had stated were proper to mention in his mother's presence. He quickly brought up the topic of estate matters that he believed the viscount had not been informed of by their agent in their usual exchanges of letters and the conversation went forth easily once more.

The only other uncomfortable moment during the luncheon was for Gilbert alone, when the viscount inquired sweetly, at the one moment when his brother had put so much cutlet into his mouth that he had to pause in his steady stream of questioning, "Not that I'm not ecstatic at seeing you, dear boy, but oughtn't you be up at school now?"

Amanda was equally as taken aback as Gilbert at the question. For though the gentleman was clearly youthful, there was so much in his manner of hearty, bluff country squire that she had forgotten that he was indeed still of an age to require schooling.

"Deuce take it, Chris," Gilbert answered when he was able to both frame the words and swallow his morsel, "I thought you knew. Well, the sum of it is that the university and I agreed to part company. That is to say, fiend seize it, Chris, I ain't no scholar and never will be. Mama agrees, and even Papa said as much when I was a tyke. You're the astute one in the family, Chris, and a lucky thing that one of us is, at that. I've no head for Greek or Latin. I help to run the estates now, you know, and I've a flair for it," he said defensively.

"We'll discuss it later," the viscount promised coolly, as his mama sat up stiffly and his brother squirmed.

But clearly, no one thing could depress Gilbert's spirits for too long, and the luncheon continued as he dominated the conversation with his constant questioning of his brother.

When the last dish had been cleared, the viscountess rose. "I think we ought to allow Lady Amanda to become acquainted with Windham House," she began to say, when Gilbert leaped to his feet and cried with approval,

"The very thing! Come, Amanda, I'll show you around the place."

"I think," the viscountess continued, as though she had not been interrupted, "that Christian should do so."

"An excellent suggestion, Mama," Lord North said with equal coolness. "Gilbert, we'll speak later, but as her fiancé, I do think I should have the honor of introducing my lady to our house."

At Gilbert's totally crestfallen aspect, the viscount continued more gently, "You shall, no doubt, grow to know her even better than I do now, for I can't think how anyone can resist your exuberance. But I can't risk having you steal her out from under my nose on her very first day with us, can I?"

As Gilbert protested his innocence in the matter of attempting to turn the affections of beautiful young affianced females, albeit with a gratified flush at the compliment upon his cheeks, Lord North went to Amanda and offered her his arm.

"Shall we take a tour, my lady?" he asked quietly, but with such underlying meaning larded into those few simple words that Amanda nodded and took his arm at once.

But she thought later, she had misread him, for there was no undercurrent of double meaning in his conversation as they strolled through the house, nor did he ever attempt to take her aside for any private conversation. He greeted the household staff cordially, and took the congratulations of cook, housekeeper, butler, and maids with the same pleased containment as they wandered through the rooms. He was at ease with them as if he had been gone only a day. But Amanda could see from their wide smiles and shining eyes that he was genuinely and warmly welcomed back to his home.

He led her through the entire house, pausing only to point out interesting or historical data as they toured. They went from wine cellar to kitchens, from state bedrooms to ballroom, with his knowledgeable commentary given in as detached and informative a fashion as any paid tour guide at the London tower.

When they had seen almost the whole of the house, and Amanda was dizzy with wonder, and hoarse with exclaiming over the beauty of the red salon or the orangery or the Chinese room or the music room, he at last paused.

"Shall we go outside?" he asked, as though to himself. "Ah no, for there is still a great deal of snow underfoot and I notice you have no pattens. I doubt my Wellington's would fit you, and I hesitate to waken your hostess from her afternoon nap to borrow hers. We shall have to leave the maze and the rose gardens for another day. I think then," he said as though the idea had just occurred to him and amused him deeply, "that I will show you to the portrait gallery. I know," he went on as he led her out of the conservatory to a long gallery lined with alternate mirrors and portraits, "that such a gallery ought to be viewed at night with the aid of a flickering taper, for dramatic emphasis. But we shall have to make do with afternoon light."

The gallery was situated in the very heart of the house, constructed parallel to so many of the rooms they had visited that Amanda was surprised that they had not happened upon it before. It seemed to her that he had deliberately saved it for last, avoiding it until their tour around the rest of the house had been completed.

There were no dark or gloomy chambers in all of Windham House. It was as if each person who had dwelt there had loved the land so much that they insisted their house open its eyes constantly to the beauty that surrounded it. Every room had windows either facing the landscape, or cantilevered so as to admit the light from every angle and direction. But even so, the force of the light in the narrow hall was so strong as to hurt the eye, for the row of mirrors threw back the afternoon sunlight in almost blinding fashion.

"This passage is the result of some ancestor's attempt to bring Versailles to the lake district," Lord North said on a smile. "Our squint lines pay the price of his ambition. The family, at least, does not hang in some deserted, musty, forgotten hallway. I find it a bit overwhelming, but they must approve of their condition, for we never have had so much as one disgruntled spirit prowling about disturbing our slumbers demanding further shade."

Amanda left his side and slowly paced the gallery, scrutinizing each portrait. There were gentlemen in ruffs, powder, and patch with their ladies in opulent dresses, ball gowns, and morning robes. There were faces from every past period of history, in every condition and stage of life. Haughty faces, delicate poetical visages, happy and thoughtful studies, proud and shy subjects; the rows of ladies and gentlemen, with their infants and lap dogs, stared out of the canvases at the lake and grounds around them.

Lord North watched as Amanda sought something from each encounter with the ancestrial portraits.

"The title," he commented as he walked along with her, "came late. It wasn't till James sat upon the throne that we could boast a viscountcy. There, that's the fortunate fellow who won it for us, the chap all in mustard yellow and flounces. He was thick as thieves with our royal highness and I shudder to think what price he paid for the honors. But there were Jarrows here upon this site, I imagine, from the beginning. I expect there were some hiding in the marshes, painted blue, and muttering darkly as the Romans first came marching across the land. It is a pity that none of the druids were handy with a brush and palette, isn't it?"

Amanda scarcely attended him. She had been gazing at each representative of his family attempting to find a match with his own unique visage. There were some gentlemen with his light musculature, a few of both genders with fair hair, but no face with his eyes, nor any with his crown of dandelion hair. As if he had overheard her thoughts, he said, from close by her elbow, "No, you won't have the distinctive thrill of seeing me, or what appears to be me, decked out in the costume of an earlier era. I know that's the staple stuff of eerie romantic novels, but as we lack ghosts, alas, so I must deny you that treat as well. But you should have expected that."

She turned to him in puzzlement but he went on, "This

last fellow here is the last viscount, fittingly enough. I came into the title when I was twenty and have never had the leisure nor the inclination to pose for any portrait. But here is his lady wife as well. Gilbert will doubtless hang beside them with the rest, 'ere long, that is, if anyone can get him to sit still long enough."

The viscountess, Amanda noted, had never been fashionable, not even in her youth when the portrait had been executed, and the artist had wisely not attempted to make her so. The portrait showed her sitting serene and dignified, her black hair about her shoulders, her figure even then wisely concealed beneath a great many folds of apricot fabric. But it was while she was looking at the painting of the gentleman Lord North had designated his father that Amanda began unwittingly to frown. The gentleman was slim, tall, and lightly made. But his hair was a light brown and in the clear light of the outdoors that he had been posed against, she could see, by peering into the picture, that his eyes were a deep chocolate brown.

Lord North had been observing Amanda's face as closely as she had scrutinized the portrait.

"Didn't you know?" he asked suddenly, in a strangely altered voice. She tore her gaze from the portrait and looked at him questioningly. He stood before her now, blotting out the sun.

"No?" he asked tauntingly. "No, I should have guessed as much. It's all of a piece, isn't it? Lady Clovelly's daughter is indeed nothing like her mother or her mother's boon companions. Then it is well that I took you for this little tour today."

He lowered his voice and looked down at her with something very much like cold anger in his gaze.

"Have you no ears, child?" he demanded. "Do you hear no evil as well as never seeing or doing it? Dear Amanda, why did you think your estimable mother was so quick to bundle me into your bed? Why me, of all the light lads she entertains? And why, little Amanda, did you think all our well-wishers were quick to cry, 'How suitable!' 'How perfect!' and comment upon how well matched we were? Did you never ponder it?"

Amanda could only shake her head. She could not understand his bitter mockery, for his face was as chill and composed as that of any painted portrait upon the wall, and his voice was heavy with sarcasm.

She looked at him in alarm, as he seemed so furious with her. She did recall random tatters of gossip about him that had come to her ears, but they were only bits and pieces of talk that she had forgotten, or caused herself to forget after they had made their plans. She knew he was said to be profligate, immoral, and abandoned. She had refused to countenance a true alliance with him for that reason. And as all the members of his wild set had a nickname, she also knew that he was referred to jestingly as "The Vice-Count North." But although she now had a glimmering of a dreadful idea, she still dared not imagine what he was implying, not here with him staring at her as though into her very mind.

She stood before him, twisting her hands in the folds of her azure skirts, her huge tilted eyes blank with dread, her curly head raised to meet his gaze. She seemed to him like some fragile sprite pinioned by the shafts of sunlight as she awaited his next words. He found himself perversely growing even angrier as he realized that in this, too, he had misjudged her.

"Why it's a delicious bit of tattle, Lady Amanda," he said savagely, "this business of our engagement. One of the Amberly Assortment to wed the base Lord North. Exquisite irony. You have totally missed the joy of it. It was there in my mama's face, and if you had tried, you could have certainly read it in Gilbert's open countenance. It is here for you to see, Amanda, only open those great gray eyes of yours to look at it."

He swept his hand to encompass the whole of the passage, then he took her tousled head between his two hands to hold her fast and look down into her apprehensive eyes.

"Amanda, my dear fiancée," he said with a twisted smile, "my reputation is based on more than mere rumor. You ought to have paid attention to those rumors instead of holding yourself above them, for they are nothing but the truth. I can see now that you know it, but you dare not voice it. Yes, I am one of those unfortunates we were discussing so amiably the other night. One of those you were so quick to disassociate yourself from. Twice you denied it, I believe. But I admit it. I am one of those chaps from your little picture book. I am a by-blow, sweet, a fellow from the wrong side of the blanket, a child of the mist. No, as I am a viscount, I expect I am rather higher than that, I am a lord of the mist. And all the world knows it but you. That is the great jest we've all shared. Amanda, my dear, don't shrink from me, for I am already like a member of your famous family," he said caressingly now, as he lowered his head. "Dear 'Manda, I am a bastard," he whispered against her lips.

IX

The study had a large bow window which presented a fine view of the lake and the mountains in the distance. Since the lady seated at the rosewood desk paused, pen in hand, while she gazed out at the few birds that wheeled and spun in the distance, a viewer could be forgiven if he guessed her a poetess waiting patiently for inspiration to strike from the blue. As the young woman also wore an abstracted air, while her petal-pink gown bore spatters of ink and almost a sheaf of papers lay crumpled about her, one might also have concluded that her muse was not in a cooperative mood.

Amanda at last turned her head resolutely from the bright winter prospect and set her pen to paper again. For all her morning's labors, the letter to Giles had only progressed to a total of two pages and there was more, so much more she wanted to include. But she could not write the simple two lines that would have said it all and had instead to couch those plain phrases in so much roundabout that she was only half done with her chore. She found herself wishing that she had the sort of bond of communion with Giles that could have enabled her to merely write: "I have made a dreadful mistake. Please come and fetch me home immediately. All my love, Amanda."

She sighed so heavily the piece of paper she was writing upon stirred beneath her hand. It was so much simpler for her to simply say a thing directly rather than to attempt all this subterfuge. That night at the Fox and Grapes, Lord North had written an excellent letter with ease. But then, she thought, frowning at the very idea of her mock fiancé, hidden meanings and deceptive wordings seemed to come to him as naturally as breathing. So it was that the words that intruded upon the silence exactly matched her unspoken complaints.

"Wouldn't it be simpler and less time-consuming to simply scrawl 'Help!' in huge letters, sign the thing in tears, and post it to Giles immediately?" Lord North said, as he strolled into the room and over to her desk. "But that, alas, would most likely cause the poor fellow to run for cover thinking you'd lost your wits entirely. It's clear you need my assistance, for you haven't the least knack for deception. You've been mewed up in here for hours and all you've done is to create enough kindling to keep the fire blazing merrily for the rest of the afternoon. I waited patiently for your summons. And when you didn't emerge, I began to entertain the nervous notion that you'd hung yourself from a convenient rafter. So pleased to see that you're not in that much distress," he added, smiling down at her as he picked up one completed sheet of paper.

"I scratched upon the door, and rapped it soundly when you didn't answer," he explained. "But I see now that you were simply too deep in the throes of creation, not self-destruction, to attend to me. Let me see what you've accomplished," he said, ignoring her glare as he began to read what she had written.

Amanda ran her ink-stained fingers through her hair and then daubed unsuccessfully at her dress as he perused her letter. Though he wore neat country garb, buff breeches, high boots, and a fawn jacket, he looked so immaculate that he made her feel a drab.

" 'Windham House is a delightful home!' I see that association with Cousin Emily has affected your speech to its detriment," he commented. "But 'beautifully situated' is nicely put. There is a great deal here about mountains, lakes, and views, Amanda; the letter smacks more of a travel brochure than a billet doux. It isn't till we are done with all the geographical detail, here at the bottom of the page, that we come to some little hint of personal distress. And 'Though the viscountess is amiable, I cannot help but think she entertains some of the same doubts that I myself have been occupied with,' is rather tame stuff, isn't it? Come, Amanda, Giles cannot be such a complete stick. Where's the fire, the longing, the regret that should be peeking through each phrase?"

Amanda glowered at him. "I am not so good at double-thinking as you, my lord," she managed to say angrily.

"Ah, so we are not forgiving, are we? I'll admit it pleases me to see you're not a complete paragon, 'Manda. I'd be most uncomfortable entertaining a saint. But allow me to point out that I never misrepresented myself. I assumed you knew the odd circumstances of my birth. It was never my fault that you did not heed the common gossip," he replied calmly.

"It isn't that," Amanda cried, stung that he could so misunderstand her. "It was that . . . it was—" she faltered—"it was that you promised you would not attempt to . . . seduce me," she concluded, abandoning missishness in her righteous rage.

"Seduce you?" he answered, raising an eyebrow, and looking genuinely blank before the light of understanding dawned upon his face. "Ah, that kiss. You consider that seduction? My dear 'Manda, I may well be haphazard in my morality, but I am not such a fool as to attempt a seduction in the family portrait gallery. Servants swarm about the house, my dear, and even if I had ordered them all away in order to commit the foul deed, I would hardly attempt to engender another such as myself beneath the very eyes of all the ancestral spirits of this house. And, 'Manda, my dear," he went on, drawing a white square of linen from his pocket, "I promise you that when I attempt your ruination, there will be no doubt in your mind as to what I am up to. I am not so oblique in my methods as I am in my letters. There's an ink smudge on your cheek," he added helpfully, handing her the handkerchief.

She scrubbed at her cheek, hoping the large white square would cover the color rising in her cheeks. It was both reassuring and lowering to hear how lightly he had dismissed that kiss. Even though she had been horrified and frightened of his anger at herself and his own state, she had forgotten her trepidations at the mere touch of his mouth. Her own lips had tingled at once and her eyes had widened at how that simple contact had scattered her wits. It had been a curiously delicious moment, those seconds before she had recovered, pulled away, and fled from him.

He seemed oddly pleased now, and said, eyeing her confusion, "So it was my actions that displeased you, not my situation? But you will have to learn to hide your feelings, my dear. It is Giles who is to think something is amiss, not my mama and brother. You clung to Cousin Emily so closely at breakfast this morning in an effort to avoid me that you almost ended up buttering her toast and getting your fingers bitten off in the process. It looks decidedly odd that you should come to visit my home and pass every moment without me. But it's not too late to remedy. Let's write something tantalizing to Giles, and then I'll take you for a stroll about the grounds. For the wind has died down and it's a clear and cloudless day we ought to make the most of."

Lord North drew up a chair and signaled for Amanda to seat herself again. "Now," he said with determination, "admittedly I'm flattered at your estimate of my home, but let's leave your appreciation of it to a sentence or two. I rather like the phrase on page two, 'North is a compelling fellow, and now I can see why he was so successful at winning my trust.' Could we not substitute 'heart' for 'trust'? So much more compelling," he concluded, while Amanda ducked her head to hide her flush, and commenced to write at his direction.

Amanda wore a thick red pellise with a stout hood, and was glad of it. For though the wind had ceased to blow with force, even the slight breeze from the lake was chillingly cold on such a winter's day. The viscount had donned a greatcoat, but his golden head was bare. He seemed to thrive on the bracing air, and after they had strolled about for a while, Amanda discovered that the motion of their walking warmed her own limbs. Soon she shrugged back her hood and let the sun warm her head as she paced in step with him.

The grounds to the house sloped down by gentle terraced degrees, to the shores of the lake. One level held a winter-barren rose garden and maze, the next some formal gardens and an ornamental pond, the third had a stone balcony that looked over the lake. Here there was a white wooden summer house, open to the air on all sides, protected only by a latticework cupola, and here Lord North and Amanda rested. It was not until she stood, her arms against the stone wall, peering over, that she realized how far they had come. Behind her, the house seemed distant as the lake itself was. Her cheeks were reddened from the cold, her eyes sparkled, and she laughed up at the viscount when he suggested that they tarry a while, as it was doubtful Cousin Emily would follow since there was nothing digestible in sight.

"Much better," he commented, noting her air of relaxation. "After our impetuous decision to wed, my family must have thought it curious that my affianced treated me like a leper."

"But won't it be more difficult when I leave if they believe me infatuated with you now?" Amanda asked.

"If they do not believe you infatuated, they will know the whole of it," he answered, leaning over the balcony and gazing down at a stand of winter-darkened evergreens, "and that would be ruinous to our plans."

Amanda did not reply, and he went on blandly, "Don't fret, 'Manda. I am not so noble as to turn my life and my family inside out just for the sake of your plight. I am enjoying this mockery for my own reasons."

When she still said nothing, he turned to face her to read her reaction. He grinned at the sight of her, for she was eyeing him dubiously, looking, he thought, very much like a curious elfin creature out of one of the books he had read as a child.

"I cannot," she said, shaking her head, "imagine why you should derive any pleasure from this imposture. Most gentlemen would have nightmares about finding themselves in such a situation. I dislike every moment of it myself, although I know it is necessary."

"Ah, but I am not most gentlemen, as you should have

realized by now," he said placidly. "And whether you acknowledge it or not, you are certainly not like most ladies. Why, Amanda, you should have been appalled by my disclosure to you yesterday. I cannot believe it is only your good breeding that keeps you from approaching the subject of my illegitimacy again. But you've accepted it as calmly as if I had told you about a birthmark, rather than a birthright."

Amanda was taken aback by his words. She had in fact spent many hours of the night thinking about his condition. But she realized he was right, the facts of his birth had not distressed her half so much as her own lack of perception had done. So she blurted, "No, but why should it upset me? I have, after all, been raised up in a family that makes light of such matters. Well, not 'light' precisely," she offered after a moment's thought. "But we have always accepted that circumstances of birth do not alter a person. I don't like Mary any the less because we didn't have the same father, and I very much doubt if she and Cecil and Alicia and James would even want to claim my papa as their true sire."

"A most unusual family," the viscount commented, as if to himself. Then he smiled at her, caught up her hand, and said, "Let us sit for a space. The summer house doesn't shield from the cold, but I should give you a chance to rest before I march you down to the lake shore."

Amanda seated herself upon a rustic wooden bench within the skeletal frame of the little house and watched as Lord North prowled its perimeters, and listened closely as he spoke to her. He did not rest at all, but paced as he pointed out details of the structure and described its summer aspect for her. His gift of speech was so vivid that soon she could almost see the heavy purple heads of drooping wisteria that hung from the roof in summer, hear the merry light chatter over the dishes of rainbow ices, and scent the fresh, cooling breezes that blew in from the lake. But he returned her abruptly to winter when he said in as casual a tone as he had related all the rest,

"I believe I owe you some sort of explanation, Amanda, for you accepted your false betrothal under false pretenses.

It's only right that you know the whole of it, for I think that Giles, indeed everyone else in the kingdom, knows of my false position."

"It's not important!" Amanda said staunchly, gazing at him where he had come momentarily to rest, with one booted foot up against a bench. She was going to go on about how she well knew how ridiculous matters of reputation were when he cut her off abruptly.

"Don't speak as a child," he said sternly, "it is very important. Should you have to go to such lengths, such twistings and turnings of the truth, if you were born to an unexceptional family? Why, you and your beloved Giles would have two in the cradle and another on the way if your mama did not have a penchant for bearing children from diverse affairs of the heart."

Amanda looked at him with awe. He spoke seriously and was bereft of humor.

"It is very refreshing to see such familial loyalty, my dear," he said roughly, "but as you should know, the world is very hard on those of us who are the result of human frailty. It is amusing," he went on, though he did not seem at all amused, "how very forgiving they can be of those who stray, provided they at last reform. But they are not quite so forgiving of the by-products of those lapses. Those living reminders are indelibly stained. Their existence recalls to mind weakness of human nature; they are regarded as somehow obscene, as though their breathing presence constantly conjures up the act that begot them. Let me tell you, my sheltered darling, that if Giles has forebodings about your sudden flight of romance with a rake-hell, he will without doubt be aghast at your particular choice of rake-hell. The reason we have had to be so nice in our choice of words in letters to him is that he doubtless thinks it a case of like calling to like. Even though," he said with pointed sarcasm, "you have papers and certificates and sworn testimony to the fact that you, at least, are legitimate."

Amanda could not think of an answer to this, and realized that in any case, any words she might utter now would be like an application of a poultice upon a gaping mortal wound.

"My title," the viscount said, rising to pace the interior of the summer house again, as though he found it difficult to be contained within it, "is as spurious as our loving relationship is. Oh, I am legally the viscount; my adoptive father was punctilious about that, at least. Never fear that we both stand in danger of being ordered from the house," he added, throwing a bright glance to her. "But I am not even a rash mistake of the late viscount's. In fact, I do not know what fellow is accountable for my presence upon this earth. And, as I did not even have the good grace to grow to remotely resemble any one of the family, the world knows of my condition as surely as if it had been announced from the rooftops."

Lord North walked as he spoke, and it seemed to Amanda that he had to speak. What had begun as light banter had clearly become something he could no longer contain. Wisely, she did not offer platitudes or sympathy as he told her of his state, but only listened closely to what he said and more closely to what he chose not to say. As he had clothed the naked structure in which they rested in the soft lineaments of summer with his words, so now he was able to let her see the past players and their performances upon that stage of his life that had also vanished after its brief season.

His childhood had been unexceptional, save for its having been perhaps even more pleasant than for most lads from a privileged family. He had come to his parents after ten barren years, and as an only child he had been adored by his father and cosseted by his mother. He could recall nothing that jarred his comfortable boyhood. But yes, he told Amanda with a rueful grin, there were those moments he could cull from his infancy that now stood out like markers on an otherwise pristine landscape. But they had only ruffled the surface of his content.

There was the governess dismissed when she was over-heard telling him how fortunate he was and how he should always practice to show his parents his deep gratitude. There was the cook given marching orders when she took to serving him queer stories with his gingerbread, tales of changeling children, goblin creatures exchanged for true human babes stolen from their cradles by mischievous fairies.

At eight, he had been sent tearfully off to school, to be trained up as befitted a young heir to title and fortune. When he had returned for his vacation the following year, he was told that his mother was increasing. His parents were jubilant and he returned to school elated, not so much at the idea of having a sibling, but at his parents' profound joy.

Gilbert had been born when he was ten, and he could still recall the look upon his mother's face when she exhibited his wrinkled, rather disappointing-looking brother. She wore an expression of mingled triumph and ecstatic vindication. He had neither been unduly worried nor cast down when he was not allowed to pass much time with the infant. He had only been surprised at how protective she had become of the babe, and how disinterested she suddenly was in him and his school experiences. But his papa had redoubled his attentions so even that had not disturbed him.

It was when he was twelve and home for the summer, that his life had been changed forever. His papa had been ailing, the lingering illness that would eventually claim him had begun to show its teeth. Through boredom the schoolboy had taken to playing with the infant, now a rotund, willful toddler, albeit always under his mother's watchful eye.

It was on a rainy Saturday morning that the first incident had occurred. Mama had some matters to settle with the housekeeper and Gilbert's nurse was abed with a streaming cold. He had been attempting to entertain his infant brother with some sleight of hand involving a red ball. Gilbert was monstrously spoiled, Lord North said with a reminiscent smile to Amanda; it was a wonder to him how well the lad had grown despite it. But then, because Gilbert could not have the ball, he had fallen into a rage. The child had at that time the habit of flinging himself face downward and kicking and thrashing at the ground when frustrated, while screeching continuously until he got his way. While Gilbert had been in this state, teary, red-face, and squalling, Mama had come running into the room. She had caught the wailing boy to her breast, and spat at his elder brother,

"What have you done to my son?"

He had explained the circumstance, but she had only stared at him and then marched out with the weeping child in her arms. He had thought then of what a strange thing she had said, but had put it down to her agitation and thought no more upon it.

"I was," he now said ruefully, as much to the ether as to Amanda, "an uncommonly dense boy."

Silence descended upon the summer house and Amanda stirred slightly, aware that she was growing cold from inactivity but not daring to move lest she break the train of the silent viscount's thoughts, lest she cause him to abandon his tale. But it seemed that he was only collecting the threads of it together, for soon he continued.

The next morning had dawned clear and sunny. This time, he had romped out into the rose gardens with Gilbert. Mama had fallen into a light doze upon her chair in the sunlight. Again, some small thing thwarted Gilbert, but this time when he flung himself down, he landed directly in the thorny rose bushes. "Lord," the viscount said, shaking his head in wonderment even now, almost two decades later in the icy cold of the abandoned gazebo, as he recalled that blazing August afternoon. "He served himself well for his folly." For now Gilbert had reason enough and more to squall. He arose from the bushes streaming gore from a dozen scratches, looking as though he had been flayed alive.

Mama had roused from her nap and shrieked with dismay. She clutched the shrilling, bleeding boy to her bosom and rose to face his brother. They were then of a height and he could recall, would always recall, the look of hatred and horror in her eyes. She did not shout, nor even raise her voice. But she trembled as she spoke, and her words tumbled out as though long-pent pressure released them.

"What evil have you done to my baby now?" she said in

a voice of iron. "Be wary, Christian. I will not let you harm my son."

This time he had risen to the bait.

"But I haven't harmed him," he explained reasonably. "He pitched himself into the bushes headfirst in one of his tempers. He wanted this rose I had plucked. He hasn't taken much hurt, it just looks fearful, and I am your son too, Mama," he had added, almost as an afterthought.

"Indeed, you are not," she had said.

They had stood arrested in the summer sunlight that had grown cold, the two of them so silent that even Gilbert ceased screeching and only lay, lower lip puffed out in fear, as the silence of their confrontation lingered.

"Explain yourself, Mama," he had answered, in a tone he had heard his father use, as though he had grown suddenly from twelve to forty years.

"You are not my son," she had whispered, her words loud in the quiet of the garden. "We acquired you when you were born. We had no children. We needed a son. Your father did not want Windham House falling to his brother and that wretched lot. His brother was a wastrel. Have you never looked in the glass, Christian?"

"What are you saying? Who else is my mother, then?" he had asked, not believing what he asked, nor what she answered, and having difficulty hearing anything above the roaring in his ears.

"A slut," she hissed, "a common woman. A farmwoman. Glad to sell her son for a crust of bread."

He had been as horrified by the furious, venomous attitude she projected as he was by her speech. But still he could not believe her. He thought her only angry at him and vengeful, and in his confusion he reverted to a child again.

"I don't believe you," he said, remembering that his lips had quavered almost as much as Gilbert's had. "I have never seen her. Where is she, who is she?"

"We sent her away so that her presence would not shame us. Her name is Annie Withers. She lives at a place called Land's End now. In Ashbourne. We still support her. Shall, for all her wicked life," his mama said wildly.

It might have been the telltale quiver of his mouth, or it might have been Gilbert's uncharacteristic silence, but she suddenly fell still as though understanding her words at last. A look of terror had come over her and she had fled with Gilbert, leaving him dumbstruck in the garden filled with roses and birdsong.

"She came to me the next day and apologized," the viscount said, resting now, leaning against the bare lattice frame of the summer house, "and begged me to never tell my father of her words. No, she pleaded with me not to."

Amanda dared speak tentatively. "And you never did?"

"No, he was ill. In any case, there was no need. I went to Land's End in Ashbourne and she had told me no more than the truth."

His coachman had waited in the carriage on the main road as he had walked the miles to the little cottage. A few extra shillings had bought the fellow's silence and the detour from the journey back to school. It had been a neat little cottage, set off by itself at the end of a lane with roses, more roses, growing in the front garden. There had been sheep, and cattle and chickens, and it had seemed a pleasant enough small farm holding. A boy, scant years older than himself, had been working in the garden when he had stopped to ask directions. The lad had looked up at him, and he had been shocked to see his own distinctive eyes gazing back curiously at himself. One blue and one gray eye had widened in the other's face even as his own had, when he asked, "Is this Land's End?"

"Aye," the lad had said.

They had been of a height, of a sameness, except for the fact that one head was fair and the other dark. One was dressed in collar and jacket of a gentleman and the other wore the full and baggy trousers, oversized doublet, and patched coat of a farm youth.

It was years of training and privilege that spoke next, in a voice of command. "And where is your father?"

"Got no father," the lad had said in sullen tones. "Never set eyes on him, leastwise."

The woman had come out of the house as they spoke and stood riveted as she watched them. She was a good

looking, flaxen-haired female. Even at the age of twelve he
could see that she had been beautiful, and still bore traces
of that loveliness although her form was too bulky and her
clothes, simple countrywoman's working garments.

She held a washcloth to her breasts and stared at him.

"Christian?" she asked in a low voice. "Can it be Christian Jarrow?"

Heedless now of the gaping boy, he had walked to her,
dared one glance at her wide blue eyes, then dropped his
gaze to the ground as he summoned up his courage to
demand, "Are you my mother?"

"They told you?" the woman gasped. "All of it?"

"All," he said.

"His lordship sent you?" she then asked again, stupid
with amazement.

"No, he knows nothing of it, and he is not to know. He
is ill," he had answered, and then impatient, and ill himself,
he only asked again, "Is it true?"

"Yes," she said.

He had not waited for a reply, had not even said "Good
day." He had only turned upon his heel and left. He could
hear her call after him, falteringly, "Christian," and then
more weakly, "My lord. Wait, only wait and listen," but
he had gone on.

"I have gone on a long way since then," the viscount
commented now, "and never returned. Oh, I've come back
to Windham House, for it is nominally my home, but it
has never been very comfortable for me since. Mama does
not like me very well," he said with a twisted smile. "It's
not that we fight, no, for that would be underbred. Say
only that she contrives to make me aware that I am an
interloper."

He paused, thinking on how he scarcely needed reminder,
remembering those years when he had first learned of his
condition and how he had struggled with it. He had been
drawn to creeping down to the portrait gallery at night
with a branch of candles, searching those mute and painted
faces painstakingly in the hopes that by some magical
means, he might discover it had all been a mistake. Then
there had been the confrontations he had endured at school

when he came to understand comments he had previously ignored. After he had blacked a few eyes, these accusations had become submerged, only to flow in a constant whispered underground even as his thoughts now ran. He had ceased speaking as he thought back. As Amanda dared not venture a word, it was the complete silence which prodded him back to the present.

He seemed to recall himself and gave Amanda a brilliant, winsome smile.

"Rather a better story than the tale of a naughty illustrated book, don't you think? And I have dozens more. I should have paid them back by being an excellent son as my governess suggested, but I have only gone on to illustrate how true the saying is that blood will tell. But come," he said, his mood veering again, "I have frozen you to ice, bored you to bits, and terrorized you as well, by the look upon your face."

He walked to Amanda and offered her his arm.

"No more of the past then, my dear. You've told me your tale, I've told you mine. Now we can be true co-conspirators, each with a tale to hold over the other's head. I suggest that you contrive to have Giles dredge up some personal shame to relate to you as soon as you have him in your company again. Nothing holds a relationship together so well as mutual confession. And," he added, smiling in his normal fashion again, "mutual fear of retaliation. Now I shall trot you down to our famous lake and regale you with merry stories so that you return to the house looking as though you had passed the entire afternoon in blissful communion with your beloved. Should you like to pass it that way, by the by?" he asked with such exaggerated interest that she was forced to laugh as she took the arm he offered and stepped down the flagged steps toward the lake.

There were details Amanda thought to ask him about his tale, several facts she wished to have him elaborate upon, but he gave her no chance to dwell upon them. They walked down the steep stairs and ambled along the winding paths, and he kept her constantly entertained. It was as though he had never spoken of his intimate life to her, so complete was his absorption now in their merriment.

He displayed yet another aspect of his quicksilver personality as he boyishly mimicked the fat, plodding sheep and assigned them nonsensical names and histories. When he was done with that, he mocked the soaring bird's cries so well that they circled back again and again to discover what manner of creature it was that had called to them.

When he guided Amanda to the shore, they tested the thin ice at the brink with their toe tips and then he showed her how to skip stones across the lake's broad blue back. It was not until the sun had begun its early descent that they paused in their wanderings to watch the echoing glow of its light trailing across the water.

They were far from the house and from any human habitation. As they stood upon the shore, they laughed together and their laughter met and echoed until it sounded as though the whole winter-locked world was amused with them. Amanda had thrown back her head in gaiety, and in that second she perceived that his face had grown still and thoughtful. She saw the way the sun had been captured in his hair and the way his strange eyes shone like the billowing crests of the waters, and she grew still as well. He gazed attentively at her rapt face and smiled as though he had seen something enormously pleasing to him.

He said only the one word, "Yes," and then suddenly drew her toward him and lowered his head to kiss her. Taken by surprise by the abruptness of his action, she surprised herself even further by allowing herself to be pulled into his complete embrace. She rested against him, drawing warmth, incredibly sweet warmth from his lips and sheltering body. It was as if there in the icy grip of winter she had found the heat of the lowering sun upon his lips and in his blazing mouth. But then, even as it seemed that he had thawed every part of her, she recalled herself. She drew back, aghast at her unsought response.

"No," she said, shaking her head in denial, "you promised you would not."

He held her fast and brushed his lips against her cheek.

"I lied, you know," he whispered.

When she broke his hold by stepping back a pace, he dropped his arms to his sides. She stared at him, amazed at both his and her own betrayal of herself.

"I do lie, you understand," he said sweetly. "That is the truth."

Then he laughed and shrugged off the expression of concentrated ardor as easily as he had adopted it.

"First lesson, sweet Amanda," he said, now only speaking as dryly as a tutor might, "seducers always lie, your nanny was quite right about that. Second lesson, they soften your heart by enlisting your sympathy. Thirdly, they lower your defenses by wanting, seemingly, only your friendship. But they don't mean well by you, Amanda," he said seriously now, "and that they never lie about."

He put out a hand and caressed the side of her face as she stared back at him, disbelieving his chameleon qualities; so changeable, changing even as she gazed at him from lover, to liar, to sympathetic companion.

"Let us go back to the house now. You really ought to get started on another letter. And Amanda," he added in friendly fashion as he took her hand, "do tell Giles to hurry."

The letter lay open upon a broad oaken desk, and the gentleman who had just done with reading it for the fourth time stood with his back to the room, hands linked behind his back, staring out at the snowy grounds. At length, he turned and walked decisively to the desk. He was a tall, well-set-up gentleman, dressed soberly and comfortably. Although not a handsome fellow, there was that in his plain open countenance that drew the eye and inspired confidence. He took up the letter and read it briefly once again, and then took it to the hearth where a fire rumbled comfortably against the chill of the day. With one exasperated gesture he crumpled the letter and flung it upon the flames. But in the next moment, he dropped to one knee swiftly and snatched it out again. He blew the flames from its margins and lay it back upon the desk to straighten it.

He was never a fanciful fellow, but as he attempted to brush the cinders off its singed edges, he could not help but think that so might a letter appear if it had been composed and sent by the devil's own hand.

X

The guests seated at the long dining table sipped their wine, pronounced it excellent, and dutifully waited for the servants to fill their cups again for yet another toast. As Gilbert had given the first to his brother and his fiancée, now it was the prospective groom who stood to raise his glass. He held his head high and flourished his goblet.

"To my singular stroke of good luck at finding such a treasure," he said as he gazed at Amanda. "A treasure that I did not know I was searching for, but discovered I could not live without. A treasure that lay waiting for me like some priceless pearl upon its rich sea bed. To Amanda," he concluded with a quirked smile.

"Here, here," some of the gentlemen concurred as they rose to salute his lady as well.

Amanda ducked her head and prayed that it appeared as though she were overcome with the idiotic shyness commonly attributed to future brides. It was too much to hope that he would have left off mentioning beds in his public praise of her. She wished that she did not flush so readily, for by now she knew him well enough to know that her aghast reaction to his hint at the truth of their meeting was precisely what he had been angling for. She could only hope that the other guests would attribute the twin spots of high color upon her pale cheeks to coy pleasure rather than the fact that she felt like a thief caught with her hands dripping stolen gems.

For if she had felt unhappy about their imposture before, when she had first arrived at Windham House, the subsequent weeks she had passed here made those first moments seem as innocent as a schoolroom prank. It was, she had discovered to her sorrow, no easy thing to live a lie. And as her worst sins, before the viscount had entered her bedroom and her life, had been only those of omission, the commission on a continuing basis of a monstrous deception had made her supremely sensitive. She felt as though her sensibilities had been sandpapered, so acutely did she respond to every nuance of speech directed to her.

Amanda looked to her hostess, who was now nodding politely to the toast being made by their vicar. It was curious that the one person she had imagined she would feel the most uneasiness with was the one whose opinion, it transpired, made the least difference to her. For the viscountess, while unfailingly polite, had never exchanged more than a bare minimum of words with Amanda in the time that she had sojourned here. And even the most exquisitely sensitive ear could not have picked a wrong note from any of her comments. The viscountess had accepted her as it seemed she accepted all that was about her. Her demeanor was equally flat with Lord North as it was with Amanda and all her servants and guests. Only Gilbert could draw some spark of emotion from her eyes or lips.

It was that young gentleman, who now seized up his glass to toast his brother once again, who made Amanda feel the most wretched. For Gilbert was as honestly and openly thrilled about the forthcoming marriage that was never to be, as she imagined he might be about his own. He obviously doted upon Lord North and approved of Amanda as wholly as he approved of a sunny day. He had attached himself to the two of them, and as Lord North dryly commented, could only be peeled off when they had cause to be alone by outright threats or bold appeals for the right of privacy enjoyed by a besotted couple.

Amanda liked young Gilbert enormously, and thought of him very much as she did one of her own younger brothers. The thought of his dismay when she parted from Lord North sank her spirits. Now, as she watched him beaming upon his brother, she wondered again as she often did, just what his reaction might be if he knew the truth not only of the falsity of her position, but of the absence of any real physical relationship between himself and Lord North as well.

Very much like a player at charades who wonders why the others have not guessed the answer to a riddle that seems obvious once one has been told the answer, Amanda, glancing about the long table, wondered how anyone could not instantly discern the truth of Lord North's position. The discrepancies of face, form, and personality between the two supposed brothers was so stark as to be almost comical.

The viscount, at the head of the table trading quips with Gilbert, was a stereotypically lean and elegant figure of a nobleman. He, the false son, was the one with the patrician bearing and personality. Gilbert, who sat facing him, was as swart and stocky as a plowman, and while he had a good enough head for figures and a heart as wide as his great chest, his conversation and demeanor were as rough and honest as that of any worker in the fields. As they stood thus, the golden-haired rapier-witted viscount born to a farmwoman, and the last of a long line of gentlemen looking even in his evening finery as though he had just come in from the barnyard, Amanda realized that if it were not for the viscountess, it would have been Gilbert who would have been labeled as an imposter.

Which of the guests, Amanda mused as she drank her wine, realized that their host was not born to his position? Then, looking up as if in response to an unspoken command and meeting the viscount's mocking glance, she wondered which of the guests did not.

The dinner had been given this night in order to celebrate their engagement. Aside from the obvious difference in the number of invited guests, it would have been hard to find two more dissimilar parties than this and the one that Amanda's mother had presided over. Although the countess's party had included those souls whose very presence might have staggered most gently reared young females, Amanda had been able to sail through it with a minimum

of discomfort. She might not have greatly cared for those
in attendance, but they were the stuff of her childhood
experience and she accepted them as one accepts a duty
visit to an unpleasant relative.

But though there were only sixteen in all at the viscountess's dinner table, in contrast to the hundreds at
Kettering Manor, they amazed Amanda all out of propor-
tion to their actual number. There was not a famous name
among them, and no one of a rank higher than their hosts'.
No gentleman present leered at Amanda, much less dared
a pinch. Though some of the females were comely, not
one ogled a masculine tablemate, nor fluttered her lashes
or fan in unmistakable invitation.

As the dinner wore on through soup, fish, and fowl, the
conversation tended toward crops and politics, never touching upon license or indiscretion. As the lamb gave way to
beef and rolled forward toward veal, sermons and fashions
were discussed, with never a mention of scandal or folly.
When the last sweet had been nibbled and the ladies
retired to the parlor, the gentlemen raised their glasses of
port to congratulate the viscount on his charming lady and
future happiness with never a speculative word about her
desirability and past experiences. And the ladies clustered
about Amanda and quizzed her about her dressmaker with
not a whisper about her fiancé's sexual prowess. Amanda
was astonished.

As she listened to the wives and daughters of the local
landowners, she could scarcely believe her ears. These
gentle well-bred creatures were realized objects from her
most fervent dreams of future peace. Such were the friends
she imagined she would have herself when she was at last
wed to Giles. These were the sort of people whose existence she had envisioned solely from her talks with her
schoolmates. For a certainty, Mama had never entertained
such proper ladies, and as for Papa, he had long since
abandoned entertaining anyone but hunting cronies as apt
to drink themselves into sullen oblivion as he himself. So it
was that when the gentlemen joined them at last the viscount was surprised to see Amanda, her face blissful,

blooming among the local flora as a rose among common thistles.

They passed the evening in listening to little Miss Protherow playing at the spinet, while in turn Gilbert, Sir Butterworth, and Major Wells sang accompaniment. After Mrs. Whitchurch had sung a particularly affecting air having to do with love and sacrifice, the vicar, Mr. Morley, told an amusing story that was almost a parable about marital fidelity. After gentle applause, the company split into little groups and the chatter became more general.

Amanda enjoyed herself thoroughly. It was toward the close of the evening when she found herself alone with Mrs. Burnham, the squire's wife. Mrs. Burnham was of an age with Amanda's own mama, and of all the ladies present, she was the one who most resembled those females that Amanda was best acquainted with. For Mrs. Burnham, although stout, had a gown cut less for function than fashion, and her hair was of a vibrant golden hue that hinted more of an origin in bottles than birth. As the lady came close to chat with Amanda, it could be seen that she was older than she had appeared from across the table, as her skin was covered with a great deal of powder to conceal its lines, and her lips were more encarmined than the ingestion of strawberry ices could have accounted for.

When Amanda had done with telling the lady the tale about meeting with Christian, the one that he had approved and that she had never deviated from, Mrs. Burnham smiled pleasantly.

"What a fortunate young woman you are, to be sure," she said softly. "Christian is unique, is he not?"

As Amanda nodded her agreement, peripherally disturbed by some note in the other lady's voice, Mrs. Burnham went on, "As I have good cause to know—" she sighed reminiscently— "for we were once very good friends, he and I."

"And no longer?" Amanda asked, wondering whether this lady had exchanged some harsh words with her neighbor and sought now to repair the matter through his fiancée.

"Oh, we are yet friends," the lady sighed, and then

added further in a low voice, although she and Amanda were far from the other guests, "but mere friendship is sad stuff indeed, compared to what we once were to each other."

The viscount was across the room from Amanda and the squire's wife, discussing village affairs with some of the other gentlemen, but his gaze had never wandered from the pair. Now, as Mrs. Burnham bent her majestically coiffed blond head to confide to Amanda and he saw the younger woman's face slowly leached of color and gladness, he stiffened. Murmuring a half audible excuse, he left the gentlemen and made his way rapidly to the ladies. As he approached them, he could not hear what Helena Burnham was saying, but from the aspect of the couple, he could not shake the image of a great tawny lioness bringing down some delicate, fleet-footed creature to feed upon.

The squire's wife noted his approach and she broke off her conversation with Amanda, to cry, with patently false enthusiasm, "Ah, North. Lady Amanda and I have been having the most delightful *tête-à-tête*. You are a lucky fellow, and you must be sure to bring her around to our home frequently so that we can strengthen our friendship, for we have such a commonality of interests."

"I doubt that, Mrs. Burnham," the viscount said with a charming smile that caused the lady's eyes to widen, even as his words froze the smile upon her parted lips, "for Amanda, sad to tell, has little interest in ancient history and I know that is your specialty. Now, she has quite a flair for writing, in fact spends hours at her desk composing the most delightful fictions," he went on, oblivious of the squire's glowering wife, as well as Amanda's guilty start, "and if we can get her to give up the composition of letters and begin some more major work, we may yet hear her praises sung by the highest critics. But alas, writing is such a solitary persuasion, I doubt she will have any time for purely social visits," he concluded with an expression of remorse, as he tucked Amanda's clenched fist under his arm.

Mrs. Burnham stood for a moment, and then inclined

her head with a wry smile as though to acknowledge a true hit.

"Ah, well," she said with resignation, "so be it. I did but try. I see that dear Henry requires my attention. Good evening, North, Lady Amanda." And nodding her head, she made her way with great dignity to her husband's side.

The viscount did not even pause to gauge Amanda's reaction. He led her immediately to the window enclosure where there were no other guests to overhear. Only then did he say ruefully, "Come, Amanda, you can skewer me later. But for now, I beg you, let it pass. I'll have conference with you when the guests have gone, but Helena will have been triumphant if you look so stricken. This is a country set and their revels will soon be ended. Bear with it only a little while longer and attempt to show some gladness, please."

But when he looked down at her, he saw, to his surprise, that all traces of her dismay were vanished. She only betrayed her emotions when she spoke to him through tightly clenched teeth.

"But, Christian," she said sweetly, "only prepare me please. How many other of your lights of love shall I encounter this evening? Is the vicar's wife among their number? And the major's daughter and Sir Humbert's mama?"

The viscount grimaced, but as the first lady mentioned was such a pillar of respectability that the entire village wondered how she had produced her five children, and the other two were variously a dewlapped female resembling nothing so much as a turnip wrapped in purple gauze and an ancient so debilitated that the company drew in its breath whenever she paused in conversation for fear that she had breathed her last, he soon grinned happily.

"Of course they are," he answered calmly, as he led her toward the center of the room. "How could I have passed them over?"

Amanda, Lord North, Gilbert, and the viscountess stood at the door and bade their guests good-bye as the ancient tall-case clock in the hall struck eleven. The viscountess paused to exchange a few words with the others but left

for her own rooms before the minute hand had crept far
past its zenith. Though Gilbert, still buoyed by the
festivities, announced that he was ravenous, wide-awake,
and eager to exchange impressions of the evening, his elder
brother told him simply that he desired some time alone
with Amanda. Gilbert shrugged philosophically, made a
few sallies about discretion, reminding them of the servants who would be swarming about the place setting it to
rights, and then took himself off to the kitchens to see
what tidbits he could forage that he hadn't had time to
devote proper attention to in the course of the evening.

It was not until Lord North had escorted Amanda to the
study that he spoke.

"I was very young, you know," he said without preamble,
as he shut the door.

As she did not answer, he went on, wandering to the
desk and picking up yet another sheet of yet another letter
to Giles, "And though it might be ungentlemanly to say it,
Helena was both the instigator and the games master. But
then, I am hardly a gentleman, so I shall say it."

He chanced a glance toward Amanda and noted that she
stood and scarcely attended to him, an expression of anger
now clearly discernible upon her face.

"Come, Amanda," he said with some annoyance, "surely
the fact that I had a misspent youth, which you surely
could have guessed, cannot have cast you into a rage? It
was an eternity ago and I have not, would not, embarrass
you by similar entanglements while you are under my
roof. Credit me with discretion, if not with proper
deportment. I'm amazed at your reaction. I'll swear I did
not think you such a prig."

"Prig?" cried Amanda with such force that the viscount
found himself taking a pace back. Her piquant face, which
he had seen in attitudes of quizzical amusement, curiosity,
and even sorrow, was now set in an aspect of fury. But
since, he reflected, it was not a countenance made for such
a vehement emotion, she looked not half so menacing as
tempting to him, though he was wise enough not to comment upon that fact.

"I tell you, my lord," she raged, now giving her emotions full sway, "that it takes a great deal to shock an Amberly."

Privately, the viscount doubted this very much, but he said nothing, knowing she must go on to her full length of anger, uninterrupted. He readied himelf for accusations about his licentiousness and profligacy evinced from the cradle and fostered onward. But her next words caused him to drop his cold, amused aspect.

"I saw the cut of that particular article when I first laid eyes upon her," Amanda lied, "and what she said did not discompose me in the least, I assure you. In fact, had she told me that you and she headed up a hellfire club in the local church, I should have not turned a hair."

Realizing that she had perhaps gone a bit too far in her protestations of sophistication, Amanda dropped her gaze from the viscount's amazed eyes and bit her lip.

"But then why are you so enraged?" he asked, dumbfounded, for once with none of the amused certainty he affected.

"Because she ruined the evening," Amanda blurted.

"Ruined the evening?" the viscount echoed. "But what was there to ruin? I thought you bored to extinction, and who could have blamed you? Only Cousin Emily could enjoy such a gathering. Even Mama, I assure you, held it for propriety's sake alone. Gilbert, of course, finds pleasure in any gathering of more than three, if there is enough food present. But this was merely a simple country evening passed with neighbors and local lights. There was not a witty word uttered nor a new tale told. I can see that Helena's spiteful confession might have overset you, although that occurred in my heedless youth rather than my heedless adulthood, but I cannot envision what you considered ruined."

"It was not tedious to me," Amanda said earnestly, attempting to make him understand her never-spoken vision of content. "I had the most pleasant time until she spoke. It was just the sort of evening I had always dreamed about. Surrounded by neighbors and friends, talking about inconsequential stuff of everyday life, with no one trying to top another's anecdote or attempting to add a scurrilous detail, and no one vilely drunk, and nothing but the kindest construction placed upon one's words or actions. They were all so respectable," she said at last, still feeling that she had not explained the whole of it, "and they treated each other with respect. Can't you see?"

He stood very still and then said, as though from a great distance, "I am beginning to, Amanda."

"And then when that overblown creature began to whisper about your liaison with her, she quite shattered it all," Amanda said sadly.

"But my dear," the viscount replied softly, "they are not paper people. You have idealized them far too much. I should think that there is as much baseness and secret shame in their make-up as in any other person's. Just as there must be some unspoken decency and value in the affairs of those you most dislike and are accustomed to meet."

"Perhaps," Amanda retorted, "but I hadn't wished to know if it were true. And surely it cannot always be so. There must be those people who live their lives in tranquillity, with loyalty and honor." She was annoyed at what she perceived to be his patronizing tone and so went on heedlessly, "I can fully understand that you may not wish to admit it, my lord, but I prefer to believe that all the world is not so vile as you would have it."

The viscount bent his glowing head as Amanda gasped at the way her words had come out. Before she could soften them, he said mockingly,

"Perhaps. But then, you certainly can understand that I don't wish to know it, if it is true."

Amanda attempted to amend her rash statement, but he cut her off.

"Think nothing of it, 'Manda. I have made my own bed, it is only natural that I should choose to have the whole world lie in it with me. At any rate," he went on, with that worldly bored note in his voice that made her feel like a chattering child, "your illusions about my neighbors are not my concern. I am only pleased that you aren't going to rake me over the coals for my past peccadillos. And since

you clearly are not going to oblige me by adding to their
number tonight, I bid you good evening."

When he had left her with a courtly bow, Amanda felt
very much like striking something. But since all the objects
in the room were alarmingly solid, she took up her pen
instead, and commenced to add to her latest message to
Giles. She had not written more than an uninspired line or
two, so preoccupied was she with continuing the unfin-
ished discussion with the viscount in her own mind, this
time with witty answers and clarity of expression, when
Gilbert popped his head in through the doorway.

"Oh, how marvelous!" he said happily, strolling into the
room still chewing upon the remnants of an iced cake he
held in his hand. "I hadn't hoped to find you alone and
awake. It's so hard," he complained as he settled himself in
a chair, "to get to bed after a party, don't you think? I
think," he volunteered, ignoring her silence, "that parties
should go on till everyone drops from exhaustion, because
it's clear that no one goes right off to sleep after attending
one anyway. Why should we all sit in separate rooms and
rehash things alone, when we could still be together?"

He frowned as he pondered what he had said and then
went on, "Christian used to sit up with me in the old days
but the gudgeon's off to his rooms without a word tonight.
Looked in a foul temper, too. Did you two have a lovers'
spat? Well, I shouldn't worry about it, for I expect that's
the way of it. Not that I've ever been in love myself, you
understand, but I'm quite looking forward to the experience.
Except that there aren't any interesting young females in
the neighborhood, save for Becky Hobson, and she's walking out with John Saunders, anyway. Do you have any
sisters by the by, Amanda?"

Amanda had gotten used to Gilbert's manner of expressing himself in nonstop fashion. He often spoke thus, as
though the simple piling up of each idea as it occurred to
him could be construed as conversation. But he was always amiable, and she always welcomed his company.
The fact of his physical presence at Windham House had
made her visit far more enjoyable. His constant attendance
upon her and his brother blunted the viscount's seductive-

ness. Perhaps it was only that even that gentleman could not bring himself to attempt a young woman while his brother was looking over his shoulder, but Amanda felt that there was more to it than that. Lord North might be a careless fellow in many ways, but he seemed to be very careful of Gilbert's good opinion. When the three were together, the viscount treated Amanda more as a unique person and paradoxically, in many ways, she had grown to know him better with Gilbert at their side than she had when they had been alone. So she lay down her pen and smiled at Gilbert. She looked at his hopeful, square, and honest face and said hesitantly,

"Yes, Gil, I do. Two, in fact. And Mary's rising eighteen now, too. She's a dear, clever girl and very lovely as well. But Gil," she said softly, not wishing to dim the eager look in his eyes, "she is like me, an Amberly. I don't know how much gossip you have heard, I've never mentioned it to you but now that you bring it up, my family has a rather—ah, widespread reputation."

She had never discussed anything personal with Gilbert, nor had he ever offered up any but the most inconsequential conversation to her. In either case, he seldom waited for anyone's reply to his discourse. But tonight she was weary and unsettled, and curiously, having been dampened by the viscount, she felt brave and forthcoming with his brother.

"Oh, you mean the fact that half of your lot is illegitimate?" Gilbert said cheerfully, as though he'd just said "freckled" or "musical." "Why, we don't live in the antipodes, 'Manda, only the countryside. But that don't make any difference to me. A chap's got enough to do to account for his own actions, never mind apologizing for his ancestors'. She's pretty, you say, and bright as well? How tall is she? Wouldn't do for a chap my size to court a beanpole, we'd look foolish. But if she's of a height, that wouldn't be so bad. Becky Hobson's only a few inches my better and she made much of it," he brooded.

"You speak so easily of it?" Amanda said in shock.

"Of what?" demanded Gilbert, thinking darkly that her sister must be a giantess, from the horrified look upon

Amanda's face. But recalling the conversation he relaxed. "Oh, about your family? Certainly I do. Why are you so astonished? You said yourself that your reputation was widespread. Lord, I haven't said anything amiss, have I? Chris would have my head. He's the best of fellows, but I wouldn't wish to stir him up."

He looked so anxious that Amanda assured him she did not take any of his comments wrongly, but she added, with a note of wonder, "But Gilbert, if you have heard of the Amberly Assortment, why should you wish to align yourself with us further than we are already linked? I should think one disreputable blot on the family's escutcheon would be enough for you."

She was astonished at his reaction to her bemused comment. He rose from his seat ponderously. He loomed over her with his hands clenched, and she was both startled and suddenly afraid of his totally uncharacteristic anger.

"I know you're promised to Chris," he said coldly, no longer the playful young man she knew, "and indeed I like you very well, 'Manda, and was exceeding happy Chris had found you. But I'll not countenance your holding his birth against him, no matter what the cause. You may have had a tiff with him, I cannot say, that's between you two, but he is my brother, no matter what idiot gossip may hold. Indeed, no bond of blood could make him more my brother than he is, and as I love him, I'll not heed a syllable about a thing in which he had no fault. I'm not saying he's led a blameless life, but in his birth, at least, he had no part. I'm surprised at you, 'Manda," he said in the manner of a disapproving elder.

"But Gil," Amanda defended herself, "I was referring to my own family, and the fact that I was surprised you'd even countenance having another such as me beneath your roof. I never spoke of Christian."

The swift change that came over Gilbert was almost pitiful. Within moments he was abject, begging her forgiveness, pacing the room, knocking a fist against his head, and damning himself for a fool. In her attempts to calm him, Amanda said, "Gilbert, I did not know you even knew the truth about my family, much less about Christian. Why, I myself did not know about him until I arrived here," she explained.

He stopped his pacing and looked at her.

"I don't wish to hurt your feelings, 'Manda," he said gruffly, "but a blind man could see it. It's common enough gossip, and I've never questioned it myself. I've known it since I was a tyke, and then I had at the baker's boy for telling me about it. But it don't make any difference, don't you know? He's been all the brother a fellow could want. Too much of one, sometimes," he said, thinking aloud, "worrying for my schooling, taking care of the estates, and seeing to our welfare. I've no wit for that sort of nonsense. And well my father knew it. Why, when he was breathing his last, he told me he was glad that Chris was to have the ordering of things when he was gone. They were two of a kind, companion spirits. He called him 'son' when Chris came in to bid him farewell. Even at the last, I heard what Chris whispered to him. He offered to give all over to me, but father summoned up enough strength to declare that he was the rightful heir. And so he is."

Gilbert subsided for a moment and then added morosely, "I cannot say why Mama dislikes it so, but then, I've never understood women at all, 'Manda, I'll confess that to you even though you are one of their number. No offense intended," he put in quickly.

Amanda assured him that none had been taken, and she passed the next few hours placating him by discussing those subjects dearest to his heart: the party, Amanda's sisters, and Lord North's nobility of character.

When the candles had guttered low, Gilbert rose and stretched. "Now, let's keep our meeting to ourselves," he said thickly, "for I don't want Christian to rate me for keeping you up till all hours. I just dropped in to see if I could mend fences. When I saw his face and then yours, I sank, 'Manda, I truly did. But I can see that it was just one of those lovers' misunderstandings that you'll doubtless clear up by morning. It wouldn't do for you two to part," he went on as he led her to the door, "for you're perfect for him, you know. I'm happy for it, for if ever a fellow

needed someone to call his own, it's Chris. I feared he'd
never wed, you know," he added on a huge yawn. "I think
he had some maggot in his head about not wanting to
marry for fear of cutting me out of succession. Ain't that
just like him though?" he laughed wonderingly. "Giving
up his whole future for my sake? But I wouldn't have it. I
planned never to wed until he did. Can't you just see the
two of us? Two stubborn old bachelors sitting here in
cobwebs until we shriveled?"

As he bowed over her hand at the top of the stairs, he
chuckled richly.

"But you've solved the problem, 'Manda, and I'll dance
at your wedding till my shoes wear out. With Mary, I
think," he mused, "the little one with the freckles you was
telling me about. Thank you, 'Manda," he said feelingly,
and went off down the corridor to his rooms, whistling
softly, vastly content with himself.

Amanda lay awake in her great bed fretting till the
turning of the night about how many people would be
wounded by the successful conclusion of her schemes.
And she fell to sleep at last after wandering in that nether-
land between consciousness and repose wondering at how
many scars she herself would bear no matter how it turned
out.

XI

Even in midwinter, the forest was alive with light. The trees were powdered in snow, the bracken underfoot was hidden beneath white mounds, and wherever there had been moisture some unseen hand had transmuted it to glittering ice. The landscape lay spangled and translucent under a sharp winter's sun. The riders' voices rang clear in the cold air; they did not hurry down the paths as they might have in some more clement season. They knew that the most sure-footed mount might have a misstep since even innocent hillocks could conceal the sheerest stretches of treacherous ice.

Amanda was enjoying herself very much, even though she might have preferred it if the excursion had been taken on foot. For though she was a good rider and had known some amiable horses in her time, she preferred to think of the beasts as either transport or pets, and did not think much of them as recreation. She confided this to the viscount, who rode at her side, along with the notion that she had always thought it a pity that one couldn't ride dogs. They, she affirmed, might be the best sort of creatures to take excursions upon, being entirely less haughty and willful companions.

Lord North agreed, and only commented upon how diverting such sport might be if one's mount spotted a cat while riding. Gilbert, who rode on ahead of the pair, tossed back a reprimand over his shoulder to his brother, for he allowed as how Amanda had the right of it and only think of the sort of hunt one could have if one's steed could not only pursue but also tree one's prey. When the viscount agreed and then speculated upon the result of patting the noble beast in appreciation and then having it fall to the ground in delight, waving its feet in the air so that its stomach might be scratched, the three laughed so heartily that the vibrations of their merriment dislodged bits of snow from the overhanging branches. The resultant miniature storm created by their mirth only caused more of it, and the forest echoed to their boisterous laughter.

Amanda wore a habit of rich red-brown, with a hat that sported a jaunty partridge feather. Since a dollop of snow had fallen on that brave feather and now was melting down in a trickle upon her head, Amanda swept off her hat and upended it to dislodge the snow. Her spice curls shone in the sunlight and her gray eyes reflected all the dazzling winter white. All three of them were enhanced by the clean light, the viscount of course, with his brilliant hair and jeweled eyes, was an acknowledged creature of the element, but even dark Gilbert's hair and form stood out in bold relief against the purity of the scene.

So Amanda would always think of this place, from the viscount's house to its surround, as some magical prism endlessly casting sharp and gemlike images. When Gilbert cried a great haloo, and pointed ahead, she saw the lake before them, broad and blue and white, seeming like some great diamond- and sapphire-filled bowl. She left off attending to her ruined hat and cried, "Ah, this must surely be the most beautiful place on earth!"

Lord North said nothing, but only looked at her and not at the lake at all. Gilbert, however, ever one to take things literally, said only that it was very nice to be sure, but in his opinion not a patch upon Hollyhedge, their estate in the gentle Cotswalds. Their piece of the Avon there, he allowed, while not so mighty a spectacle as the lake, was a more manageable bit of scenery and more to his liking. Amanda was surprised when his brother replied in a cautionary tone that this riding excursion was not a proper place for Gilbert to go off riding on his favorite hobbyhorse again. When Gilbert subsided into glum silence, the viscount added that they had been all through that particular subject and would not discuss it again, no matter how deftly a fellow might think he had brought it up.

Never one to remain in the sullens long, Gilbert, obviously dying from inactivity as they had been sitting still upon their mounts for the space of two minutes, spied Amanda's devastated feather.

"Ho, 'Manda," he cried, "that bit of plumage is done for. Tell you what, I'll go scout the edges of the lake for some partridge. See if I don't find a covy. We can come back later and flush a dozen of them and have your hat back in fine fettle again."

Before Amanda could protest that she did not fancy adorning her head with fresh-plucked feathers from some still warm carcass, Gilbert was off down the trail happily hunting down the traces of a bird fine enough to embellish a fair lady's hat.

"Let him go," the viscount said benignly, "for he's fretting for some exercise. We two elderly parties set far too slow a pace for him. He'd hunt raspberries in the snow if he thought it would give him an excuse for activity. I doubt there's a partridge in the land dim enough not to elude the racket he's making, so you'll not have to worry about having to sport gory feathers upon your hat."

Amanda chuckled, and they rode on slowly, pacing their mounts easily along the path around the lake. They chatted absently on a variety of unimportant trivia, but so pleasantly that Amanda felt all her constraints slipping away. Here in the sun and the air the viscount did not dwell conversationally upon her charms, or upon his motives pertaining to them, and this lack of threat freed her tongue.

"Why," she said at last, "do you not stay here more? For I can see how very much you love this place and all that is upon it. If I had such a love for my home, I should not leave it so easily. You have been gone for two years and yet it seems as though you have recalled each tree and rock as though you've held them in your mind's eye constantly."

But at those innocent words, his face changed and he assumed the bored, laconic drawl of the salon again. "So I have," he said, "and so, I imagine, I always shall. But it is not mine, and never was. I am only a cuckoo in this palatial nest. My true home is in some barnyard, I expect. Even now, if it were not for fate's intervention, I should be mucking out a stable, or winnowing winter wheat, or ministering to a pig. This is Gilbert's legacy, and I only tend it for him. His father entreated me to keep the title and the land. I do, for I promised, but I feel a usurper doing so. Though Mama resents my very presence, Gilbert loves me well. But I cannot say why, for if I were he, I should not. So every now and again," he went on more lightly, as though recalling how very nearly he had begun to speak his true mind to another being, "I take a little jaunt to the continent and disport myself as a fellow of my caliber should."

They rode on in silence, Amanda realizing that there were as many deceptively innocent patches in their conversation to avoid as there were under their mounts' hooves. But the viscount seemed reluctant to let the subject go, and soon he said, in a constricted voice as though he had been trying to shape the words into an entertaining fashion but could not quite do so,

"He keeps harping on the subject of Hollyhedge, for now he thinks that I'm to marry, he wants to take himself off there and set up his own household. It's a well enough site, a particularly choice holding in fact. But this is his home, and I cannot understand why he does not love it as I do."

He fell silent again and in an effort to change his mood, Amanda said brightly, "He thinks the world of you. He's forever singing your praises to me."

"Ah, yes," Lord North smiled, "was that what you and he were doing till late in the night? I wonder that you did not drop off to sleep immediately he began. That's the only way to discourage him, you know."

Again, Amanda was surprised at how much that transpired about him the viscount noticed even when he seemed to be the most oblivious. The thought that came to her mind came to her tongue instantly.

"That must be why you were such an excellent spy!" she exclaimed.

The viscount let out such a peal of true laughter that his mount's ears flattened back.

"Oh lord," he laughed, "what mare's nests has Gil been exhibiting to you? What I told him was no more than the truth, 'Manda. I did try to be of service to my country, to be sure. And I did carry a few messages from Elba to Sicily and thence to Vienna. At first, you see, it was most effective double-thinking, for the powers-that-were thought it supremely amusing to use a fellow everyone would think too conspicuous to be a spy, as a spy. But once our foes twigged to the scheme, my role was done. No, my dear, I passed most of my time in Vienna just as you would think, in wenching and gaming and sport and wenching."

He gave Amanda a glittering smile.

"It really is a great pity, Amanda, that you are not tempted to try what I am best known for. I feel rather like a master chef forced to keep company with someone who dines only on vinegar and water. For what I most enjoy you seem to appreciate the least. But," he continued, with a sidewise look that caused Amanda's hands to tighten involuntarily upon her reins, "I am eternally optimistic. And there may yet come a day when you are willing to try my wares."

Amanda made such a brave show of trying to change the subject that her very efforts had him merry once again. She was enormously relieved when a crestfallen Gilbert rode back to report that all the deuced partridges seemed to have flown south for the winter, or had been poached out of existence from the very planet.

They rode back to the counterpoint of Gilbert's incessant plans for luncheon, as the ride seemed to have whetted his appetite beyond merely mortal limits. He was still musing aloud about his expectations of game pie, and brooding as to whether his chief competitor in the larder at Windham House, Cousin Emily, had snabbled up all that excellent Stilton, when they arrived in the courtyard. They gave their mounts to grooms and entered the main hall again.

The viscountess surprised them all by coming to greet them. In the natural order of things, she kept to her rooms or her own occupations most of the time, meeting them only at table or occasionally sitting with them in the long evenings. But now she came to them readily, almost blithely.

"We have another guest," she announced in sprightlier tones than usual for her. "A friend of Lady Amanda's, I understand. A friend from home. I made him welcome in your absence."

Amanda stared at the figure who emerged from the salon behind her hostess. The gentleman was tall, neat of person, and wore a bland expression of politeness.

"Giles!" Amanda breathed. "Oh, Giles!" she cried.

Amanda had the sudden wild impulse to race forward to embrace Giles, but fortunately she recalled herself before she could so disgrace herself. Even had she been alone with him and not engaged to wed another, such a rash show of emotion would have been incorrect. It was the sight of his quiet, watchful face which checked her before she could commit such folly.

Constant association with both the viscount and his brother had made her careless. For Gilbert was forever patting her absently, as though she were a favorite spaniel, as he did to all those he considered his familiars. The viscount, she now realized, also somehow always managed to contrive to touch her, even if it were only the slightest brush of his hand against her cheek.

Giles had always reserved any show of physical affection toward her for times late in the evening when they were quite alone, and then, only after a lengthy prelude of quiet talk.

Amanda put out her hand and smiled as Giles took it.

"Giles. How delightful to see you. What brings you to Windham House? Nothing is the matter at home, I hope?" she asked with some trepidation, not daring to believe her letters had been successful, and now envisioning disaster.

"No, nothing is amiss," he answered in his cool, even voice. "It was only that I had some business to attend to locally and decided upon the spur of the moment to have a look in at you, so that I might report upon your condition to your papa."

Since Amanda knew that her papa, in all likelihood, had

not even yet realized she was gone, and in any case was not in the habit of inquiring about her or chatting with Giles about anything but the merits of a particular vintage or fox run, she flushed with pleasure. Giles's pointed stare recalled her to her surroundings once again.

"Giles, where are my manners? Please let me make you known to Viscount North," she said. "Christian, this is a near neighbor and a dear friend of mine, Sir Giles Boothe. And this is his brother, Gilbert Jarrow. Gilbert, Sir Giles Boothe. And the viscountess, I am sure you have already met."

"But we've not yet been properly introduced," Giles corrected her quietly, as he took the lady's hand in turn.

The viscount had been standing at Amanda's side, and now he placed his hand upon her shoulder in proprietory fashion as he said sweetly, "How very pleasant for us that you have come to pay Amanda a call. Since you have come this far, it seems wasteful for you to hurry off. I hope you will be able to stay for some time. Please give us the pleasure of your company for several days, Sir Boothe."

Amanda held her breath until she heard Giles say in reply, "So kind of you, your lordship. I should be delighted to, if it is no bother."

As the viscount reassured Giles, Amanda let out her breath. As she looked about her, she could not escape noticing that though they all wore polite smiles, it was only the two ladies present, herself and the viscountess, who seemed to be genuinely pleased at the turn of events.

If the object of her series of painstakingly devised letters had been to lure Giles to Windham House, then she had succeeded. But if, Amanda thought morosely as she sat to dinner a few nights later, her object had been to spur him to attempt to dissuade her from her forthcoming marriage, she could be counted a dismal failure. For she had not even been able to get him alone for private speech above the space of a few moments. And those few words he had spoken, which she had gone over in her mind a dozen times since, could only be construed as mildly hopeful to her cause at best.

The very first evening he had come, he had met her in the hallway as they were going in to dinner.

"Amanda," he had said carefully, "your letters prompted this visit. As your friend, I felt that I could not rest easy until I had assured myself of your well-being in person."

Then they had gone into dinner, whereupon he had been swallowed up in conversation with Miss Emily and the viscountess. Since that night, he had gone riding with Gilbert, strolling with Lord North, shooting with Gilbert, and touring the countryside with herself and Lord North. The rest of his time had been filled with playing at cards with the entire company or discoursing with them.

Now, looking over the centerpiece of hothouse flowers at him, she felt frustration at how she was hemmed in by the very proprieties he represented. As an engaged female, she could not very well seek him out and draw him to her side alone. Giles was not the sort of fellow one could be that easy with. Such an action would have startled him as much as it might have persuaded him of her unhappiness, for Lord North played the doting cavalier as though he had rehearsed the role since childhood.

Amanda bit at her lip and ignored her fruit compote. To be sure, Christian could not suddenly turn upon her and treat her vilely here in the midst of his family. But his portrayal of a smitten swain did nothing to advance her purposes. Although Giles remained expressionless whenever Christian ran his hand absently across her arm, traced a wayward curl, or held her about the waist before assisting her to mount, she knew Giles must think she had run mad to compose such doubting letters to him when her new fiancé showed such fond courtesies to her. She could only hope that he understood that her infinitesimal leap of shock each time Christian touched her was caused by her dismay, not her pleasure.

She let her dish be removed untouched as she observed Giles and the viscount as they chatted together. Any other eye, she decided glumly, would have found Giles overshadowed by his host. Though both men were slim and straight and wore sober, correct evening dress this night, there was that in the viscount's bold coloring and aspect that made

him seem theatrical. Giles's steady dark gray gaze might
look, she conceded, ordinary when compared to the
viscount's changeable varicolored eyes. Neatly brushed
brown hair might pale compared with that glistening golden
crop. And Giles's precise, toneless speech might strike the
ear as commonplace when compared to the viscount's
amused and dulcet tones. Giles was a few years older,
admittedly, and nothing in either his aspect or his countenance denied that fact. But there was, she thought loyally,
certainly nothing in that reserved countenance to dislike.
He even had, she remembered, as she sought to find
advantage for him, a few inches of height over the viscount.

But, Amanda thought, stabbing into her cream cake,
Giles had not honed his humor against the diamond wits
of the land and continent for decades. He had not danced
attention upon a score of light ladies, nor had he tutored
himself to be as universally pleasing as a fellow whose
confessed avocation it was to play upon the sensibilities of
weak-willed fellow creatures had done. It was because of
Giles's very plainness, his unexceptional steadfastness and
respectability that she had originally been drawn to him.
She sighed and laid aside her cake fork as the viscount
threw back his head to laugh and Giles permitted himself a
smile at the same jest. If Giles had cultivated the same
aspect as the viscount, she should not care for him in the
least, she reminded herself.

When dinner had done and they were all assembled in
the salon again, Gilbert suggested a hand of cards. Amanda
looked forlorn even as all the others readily agreed. As
Gilbert rummaged through a drawer to fetch the cards,
Amanda wondered if she would not have to resort to slipping through the corridors in the depths of night to seek
out her erstwhile suitor for a private talk.

"I suggest," Lord North said easily, watching Amanda's
reaction to his words with an expression of vast amusement,
"that we four family members play the first hand and let
Amanda and Giles catch up on old times together. We've
been such good hosts that I fear they've not had a chance
to exchange a bit of gossip."

Giles said properly that he would be pleased to play

immediately, but there was no question that the viscount alone constituted a majority in his family. Soon the four relatives were playing at a table set near the fire while Giles and Amanda were seated near the window together. They were far enough from the others for private converse, but still, for the first moments they had nothing to say to each other at all.

Amanda could have wept from sheer frustration. She wanted to have Giles's ear privately, but the manner in which the viscount had provided her with that which she had most desired had made the moment even more difficult. It was hard not to feel as though she were betraying him by what she most wanted to say, and she could not shake the feeling that she was committing some sort of verbal adultery, when her unsuspecting fiancé had made such a magnanimous gesture.

"You seem pleasantly situated here, Amanda," Giles said at last. Amanda had then to leave off her ruminations and think out her next words with painful concentration.

"So it would seem," she replied inconclusively, to buy time to frame her utterances concisely.

"I only came here," he went on, picking up a round paperweight and turning it in his long fingers, "because your letters implied some doubt as to your circumstances. We have been friends for so long that I felt it would be remiss of me not to play the part of elder brother—that is, if you needed counsel."

Amanda stifled her mental protest of "Not elder brother!" and instead said quietly, "I have been treated very well here, to be sure. But Giles, I do need counsel. I could scarcely ask Mama's advice—Christian is a pet in her set. Nor, as you know, could I broach the subject to Papa. I'm very glad you have come."

"As I thought," he said, nodding his head sagely. "But then, Amanda, you can scarcely expect me to speak against my host while I remain under his roof."

Amanda sat back and fell still. He was quite right as usual. All the things she was about to say died on her lips.

"But I can say," he stated softly, "that I think it unwise for any female to make a decision that will shape her whole life so precipitously. Or for any gentleman to do so either," he added.

"But especially in your case, Amanda, with your background," he continued blandly, "it seems unfortunate that you raced to such a decision. Still, I find myself wondering how much of the matter was due to your calm thinking, and how much was because you found yourself dealing with a type of person you had little experience of. I do think my trip was not in vain. We shall talk more later. Only know that I have your best interests at heart, and shall attempt to guide you honorably," he concluded.

Amanda had to be content with that utterance about her future. For Giles soon turned the conversation to precisely that which the viscount had mentioned, gossip. She learned of all the doings of her neighborhood, from dogs littering to barns burning, but nothing of the workings of Giles's heart. Soon she was able to rise and rejoin the card players when they summoned her, knowing all that she had no interest in, and nothing of what was her paramount concern.

Throughout the rest of the evening Amanda noted how Lord North observed her with heightened consciousness. When he let his fingers linger against hers, or touched her shoulder, or bent his brilliant smile upon her, it was the fact that she knew Giles was watching as well that made her breathing quicken and her eyes widen. The game that went forward around the gaming table was far more exciting than any of the cards dealt. But that game had only three players, and each concealed his hand from the others well.

When the others had gone off to their beds and Lord North had disappeared into the shadows of the hallway, once again Amanda had a second of privacy with Giles. He took her hand and said softly, "Perhaps we can go for a ride early tomorrow morning, Amanda. Before the others have arisen. Even with a groom attending us, yet we can talk."

"Oh yes, Giles," Amanda concurred.

"At seven then," he said before he made his bows and left her.

She stood at the bottom of the stair, gazing into the direction he had gone.

"How romantic," a drawling voice intruded upon her thoughts. "How greatly daring. What ardent fellows you become entangled with, Amanda."

She wheeled about to face the viscount, who was standing with a decanter and a glass in his hands.

"He can scarcely do more while he is your own guest, my lord," she said heatedly, feeling oddly embarrassed by Giles's proper demeanor and curiously finding herself defending that which needed no defense.

"Oh, I have no complaints," he said happily. "I am a very willing cuckold, remember? It is only that it intrigues me to observe the mating rituals of the respectable. Perhaps I can learn something. Only think, never an impassioned word, not one delicious, hurried, clandestine kiss. It is just that one has to take great care not to stand in the direct line of sight between the two of you, or else risk being blistered by the heat of your stolen glances. And sighs! Lord, one could steer a boat across the lake on the collective strength of those unbottled sighs."

Aware that she was being mocked, and somehow now, with Giles beneath his roof, acutely aware that she and her purported fiancé were alone in the darkened hallway, Amanda felt anxious. She sought words to dispel the nervousness his nearness and his powers of observation brought to her.

"Abominable," she declared vehemently. "Why should you make sport of that which you helped to bring about? I cannot understand you," she complained.

She gave him one last furious look and then marched up the stairs, leaving him alone in the dim light.

"No, how should you," he said to the empty air, "when I expressly wish that you should not?"

XII

It was such an early hour that the horses left fresh track marks upon the skein of hoarfrost the sun had not yet had a chance to melt. The groom who trailed behind the two riders shook his head at the foolishness of the gentry, who would ride so early when they might sleep so late. But Giles had been right, Amanda thought; there could be nothing clandestine about a couple going for a gallop before breakfast.

Neither Amanda nor Giles could know that this was the viscount's customary favorite hour for riding, and as the groom had been specifically requested not to bring the matter up, they could not know that Lord North watched them from his bedroom window as they left the graveled front drive. They rode in companionable silence for a while, for the quiet was so immense that any sound they made might travel easily to the groom's ear. Thus, the first part of their ride was filled only with equestrian sounds: the snorting exhalations of the horses, their hoofbeats, and the creaking sway of the saddles. Even the birds, who were generally subdued of a winter's morning, were as yet completely mute.

When they reached a prospect that looked out over the lake, Giles at last requested Amanda to dismount so that they might stroll the narrow path's perimeters. They gave their mounts to the groom to walk and went on together alone.

Giles was a study in flint tones this morning, Amanda noticed, from his riding jacket to his breeches. The color suited him and she thought he looked distinguished, clear-eyed, and handsome. He appeared every inch to be precisely what he was: nobleman, local magistrate, and authority, at least in her small corner of the kingdom, on all that was just and seemly. She had always considered it a great honor that such an admired gentleman paid court, however tentatively, to her, and now as always she deferred to him and kept silent to await his invitation to speak.

She was glad that she had worn her cherry-colored habit, for he had said when he had first seen her that she looked very nicely. That was a great compliment from him, as he was a man of few, always well-considered words. But he spent no further time with idle chat and said at once when he felt the groom was out of earshot,

"Do you plan to marry North, Amanda? Are you deep in love with him?"

She did not reply straightaway, for if she said a bald "no," he would think her a fool to have gotten involved to the extent that she had. Neither, of course, could she possibly say "yes." So she said, at length,

"I do not know, Giles. Indeed, that is why I wrote to you so often. It wasn't only to get your thinking on the matter, it was also done in the hopes that seeing the thing set out in bold letters might give me a clearer idea of how I was to go on. But I do not know."

"Then you should not wed him," Giles said sternly. "For matrimony is an estate that should only be entered into wholeheartedly. There are enough mistakes made by those who feel sure of success; there is little chance for happiness when there is doubt from the onset."

Although these were the very words she had been hoping to hear, Amanda felt she ought to offer protest.

"But Giles," she said, looking down at her toe tips as she paced, "it seemed the right arrangement at the time we decided." And so, she thought wryly, it had been.

"You have not," Giles began, then hesitated before he plunged on, "you have not committed yourself to an irremedial extent, have you?"

Amanda paused and looked at him. She could not quite

understand his words, so he went on, his usually composed face looking rather strained. "That is to say, Amanda, if I am going to advise you, I think I have the right to know, you have not . . . given yourself irrevocably to him, have you?"

It was his acute embarrassment, evinced by the fact that he looked supremely uncomfortable and did not meet her eyes, that made her realize what he was getting at.

"Oh no!" she cried, so loudly that he swung his head around to see if the groom, who was a distant figure behind them, had heard. "No, of course not. Why, whatever do you think of me?" she went on, now growing a little heated.

"I think you are an unworldly female," he said, his expression composed again, "and I think North uncommonly adept at seduction. I thought so from his reputation, I thought so from the tone of your letters, and now I have met him, I am sure of it. Oh, he is intelligent, and charming to a fault—indeed, he could not be otherwise to have earned such a name for himself. But you are no match for his wiles, Amanda."

She began to speak, but he cut her off with an uplifted hand.

"You asked me to tell you my mind, and so I shall. You cannot blame me if you do not care for what you hear. I will speak my piece, and then be done. But obligation to one's host or not, I did not ride all this way just to return with my thoughts kept to myself."

They halted in their steps and he faced her as he spoke. He seemed almost to be lecturing, and she did not breathe a word lest she misconstrue one word of his discourse.

"When I first heard of your engagement, Amanda, I tell you truthfully I was wounded. Not only that you had promised yourself to a stranger, but that you had not thought to speak to me about it first. We have known each other for several years now, and I thought at least you owed me that courtesy. It was hard, Amanda, to read of it in the papers. Your letter made it no easier," he scolded.

She bowed her head. He nodded and then continued, "At first I was very angry. I thought that I had been entirely wrong in my assessment of you and wondered at how I could have been so blind to your true nature. I confess, I wrote you off and considered my judgment sadly deficient. But then, as I began to receive your letters, I saw that all was not what it seemed at first stare. Clearly, you were confused, and already beginning to regret your rash decision."

Amanda kept her head low and so could not see the triumph briefly flare in his eyes. Nor could she see his face soften as he observed her contrite expression.

He took Amanda's arm and began to walk forward with her again.

"I do not think you should wed him," Giles repeated while Amanda kept her face averted so that he might not see the eager hope with which she received his judgment. But he was too involved with picking out his words to note her reaction this time.

"I have thought about it at length. North is entirely too jaded a creature for you, my dear. It would not be long before he would be off about his philandering once again. He is sadly unsteady in nature. It is true," Giles said expansively, taking note of the fact that she had not raised a protest to his assessment of her fiancé, which he felt she must have if her heart were truly involved, "that the fellow cannot help himself. It is the way he was born, it is the way he will go on."

"What do you mean?" Amanda asked, raising her head.

"You are unworldly, Amanda," Giles said comfortably, "but by now even you must know of his condition."

"You mean," she said, stopping short and causing him to do so as well, "because he has the reputation of a rake?"

"I mean," Giles said, shaking his head because of the unfortunate words he must next utter, "because of his very birth. The fellow is base-born. Not all the accouterments of gentility can alter that."

Amanda's eyes widened. Giles had never mentioned that matter as pertained to her own family, and she was amazed that he would bring up the viscount's circumstances. As though he realized that, he went on, "Surely you have suffered enough because of your own mama's actions that you need not seek out such another for husband?"

There was both everything and nothing wrong in what he said, so Amanda could not reply at once.

"Do you think that I have not witnessed your own struggle to surmount the infamy in which your name is mired?" Giles asked with a wintry smile. He stood to face her and took both her hands in his and raised them as though they were children about to play at London Bridge. Then he said earnestly,

"I believe that with time and care you will succeed. But never if you align yourself with North, for he has never attempted to deny his birthright by word or action."

Amanda could only ask bluntly, "But Giles, there are far more base-born members in my own family. Are we not two of a kind?"

Although he dropped one of her hands, he still held one securely as he replied, "You should not equate yourselves. You're legitimate, Amanda. You can still surmount the obstacles that your family has erected about you. North cannot. The world knows what he is. I wonder if you completely realize that. Did you know that aside from being jested at as the 'Vice-Count North,' he is known in some circles as 'Fitz-North'? Even if he improves his behavior, yet he can never escape that particular epithet. It's common knowledge that his parentage is more anonymous than that of the cattle in the field, for at least the well-bred among them have documented pedigrees. Perhaps if he wed some female of good family, he might come to have his children's children accepted. But if you two married, it would be disaster for both of you. It would only illustrate to the general run of society that the apple does not fall far from the tree."

As Amanda stood and gaped at him, speechless by virtue of all the speech which vied for predominance in her thoughts, he went on, "Similarly, if you should wed a gently born fellow, in time your past might be forgotten. But it is not a thing which you, or he, if he has any wit, ought to rush into in any case."

"Giles," Amanda said, disengaging her hand from his

with a note in her voice quite different from her usual tone, "surely you do not believe that one must suffer for the sins of one's parents? For if so, I wonder that you bear me company. For some of my best friends," she laughed shakily, "and kinfolk, too, are bastards, you know."

His expression did not change, though Amanda felt that she had let a monstrous thing fly from her lips, and had split the world in two with her plain speaking. He only nodded as though satisfied in some strange fashion, and said, "I understand only that the company you have kept of late has influenced your mode of expression. And to its detriment, I might add. This is not you speaking, Amanda; this is the overlaid veneer of sophistication you have adopted to please North. But since you have chosen to be so free of speech, I shall be as well. The world is well aware of love children, it has been so since the dawn of time. But the world has rejected them since then, and with good cause. We remember William the Conqueror and Leonardo, but recollect that we recall them as much for their state of grace at birth as we do for their genius. Rightly or wrongly, bastards are outcasts, Amanda; they are mongrels in a world that values good breeding."

"I should like to go back now," Amanda stated flatly, afraid of hearing more. She had wanted him to discourage the idea of her marrying the viscount, but she had never wanted the reasons he put forth to be given to her.

"But, Amanda," Giles said quickly, staying her by holding her arm firmly, so insistent on what he had to say that he forgot the presence of the groom in the distance.

"I must say further. Not only do I think you ought to break off with North, I think you should return home as soon as possible. We, the two of us, can go on just as we were. I will forget this episode. I do not believe you are irrevocably fated to become like your mama. But I believe that if you remain with North, then you are lost."

"I understand," Amanda said tightly as she wrenched her sleeve from his grasp and walked forward to her mount.

But in truth she did not, she complained to herself as they rode sedately back to Windham House. She did not understand her reactions at all. Giles had said no more than what she might have expected. It was precisely what she herself might have thought a scant month before, so she could not be angry at him. But she was enraged, though she could not fathom why, or at whom the fury was directed. All had gone exactly as hoped for.

Her scheme with the viscount had come to fruition. There was no further need for dissembling. Mama's foolish meddling had been undone, as Giles had said; all could be forgiven and forgotten. But it was not a happy end to her misadventures, for something had changed in the interim and whatever it was, it was certainly not Giles.

It was at three in the afternoon, while the other ladies were napping and Gilbert had cornered Giles for a game of chess, that the viscount finally ran Amanda to earth in the study. She was seated at the desk writing furiously when he entered the room, shut the door behind him, and paused before her.

"Behold me ill with anticipation," he cried. "I have been in a fever of anxiety. How did it go this morning? You and Giles were sublimely indifferent to each other at breakfast and at lunch. But Hodges said you were holding hands during your excursion at dawn. Judging from your pattern in the past, I assume that was your version of ecstatic lovemaking. Has he offered? Am I to gnash my teeth and rattle sabers when he confronts me with the news of your defection?"

"It was as you had thought," Amanda said impassively, ignoring his histrionics.

"Then he has offered? Then I am lost?" Lord North said merrily enough, though he turned to face the windows.

"He only offered his advice," Amanda said, "and that was that I leave you and this place and go home again. He added that we could go on as we were before Mama slipped you into my bedcovers."

"Now that," Lord North said, turning to grin at her, "he did not say. But no offer? That does surprise me. We shall have to cook up something quickly, so that you do not leave here ringless. Gilbert's been nasty enough about the fact that I never gave you a precious token of my devotion; we ought to see what we can do to make Giles come across with something faceted for you."

"You needn't cook up anything," Amanda said, putting a finishing flourish on the letter she was writing and standing. "I shall be leaving here as I came—ringless."

"Ah, that rankles, does it?" he said, walking to the desk. "But I could hardly offer you one for fear you'd fling it back into my face. What's that you've been penning, then? Since you've already gotten Giles here, I assume it's a suicide note to commemorate your failure in netting him. No," he said holding the letter to the light, "I see it's only an excruciatingly polite thank you to my dear mama for all her kindnesses. You needn't have bothered. Your exit will be thanks enough for her. She's been wretchedly unhappy since you set foot in Windham House. The thought of you thwarting me in my attempt to spawn legal brats will far exceed any gratification she could receive from a mere note."

He put the letter down and watched as she scrubbed ink from her hands with a penwiper.

"Why leave before anything is resolved?" he asked idly.

"Nothing will be resolved for some time," Amanda said, avoiding his eye, "so there's no sense in my remaining here. It is enough that we have been able to mend matters; the rest will take time."

"I see," the viscount said thoughtfully, "he plans a wait of five years so that he may be sure you don't err again, perhaps two more to ensure your penance, then a three- or four-year engagement to be absolutely sure of your steadiness of character. You will wed from an invalid chair if you're not careful, Amanda. You'll have to listen to the vicar through a hearing trumpet as well. I can just envision a decrepitated Giles attempting to wedge a ring over your arthritic knuckles as you quaver, 'I do.' Don't do it, Amanda," he said, his face suddenly still.

"What?" she asked stupidly, unsure of what he had said.

He took her by the shoulders with hard hands.

"Don't marry him," he said, his bright face strangely solemn. "It wouldn't be right. Not for you. Oh, you'll get him to the altar in due course of time, but it isn't worth it. He's not for you."

"He said the same of you," she replied, gazing into his distinctive eyes.

"He's right there. But so am I," Lord North said. "It would be hellish, you with him."

"I know you think him stolid and stodgy," she began, but he shook her gently to silence and went on abruptly, as though the words were driven from his lips.

"No, no he's not. I thought you had painted a picture of a suitor who was fair, true, and solidly worthwhile, and so he is. You are not a fool, your judgment was sound. But it's his respectability you're after, my girl, and never mind his wide shoulders and his big gray eyes. And that very respectability will be what drives you to despair. For if ever you happen to sigh over an actor upon a stage, or laugh at a butcher boy's cheekiness, or comment on any fellow's fine figure, he'll impale you with his stare. He'll never trust you, Amanda, not in his heart. In time, you'll stop trusting yourself. You'll either diminish to a Cousin Emily or outdo your dear mama for spite. It won't do, love. It would never do."

As he shook his head and smiled at her, Amanda gazed blankly ahead. There was so much truth in his words that she felt her heart constrict.

"Perhaps," she murmured, "perhaps you are right. But I'm free of my predicament. I'll go home now, Christian. My way is clear to that, at least."

"Home?" He laughed scornfully. "What sort of refuge is that? If you had had a proper home, my sweet, you would not have yearned for Giles so passionately. Do you intend to go home and collect cats or dwindle to a housekeeper for your papa when he tires of the slattern he's keeping? Don't wrench away from the truth, 'Manda, and that is that you would be better off repairing to a nunnery straightaway than traveling home again."

Having given up her brief struggle to be free of his hands upon her shoulders, she now attempted to turn her head aside so that he could not see her face. But this he did not permit. His mood seemed to turn to cruelty, so he held her fast as he went on angrily,

"You are three and twenty, 'Manda, too old for childish illusions. Shall you let your entire life pass by while you air-dream of what could be, if only, perhaps?" he mocked.

"Without illusions I should become like my mama," she cried, heedless of her angry tears. "Is that what you wish for me?"

"No, 'Manda," he said more quietly now, as though her tears had dampened his rage, "it is only *with* illusions that you could emulate your mama."

"And what is your advice, then," she asked, lifting her chin, "if I am not to marry Giles, and not to return home, and not to take up where my mother has left off? Shall I indeed hang myself from some convenient rafter?" she said bitterly.

"No," he said calmly, "but something very much like. Marry me, 'Manda, and be damned to the lot of them."

She gaped at him as though he had run mad.

"It makes perfect sense," he said, releasing her as she wiped savagely at her face with her hand. "I am responsible for your distress, or at least as much so as your mama. I proposed this scheme, and now I see it is unworkable. I offer recompense. Come, 'Manda, think on it. I, of all souls on this planet, will never throw your family history in your face. It would not bother me in the least if you had a legion of illegitimate relatives."

"I thought you never wished to wed," Amanda said, forgetting the import of his offer in the very strangeness of it.

"Why, so I didn't," he smiled. "I see you have been speaking deeply with Gil. But as I cannot give up the title unless it is over Gil's lifeless body, for so he has told me, I cannot ensure that he and his inherit the succession in any case. I can sign Windham House over to him, though, and have always intended to do so anyway the moment he himself weds. We can be very snug at Hollyhedge, 'Manda, or in my town house, or even upon the continent. I'm very warm in the pocket. Do not fear we will have to dwell in a hovel. I offer a fair exchange. I took your reputation, I

offer you mine. It isn't much, lord knows, but I think it is
far better than any other alternative open to you."

Amanda stood and studied him. Her arrested expression
was so altered, so unlike her, that for a moment he felt as
though she were a stranger coolly weighing him up in a
balance. Then she spoke slowly.

"And all this for my sake? Come, my lord. Wherever is
the advantage for you? You are not such a selfless fellow as
this, I think."

Her words were so at variance with her appearance, for
at the moment she looked so small and so young, her gray
eyes misted with tears, her little pointed chin still trembling,
that the harsh truth she spoke seemed to have come from
another's lips. He gave a crow of delight.

"Very good! You have some defenses left after all. Well,
I shall tell you, sweet. Wherever in all this world shall I
find a female who is at once gently bred, literate, comely,
and pure, who will not forever hold my birth against me?
You have grown up considering my state commonplace.
You are quite unique on this island England. I should have
to go to Arabia, at least, to find another such. For there,
gently bred females are accustomed to seeing their fathers
sire multiple offspring from diverse females. Only then, I
should have the trouble of teaching my bride not to eat
with her fingers, to say nothing of the language barrier.
And I refuse to harbor camels," he laughed.

He looked so merry, so alive and enthusiastic, his face
lit with such mischievous joy that it seemed he was propos-
ing some schoolboy lark, rather than marriage.

"And I am of an age to wed, past it, actually. Unlike
Giles, I cannot see the advantage of waiting until my dotage
to exchange vows. I cannot fancy myself being as toothless
as my own firstborn when that happy event occurs. You
have told me that you don't wish to follow your mama's
lead, and I readily believe you. I don't have to let a decade
crawl by as I closely observe your honesty. Come, 'Manda,
don't you wish to kick dust in all their faces?"

He gazed down at her and went on, as though he
wished to carry her along by the sheer exuberance of his
reasoning.

"You cannot be so noble that in some secret part of you you don't wish to see Giles confounded by your marital happiness, left to cursing himself for a fool for not snatching you up when he had the chance. And I confess, I have the most base desire to see my mama wail at my wedding. Let's do it, 'Manda," he urged her with a grin.

"You would wed me," she said carefully, "because you owe me recompense, because we share a shameful heritage, and because we can confound everyone by our union?"

"You want more than that?" he asked, cocking his head to one side. "We have more than that. We get on very well together, you know. We make each other laugh. Not enough?" he asked curiously as he saw that her face was grave.

"Greedy thing," he laughed low. "You shall have even more then."

He pulled her into his arms. "We have this as well," he whispered in a low voice as he kissed her. His kiss was long and deep and thorough, and she never for a moment sought to escape him. By the time that he drew back from her with a wondering exclamation, he realized that for once he had gotten back in full all that he had given.

After he had waited quietly without receiving a word of her reaction, he asked softly, "You see?" He looked at her expectantly, this time without using the many words he could usually call up so easily. Instead, he only touched her cheek gently and asked again, "You see, 'Manda? It is an excellent idea."

Amanda stood stone-still, wavering slightly, her eyes half closed. She looked lost until at last his words and touch called her back to him again.

"Oh I see," she answered finally on a shuddering sigh. "I see clearly now, thank you."

Then she straightened her shoulders and gave him such a blazing look of fury that he blinked. "I see that you and Giles are kindred spirits, for all your outward differences," she said vehemently. "You are opposite sides of the coin, but you are both cast from the same metal. He has not offered for me because I am my mother's daughter and you have offered for me only because I am my mother's daughter. There is your commonality. There is the one most important thing about me for both of you. For if Giles would have wed me years ago if it were not for Mama, I doubt you would even consider me for your wife if it were not for her."

"Well, it won't do," she cried as she stepped away from him. "It will never do," she said furiously as she stalked to the door.

"I am Amanda Amberly, and I am myself. And if neither of you can forget for a moment that I am one of the Amberly Assortment, then I say the devil fly away with the pair of you. You do kiss very well, my lord," she added fairly as she opened the door. "But there's more to marriage than that, I think. I am leaving Windham House, and you are free, and Giles is free, but most of all, I am free."

"But where shall you go?" he asked in honest perplexity.

"Why to the very place for me," she said, her head held high, "to the only one whose presence accounts for all my desirability to you and lack of desirability for Giles. To the one neither of you seems to be able to get out of your minds for a moment when you think of me. I'm going home to my mama, of course."

After curtsying very deeply and respectfully, she left the room hurriedly with all the calm dignity she could muster—except she did slam the door behind her till it rattled on its hinges.

XIII

Amanda paced the morning room as she waited for Miss Emily to be done with her breakfast so that they could be on their way at last. It had been three days since she had made her decision, and now all that remained to be done was to make her last good-byes to Windham House and its occupants. That it was only she and the viscount who knew that these were to be quite final farewells only made her task more difficult.

She had already had her last words with him. Although she had passed the previous days attempting to avoid all the inmates of Windham House by pleading so much physical infirmity that they could have been forgiven for imagining her on her death bed nightly, she had suffered through one further private interview with her host.

Lord North's demeanor had been cool and detached and he had only asked if she might reconsider her decision. When she hotly denied any such possibility, he had merely shrugged. He had listened to her plan of action quietly, his face so composed throughout her recitation that she had difficulty recalling the warmth and brightness with which he had previously attended to her.

When he at last suggested reasonably enough that she be the one to place the notice of their "disengagement," as he termed it, in the papers so that he would not appear to be a complete bounder, he had seemed so distant that Amanda could scarcely believe that she had ever seen that vulnerable, hungry look upon his face when he had done kissing her.

As he calmly informed her that he thought it only fair

that she take Cousin Emily back with her, if not for
propriety's sake, then at least as an act of charity toward
the poor inhabitants of Windham House, Amanda could
detect nothing but ironic amusement in his light voice. She
marveled at his attitude. For if she could not as yet forget
the extravagant sweetness of his lips upon hers, as much as
she attempted to, then it seemed that he did not even recall
there had ever been such intimacy between them. She had
to conclude, when he left off the interview by casually
wishing her well, that practiced rakes such as he had
conveniently dim memories or at least never looked backward upon pleasure, only forward toward the acquiring of
more. She found the possibility that he had not derived as
much from that embrace as she had too lowering to
contemplate.

Now, as Amanda fretted and wondered at how many
more cups of tea and racks of toast Miss Emily would
consume before she deemed herself equipped for travel,
she thought that at least she had acquitted herself well at
that last hurried meeting with her former affianced. For
she had not let her eyes dwell upon his face when she
promised that her public announcement of their engagement's dissolution should be made only after she had left
Windham House forever. And she had never once let her
voice falter as she had agreed that keeping the news from
Gilbert until she was far away enough in person and
memory from him to blunt the blow was the kindest
course.

Last night Gilbert's eyes had grown wide as saucers and
she glimpsed the child behind the man when she had
announced at dinner that she wished to return to her
mother's house for a space. When Lord North had followed up that pronouncement by pleasantly agreeing that
he thought a young woman ought to be alone with her
mother for a time, Gilbert had actually laid down his fork
in the midst of attacking his favorite meat pie.

Those simple twin announcements had in fact created a
vast stir about the table. Giles had stiffened and stared
hard at her before he regained his composure. The viscountess had enough years of control and breeding to

allow no more than a flash of wild eagerness to come into her eyes before she had quickly lowered her gaze over her pleasure. Miss Emily had gone on eating, only pausing to announce that she would be delighted to see the dear countess again, but Gilbert had neglected his meal entirely and had passed the dinner hour looking accusingly at both his brother and Amanda in turn.

After dinner, Amanda successfully eluded the entire company by again fleeing to her rooms, but not before she heard Giles's disclosure. For he flatly stated that as Kettering Manor was on his route home—only off it, he conceded to Gilbert's outraged stare, by some mere fifty miles or so—he would be pleased to accompany the two ladies to their destination. As the viscount raised no protest and Miss Emily immediately expressed her delight, Amanda remained mute about the acquisition of an escort.

Amanda mentally unpacked her traveling cases now to be sure that she had left nothing behind. She had just located her paisley shawl in her mental luggage when a triumphant exclamation shattered the silence of the morning room.

"Aha!" Gilbert cried as he stormed into the room. He stood gazing at her, his fists on his hips, his legs apart, glowering as though she were a prisoner in the dock and he, the king's prosecutor.

"I've run you down, 'Manda, and I shall have my say," he threatened. "Chris is mute as a stone on the subject, and what with your headaches and toothaches and brainstorms and lord knows what else, you've been playing least in sight with me. But I've steered Cousin Emily to the ginger preserves and bought myself some time with you at last. Now what's this all about, my lady?"

Without giving her a heartbeat of time to answer, he walked up to her and continued, all anger gone and only a petulant expression upon his face, "It's clear as ice to me that you're giving Chris the final push, and for the life of me, I can't say why. Why, you two suit, 'Manda, you suit right down to the ground. I know the fellow's got a shocking reputation, but you knew that when you promised yourself to him. You were wise enough then to know that it's not all his fault. The chap's got such a pretty phiz, he can't help it if the ladies fling themselves at him. He's not made of granite, you know, but I'll wager he hasn't cast a glance at any but you since you've met. No, and neither will he in future, for I know the chap, and he's as solid as a rock beneath that damnable care-for-nothing air of his."

Gilbert went on in his usual fashion, attempting to put all his arguments before her in one breath.

"And I've eyes in my head and I never saw nor heard any insult given to you, and he could cut glass with that tongue of his if he'd a mind to. Why, he's leagues in love with you, 'Manda. And if he's overstepped his bounds in his ardor—" and here Gilbert had the grace to flush before he said hurriedly—"not that it's my place to know or speak of it, but it would only be because he's an affectionate sort of fellow. But the moment you tie the knot, he'd be yours forever. He won't take up with another female, if that's what's concerning you. For he's not a sneak, nor unfaithful in any of his dealings. Why are you running out on him, 'Manda?" he concluded unhappily.

"I'm only going home to Mama for a visit, Gilbert," Amanda said, but her voice was so weak and insincere that it sounded hatefully cozening, even to her own ears.

Gilbert's lips set in an angry pout as he declared, "And going back with that stick Sir Boothe to hold your hand. The Friday-faced fellow hasn't an ounce of life to him, 'Manda. Ah, I cannot understand this. Mama's in alt at your leaving, but then she's never been fair to Chris. I'll say it and be glad. She's aces high on me, and I'm not a patch on him. It ain't only that he's no blood of hers, I'll venture. It must go deeper than that. Perhaps it's because Papa doted on him. The two were like peas in a pod. Always jabbering together on what was catnip to them both, their books and travels and politics and what not. Yes, and I'd stake my life that Papa wouldn't have let you just sail out of here and out of Chris's life. No, he wouldn't, and I wouldn't either if I had an idea of how to stop you short of crippling the horses."

Gilbert subsided into brooding, looking so woebegone that Amanda could easily believe that he had cast himself headfirst into the briars in his infancy when in high emotion. All she could do to attempt to cheer him was to offer up further paltry excuses about a daughter's devotion to her mama. She did not have to go on very long in this embarrassingly insincere fashion. Within moments, Giles came into the room, already clad in his greatcoat, and Miss Emily, sated at last, came to tell Amanda to ready herself for their journey.

Gilbert stood at the top of the stairs as the two coaches awaited their passengers. He gave Amanda a gruff good-bye, but would not meet her eyes. She felt heartsick as she turned to the viscountess's genuinely gratified and warm farewell. Then Lord North bent to Amanda to say his last. Although the day was shockingly cold, he had put on no coat, and for a moment Amanda was tempted to caution him to return to get one. As he had been working in his study, he had left off his jacket as well.

He stood before her, his white shirt cuffs fluttering in the brisk wind, his golden hair whipped across his forehead, and he smiled such warmth at her that he dispelled all thoughts of winter.

"Fare thee well, 'Manda," he said softly, "and return even more swiftly," he added more audibly for benefit of the company that awaited her departure. But then he bent his head to brush his cool lips against her cheek and whispered for her ear alone, "You can change your mind, 'Manda. You can change your mind at any time. I shall be here."

Then he assisted her into the coach, although Giles stood waiting to do so. Even to the last, as the lead coach pulled down the drive, Amanda stayed turned to watch him. In his white shirt and buff breeches, his light hair so vivid against the dim day, he appeared to be one lost beam of sunlight illuminating the stair. She gazed back at him till she could see no more, since it seemed the cold breezes had made her eyes water so profusely.

It ought to be mandatory, Amanda thought crossly as she sought a comfortable position in her corner of the lurching coach, for a couple contemplating matrimony to be locked together into a traveling coach and forced to occupy themselves with nothing but conversation for a day. If someone like Cousin Emily was included in the bargain, she was sure that a substantial portion of church income would be lost forever. She had a great deal of time to spare for such disgruntled musings, as she sat and observed her traveling companions, for she had not spoken a word for over an hour.

Giles and Miss Emily had been carrying on a most mutually satisfactory conversation steadily since they had stopped for luncheon. If, Amanda corrected herself, one could call that which was issuing from the pair conversation at all. For the discourse consisted of Giles airing his viewpoints on a variety of subjects, with Miss Emily interjecting appropriate sounds of agreement and delight throughout. Amanda's own response was not solicited, since, she realized with a sudden jolt that made her sit up straight, she seldom was asked to contribute more than Miss Emily was now providing.

As she watched the pair through narrowed eyes, Giles smiled at her, thinking her abrupt reaction caused by her enthusiasm for a point he had just made. She smiled back tentatively, guilt spurring her as much as politeness. For it could not be Giles's fault that her recent sojourn had so altered her perceptions.

They seemed to have been traveling forever and that was odd as well, for Amanda's experience had taught her that some unwritten physical law of nature always made a return trip shorter than the way forth. But on the first journey, she remembered, she had scarcely marked the hours, having been first occupied by her trepidation and then with the attentions of the viscount. She had originally marked all these same weary miles with wit, with laughter, and with lively interest. For the viscount never said a thing without expecting her response. If she had merely nodded or exclaimed about his wisdom, he would have roasted her alive. She nodded at Giles again and pushed away all inappropriate thoughts of another gentleman's intent, alert reactions.

She bore another day's travel in much the same fashion.

But when they at last achieved the inn where they were to stay the second night, she could no longer escape the lingering presence of her former fiancé. For they rested at the Fox and Grapes again. Though Amanda had a secret moment of amusement imagining the landlord's private thoughts about a female who came to his lodgings so often with a variety of gentlemen escorts, that was the only present enjoyment she had. All the rest was in remembrance of times past in his establishment.

There was no strange, intimate conversation after dinner in the private parlor, since Giles so rightly heeded convention. There was no half-frightened, half-anticipatory reaction to Giles's good night to her, for she knew he meant only to bid her good night. But there was little sleep for her in any case, since Lord North's presence was as palpable as though he were sitting in her room, helping her to keep watch through the long night.

So it was that when at last the carriage stopped in the drive of Kettering Manor, Amanda sprang forth from the coach like a jack-in-the-box loosed from its confines. She greeted her mother with outsize pleasure as that lady hastened from the hall to admit her unexpected visitors. But one look at her mama's shocked face drained all of Amanda's enthusiasm.

"Amanda!" the countess gasped, "whatever on earth are you doing here? Where is North? Whatever have you done?"

"I've come back," was all that Amanda could manage to say.

"Oh lud," the countess sighed, ignoring Amanda's companions in her distress, "you've gone and mucked it all up."

"Out with it," the countess cried, bustling into Amanda's room and flinging back the draperies to admit the morning light. "I've waited half the morning for you to show your face, and cannot bear to wait a moment longer. I understand that you could not speak last night; it's a hard journey down from North's establishment. And so I let you go to sleep with all my questions unanswered. Lud,

child, you look hagged," she said as she peered at Amanda
rising from her coverlets. "Did you get no rest at all in all
these hours?"

She had not, but Amanda passed a hand through her
curls and said, "I always look so in the morning."

The countess looked doubtful, but only said, as Amanda
stretched, "I've spoken with Emily Atkinson, and though
she is the most convivial soul, the dear clearly does not
know the day of the week. I refuse to pass another word
with Sir Boothe. Not that I've come to cuffs with him, for
I know better than that, but he's so politely disapproving
of me that I long to turn him from my door. All he will
say is that you wished to bear me company for a while and
that he accompanies you since he is returning home. But
as Kettering Manor is not on the west road, I take leave to
doubt that. What is going forth, Amanda? I demand to
know."

As Amanda's face was now immersed in suds in the
wash basin, there was no reply. The countess contented
herself with rummaging through her daughter's luggage
while Amanda vanished into a side chamber to attend to
her morning's ablutions. When she emerged tying a sash
about her robe, the countess seated herself in a chair by
the window and motioned Amanda toward its twin facing
her.

"Now," she said curtly, "not a bite shall you eat nor
shall you leave this room till you have told me what has
transpired."

Amanda toyed with a tassel at the end of her sash and
observed her mama. The countess sought to maintain a
stern expression, but a look of concern kept crossing her
delicate features. Amanda tried to temper her next words.

"I have left North. It was a sham, Mama. I could not
keep it up any longer."

"He offered you insult?" the countess asked fearfully.

"Oh no," Amanda sighed, "never, not really, no never
in words." She paused as she realized that he had never
truly insulted her in actions either. He had passed so much
time in warning her of his base intentions and she had
spent so much time imagining what he might do, that it

had not occurred to her until now, as she sought to explain it, that he had actually never wholeheartedly begun the seduction he was forever warning her about.

"No," she said at last, wonderingly, "no never in actions, either. He was a gentleman. Or at least as much of a gentleman as he could be," she temporized, wondering if a true gentleman would kiss and cuddle a lady who was a guest beneath his roof. But then, she wondered if a fiancée, mock or not, was considered quite a lady guest.

Her mama watched the puzzlement chase the astonishment across Amanda's face and then asked again, "He asked you to leave, then?"

"Oh no," Amanda corrected her immediately. "In fact, he asked me to stay on. He asked me to marry him, in fact."

"And you would not?" the countess asked in confusion. "I cannot understand. I thought you two so well matched, that is why I brought you together. In a manner of speaking, of course," the countess added hastily, her face becoming rather red. "For it was my silly mistake about the gray and the blue rooms which accomplished the thing prematurely. I had every intention of introducing you properly at the first possible moment. For I know North of old. He has a dreadful reputation, but I swear he is one of the best fellows I've ever met. He's very honorable in all his dealings, and witty," she continued, hastily sliding over certain aspects of the viscount's reputation. "Wise enough for your most exacting standards, young enough to be flexible, but old enough to know his mind. Wealthy, and handsome as sin. What is there to dislike in him?"

Amanda sat without replying and tangled the tassel upon her sash as her mother awaited her answer. Finally she said in a very low voice, "He does not love me."

"Ah," said her mama with a world of comprehension in the syllable. Presently she asked slowly, "But my child, North was never a one for conventions. He would not have proposed marriage for respectability's sake. Now why else should he have offered for you if his heart was not involved?"

Amanda stood and turned from her mother. What she

had to say now was a thing she had never mentioned to that lady.

"He told me he offered because we had so much in common," she said in a low voice. "You see, because of my history, he felt that I could never fling his dishonor in his face. Oh, Mama," Amanda said desperately, wheeling about to face the countess, "he is base-born, I'm sure you know of that. And it is a thing which eats at his soul, as well it might. Because of my experience with his kind, he feels that I would not mind marrying him. Similarly, he thinks that flaw in himself, which might prevent marriage with a gently bred female, would make no difference to me. And for that reason, and that alone, he asks for my hand. With no word of love," she said as though to herself, "or devotion or caring. Simply because we share a shame."

"You have a care for him, then?" her mother asked thoughtfully.

Amanda only made a bleak gesture with her hands, and sat again. He had been right, she thought; she was not a fool. She did have good judgment. And she had known almost from the moment she had left Windham House— although she had not admitted it to herself then—that she had left some integral part of herself behind there with him. She felt the lack of him acutely and had done so during the interminable coach ride as Giles had prosed on with Miss Emily. She had missed him constantly at the Fox and Grapes. Last night, while her aching body had demanded sleep, her active mind had pictured his bright face, her ears had retained the echoes of his soft voice.

Almost she regretted having left him now, though every reasonable thought applauded her action. Had she stayed on she might never have left. Had she wed him, she knew, it would have meant disaster for her. To enter marriage with no expectations of anything but light affection would have been to sow the whirlwind. She could not have endured the indignity of knowing she alone brought love to the union. And what if he discovered love only after he had wed her, but with someone else? She could not have borne the years of watching him disport with other females, in any case. For she would be impelled to pay him back.

How long then, until the Countess of Clovelly's daughter became even more infamous than her mama?

All this she thought, but all she said to her mama was, "It makes no matter. I came back to you to tell you I have ended it."

"And you intend, instead, I take it, to wed Sir Boothe?" her mother asked heavily.

"Oh no." Amanda laughed. "No longer. Though I expect I shall never have the chance to refuse him. Giles likes me very well, but he does not care for my name. I'm sorry, Mama, but there it is. There it always is," she said, unable to speak further, having already spoken more from her heart than she ever had done with her mama.

"I'm sorry for it," the countess answered, "though not if it prevents your taking up with Sir Boothe. For I cannot like him, and never have been able to."

"But you've only just met him." Amanda smiled sadly, feeling quite alone, realizing the impossibility of having a serious conversation with her lightheaded mama.

"No, there you are out, Amanda," the countess said calmly, "for I do know him. I've met him times without number in London. Don't look so amazed, child. I know most souls in the land even if they chose not to noise it about. Your dear Sir Boothe amuses himself handsomely when he is on the town. He may set himself up as a saint when he is at home, as so many of his kind do, but I've seen some of the birds of paradise he flies with when he is on the strut. Don't goggle, Amanda," she chided, "it ill becomes you. You may be very educated, but you've a great deal to learn. There are a good many respectable folk who point a finger at North or me and my set while they themselves have a great deal to hide."

"I've never spoken to you about myself, Amanda," the countess continued, plucking at her skirts, "because it never seemed the right time. First you were too young, and then when I turned around, you were too old. But I believe it is time now. For if you must live with my name, at the very least you deserve to know how I got it. Oh dear," she sighed, looking so prettily confused for a moment, so much like the mama that Amanda knew, that she could scarcely believe the sensible words she began to speak.

"I'm sorry for the difficulties you've had being my daughter," the countess said. "And indeed I never thought on it, being quite a selfish creature, I'm afraid. But I did not set out to scandalize myself. I wed your father as he wed me, with and upon the instructions of our families. There was no vow of love, nor was any expected, but I attempted to be a good and faithful wife.

"When you were rising four," the countess said restlessly, as though she did not enjoy her remembrances, "your father informed me that he required no further heirs. You understand," she interrupted herself to gaze at Amanda, "that meant he allowed me my freedom and did not plan to frequent my bedchambers any longer. I did not believe him, even when he took up with another female, for I was far more strictly raised than you, my dear."

The countess allowed herself to laugh at her own utterance. Then she sobered and said carefully, "I went to London and took up with a fast set. I expected that word of my behavior would reach your father and that he in turn would come to bring me home. I was," she sighed, "extremely youthful for my age. To be brief, I met up with a rake, the Marquess of Carrick, fancied myself in love for the first time, and soon had to return home to bear Mary, for he would have no part of me when I told him of my situation.

"When I returned to town, I vowed to be more clever. But then I met a gentle, good, and compassionate man, Sir Harley Kilcane. I do not apologize for my liaison with him, my dear, and never shall. If he were not already tied to an invalid wife, we should have wed. He was beside himself with both despair and delight when Alicia was born, and determined to risk his name and his reputation in divorce when James was on the way. But he was even less robust than his wife, and succumbed to consumption before it was possible. The more fool I," the countess sighed, brushing at her eye, "for I had thought his pallor interesting and the bright spots in his cheeks due to his ever high spirits.

"After that I met my own dear Bobby, and after Cecil

came, we decided to flaunt convention and dwell together. The duchess will never give him his freedom; she is content to live with his name and without him. And, to be sure, there is no longer any reason for us to wed; we rub on together well enough the way we are. Divorce is no easy thing, my dear; there are only a handful obtained every year, and those only after so much scandal and name-blackening that it is hardly worth the effort.

"So you see," the countess said simply, "I am not such a wicked lady as you may have thought. Or perhaps I am, at that. But I am not light in my affections, Amanda, no matter what you have heard, nor have I ever been for sale. Mind, I do not ask you to excuse me, only to understand me."

Amanda sat very still. The countess, construing her amazement as disapproval, said, as though defending herself, "And at that, I believe I am villified the most for my honesty. For I could never give my children up. Many of the same grand dames who pretend to be aghast at me have gone for their own little repairing leases in the country in midseason. Oh yes," the countess said sagely to Amanda. "They begin to grow a little stout and then claim an overwhelming fondness for rustication. When they return, they are slim as wands, and some farmer's family has another child donated to help with work in the fields.

"And of course, the light sisterhood does the same," the countess reflected, "for there is little help for it. The gentlemen may like to forget it, but certain doings result in offspring, without fail. I am not saying it is common practice, but it is common knowledge, at least. All are not so fortunate as I," the countess grimaced, "to have such a free-thinking husband. But still I cannot understand how any could lightly give away a child as though it were a frock one had outgrown."

"What becomes of them?" Amanda asked suddenly, her mind returning from her mother's story to her own problem, "the cast-off children, I mean."

"They are taken in for a sum by farmers and the like, I imagine," the countess replied, "for they always need an extra hand to turn to work. And I have always thought that they are kinder to their children than we who purport to be above them, for they welcome each new addition to their house, or so it seems."

"Have you ever heard of the reverse?" Amanda asked quickly. "A farm-woman giving away her child?" She would have liked to clarify her question when her mother gazed at her uncomprehendingly, but dared not say further on a subject she felt was not hers to ask about.

"Why no," her mama replied. "As I have said, they treasure their offspring, there is always some relative to take them in. And who would seek them out, anyway? Children are cheap commodities as they are so easily gotten, Amanda," the countess sighed. "I know many who would pay a king's ransom if they could purchase a good way not to have them. But that's not the point. I have told you my tale because I believe that though one's life is one's own, parents owe their children explanation at least, for any stigma that might attach to them as consequence of their actions. Have you any questions you have hesitated to ask?" she ventured.

Amanda had a great many questions about a different set of parents and their actions, but none that her mother could answer. Still, she thought she owed her mama some query in reply to show that she understood and appreciated her candor, so she put her own thoughts away to frame one.

"Mama," she said slowly, as that lady steeled herself for whatever she might choose to ask, "I do have one question that I have been told I ought to ask. As we are speaking so frankly, do you remember a stack of slim green leather volumes that you secreted in the library years ago?"

Her mother started and glanced at Amanda nervously, wondering if her daughter's mind was wandering due to all the shocks she had been subjected to. But seeing Amanda's serious expression, she cudgeled her wits to recall the volumes as Amanda, choosing her words with great care, described them and their contents.

"Lud!" the countess cried, holding one dainty hand to her breast, "I thought we had burned them all. Never say you discovered them? And if you left them there, so they remain there to this hour, for Bobby and I are not great readers," she said regretfully. "I must have them destroyed before anyone else discovers them. They are rude, and crude as well, and there is nothing but malice in them."

The countess rose and hastened toward the door, but Amanda stopped her by saying gently, "But Mama, before you burn them, there is a question I must ask about them."

The countess stopped and looked very ill at ease as her daughter attempted to frame her request.

"My child," the Countess of Clovelly began, "the verse about me was untrue, you know, and as to the others, I can hardly vouch for their authenticity . . ." Her voice trailed off in uncertainty.

"No, no, Mama," Amanda said kindly, "I care nothing for the verses. It is only that I have always wished to ask you . . . it has been suggested that I ask you . . ." She hesitated and then plunged on, a look of fierce embarrassment upon her face, ". . . about the illustrations."

"Ah," the countess replied, nodding her head sagely. She glanced at her daughter's averted eyes and then pulled herself together in a very businesslike fashion. "An excellent idea, Amanda," she said briskly, "a meritorious idea. I shall just nip down to the library and fetch a copy now. As you are three and twenty and unwed, I believe it is past time we discussed them. And then," she added slyly, with a hint of the look that had brought the gentlemen of London to their knees decades before, "then we shall warm ourselves about a comfortably burning book while we decide what to do with your future."

XIV

The gentleman packed his portmanteau rapidly. His valet, he decided, as he paused for a moment to assess the number of neckcloths he needed and then cast several in without counting them, could do a far superior job of it. But that fellow would have taken hours with the task that he was accomplishing in minutes, and now he valued time above precision. He would let Atkins pack the necessary at leisure, for he had given him his direction so they could meet up later. Now he was in a fever to be off and would not let merely fashionable considerations forestall him.

As the viscount went to his wardrobe to get some shirts, he thought with a grim smile that he had done this so often that the actions came to him without thinking. It seemed that he had been constantly traveling since the moment he had decided to return to England. But as he reached for his shirts, he realized that he had been in transit for many years before then, as well. Whenever the company had palled, whenever he had found himself in a situation that had become tedious, whenever he wished to escape something or some thought, he had pulled out his portmanteau as though he could pack all his doubts in it with all his clothes, and had gone off without ever a look behind him.

This time was no different, although it was altogether unique. This time it was not the presence of someone that he was fleeing, it was the absence of someone. Since she had left, the viscount thought, packing his shirts deep within his traveling bag, Windham House had become intolerable to him. He had walked, he had ridden, he had paced the long halls until he had realized that he must be quit of this place. Now his mind was made up, and no thing on earth could divert him; it had always been so.

It was not that he missed her, it would have been impossible to miss someone whose unseen presence was felt in every corner of his house. It was instead that he could not rid himself of her. Lord North flung an extra pair of boots into his bag with a careless vehemence that would have made his valet wince, and thought of how many manifestations of her he had encountered in the long days since she had left. That was odd too, for he was used to more static ghosts of the past haunting him.

He paused for a moment at his dressing table, his hands arrested in midair above his brush, as he mused about the phenomenon. Most persons he had locked in his mind's eye seemed to be forever fixed in one aspect, as firmly and unchangeably imprinted upon his memory as each of his family was posed and frozen in their portraits in the bright, long gallery. When a name was recalled to him, he would recall that face as it had appeared in one distinctive expression.

Gilbert would always be that beet-red furious infant, lower lip jutted out, face swollen with outrage, eternally poised as he was about to fling himself into the nettles. His mama would always come to his mind as she had been in that one moment of frantic spite. Not one of the warm, compassionate smiles she wore in his childhood could be recalled without effort. Although they customarily slid by each other carefully since he had attained adulthood, and when he surprised an emotion in her eyes as she covertly observed him it was generally one of embarrassed regret, yet he could never forget the malignant look she had borne that one day. His adoptive father would always come to his mind as he had been on a distant winter's night, as a gently smiling adversary in a chess game that he replayed frequently in his memories, with that same anticipatory look of glee upon his gentle face that had caused him to betray his move and lose the game.

Some persons he had never bothered even to frame in his memory. It would shock most of the females he had

ever known, from those partners in affairs that had lasted
for months to those chance-met bedmates he had taken
through boredom, if they could know that he could recall
them only in fragmentary fashion. Here a smile, there a
dimple, now a flash of breast, or then a moment of repletion,
he remembered them as spasmodically as he had entangled
himself with them. For as he had taken them only for
pleasure's sake, they had returned nothing but delight to
his senses and thus he bore no trace of them upon his heart
or mind.

It was not that he was an uncommonly cold fellow, but he
would have had to be wanting in wits to take any one of
the light ladies from his set seriously. He had deliberately
never sought the company of well-bred eligible young
females, knowing that he could never provide them with
the one thing they sought—a respectable name. He was
not fool enough to court mockery. But now, he had been
well paid for his one lapse.

For Lady Amanda Amberly, he thought, shaking his
head as he placed his hand about his hairbrush, could not
be contained in merely one image, nor could she be dismissed as a vagrant, fragmented memory. No, she broke
the mold, for she appeared to him both complete and in
endless guise.

He seized up the brush and hastened to cram it into his
bag. He could not fix the damned chit in his mind in one
completed final portrait and be done with her. She appeared to him in as many pictures as there were occupations in his day. He had only to enter the study and she
would be there, her face filled with concentration as she
penned one of her damned letters to another man, her lip
caught up in her small white teeth as she struggled with
invention. If he walked by the lakeside, she would pace
with him, her face turned to his, a study in attentiveness,
her long gray eyes lit with coming laughter.

He saw her bemused as he spun out his tales to her, he
envisioned her wary as he drew near her, he pictured her
valiant as she sought to conceal her distress at her situation
in life. In the night, he saw her as he had first encountered
her, deep in slumber. And then, due to his wide experience,

he was easily able to envision her as he had never seen her, without her pristine white nightshift. And then, he would rise from his bed and damn his fertile imagination.

It was not just that he desired her, he was no stranger to that emotion. It was that he desired her conversation and good opinion as well, and that was a novelty to him. He had told her about himself and it had not fazed her. Although there was a good deal more that he could have told, he had the distinct notion that though he might disappoint her, she could never fail to understand him. Perhaps it was as he had said, because she had grown to adulthood in the shadow of inherited disgrace as well, that she was able to accept him as a being apart from the label of his birth. Perhaps that did not really matter at all and by insisting that it did, he was only perpetuating the same prejudice that he deplored in others. The cause no longer mattered. The matter was that he could not forget her.

She had spurned the only offer of marriage he had ever made, and yet he was not surprised. He was too clever at cards not to know that even the best bluff might be called. Thinking on it now, as he placed the last of his toilet articles in his bag, he acknowledged that he would have been more shocked had she accepted him. For he knew even better than she had just what he had left out of his offer, having been so careful to do so. Had she whispered a shy "yes" when he had done, he would have in some corner of his mind been disappointed in her and in his reading of her character. For he had not mentioned love, nor fidelity. It had been his deliberate intention not to.

Love, Lord North thought angrily, closing up his portmanteau and looking about the room absently for any item he might have missed, *love* was not a word he had ever used, or needed to either. She had noted it; she had wisely declined his offer. He congratulated her now on a savage underbreath as he picked up his bag.

Lord North reached to open his door and found himself clutching air as it swung wide. Gilbert stood there, his expression so very nearly like the infant his brother had been imagining that it was laughable. But there was no laughter in the viscount's eyes as he looked the younger man up and down.

"Here to assist me in carting my luggage?" Lord North asked coolly. "I am not so up in years that I cannot manage by myself."

"No, and you know it, too," Gilbert said gruffly, his lower lip so extended that his speech became blurred.

"Ah," Lord North sighed, putting his traveling bag down, "so be it. Come in, brother, and open your budget to me before I leave, for I see that I shan't step a foot out today until you've unburdened yourself. But do try to hurry, won't you, for I've a horse waiting and many miles to go."

"That's just it," Gilbert said unhappily, stomping into the room and lowering himself to the edge of the viscount's bed dejectedly. "Don't want you to go, Chris, don't know how I can get you to stay, neither. But I never felt so worthless in my life, and there's the truth of it."

"I'm touched by your devotion, Gil," Lord North said sweetly, as he closed the door and turned to the forlorn youth, "but as you've mentioned your reluctance to see me depart only a few hundred times in the last days, I don't see why we should go over it again."

"Yes," Gilbert cried angrily, "and you've remained mum as a mouse to whatever I say. But I'll say it again at any rate. If I had a fiancée like Amanda, I shouldn't take myself off to the continent and forget her forever, no I should not. For that's what it would mean. You may say that it is all right for her to remain with her mama, but I say never! For Amanda's nothing like her mama, that I do know though I've never set eyes on the countess, nor do I need to. And Sir Boothe may be a stick, and no denying it, but a fellow would have to be addled to leave his promised bride alone with a chap that's got eyes for no one else but her. And finally," Gilbert said in vexation, "since Mama's so pleased with what's transpiring, I should think you'd know it was the wrong thing for you to do. She's made for you, Chris," Gilbert concluded, mixing up his mama and his brother's fiancée in one last mighty attempt to make his brother see the light.

But all that slender, expressionless, flaxen-haired fellow did was to smile and then say, softly, "Yes of course," in response to his brother's impassioned plea.

"Oh, yes, I knew you'd say that . . ." Gilbert began, but then broke off and gaped at the viscount.

"Yes, Gil," Lord North said reasonably, "you are quite right. And that is why I am leaving now."

The look upon his brother's face was so turbulent that the viscount relented. He put a hand upon Gilbert's shoulder and said kindly, "I'm going to get her, Gil. I'm leaving to go to Kettering Manor now to put an end to all this charade."

But as he put spur to horse, and waved farewell to Gilbert, the viscount wished that he had some of his brother's eternal optimism. For he did not know if he would succeed. He knew that he had his lady's interest, he knew that he could ignite her physical desire. But he did not know if that was enough for her. Plainly, it had never been enough for him.

He could only hope to persuade her by offering her that which he had never tendered to any other female, and that was a meager enough gift, he thought wryly, for it was only himself, entirely.

If he won her, he thought, as he galloped forward, it would mean that he must give up his wanderings, his constant conquests of alien flesh, his solitary life, and his devotion to only his own interests and entertainments. And as though he could not bear to wait to be free of these, his former pleasures, he leaned forward to push his mount to greater speed.

The day was clear and bright, but the journey was bumpy as the road was filled with so many frozen furrows left by other vehicles' passages. The brief winter afternoon was dimming and the occupant of the lurching coach sighed as she realized that the journey, which might have been accomplished within a day, would take yet another due to the ruts and hollows that impeded the coach's swift progress. It was as well, Amanda admitted, that her mama had insisted upon her packing for an overnight stay. For as much as she disliked the idea of it, there was no longer any doubt that her mission would take longer than she had planned or hoped.

It was only the cruelty of fate, she decided, as she snuggled down within her cape to elude the chill winds that stole within the joinings of the carriage, that prolonged her journey. For as it was a trip that was conceived in desperation, executed on a moment's notice, and embarked upon with trepidation, each hour that it wore on, wore down the weak reasons for its very being. It had been one thing to decide upon a course of action in the depths of the night in one's snug bed, and quite another to be forced to examine that decision minutely once one was already involved with it.

She glanced over toward the sleeping maid in the other corner of the coach and envied the girl from the bottom of her heart. If she could only lose herself in sleep so easily, she would be free of the thousand doubts and regrets she now suffered. Free of them, Amanda groaned as she pulled her hood over her face, as well as the biting cold that now filled the vehicle. She had only herself to blame for that as well, for she had insisted that no time could be spared and had refused to stop for a luncheon, or even for so long as to have the bricks at her feet reheated.

This very morning she had woken from the broken sleep which had plagued her since she had arrived at Kettering Manor, and had been suddenly full of resolve and determination. This journey had seemed then the only sensible, indeed the only feasible, course that she could follow. Mama, who had projected a dozen different solutions to her problems, only to have them each and every one met with firm denial, had agreed with her at once. But that, Amanda now thought, was only because the usually astute lady was anxious to see any plan go forward, any action taken, no matter how nonsensical.

Mama could not have truly approved of the scheme, Amanda knew, if only because she had not known the half of it. There were some things that her daughter could not divulge to any other being, and the real reason for this impetuous jaunt was one of them. Indeed, Amanda thought as she gazed upon the patterns of hoarfrost on the coach window, if she had been completely honest and clear-thinking this morning she might never be sitting where she was right now. But, like her mama, she too had only felt the pressing need to do something, to take some action, however foolish.

She wanted to see Lord North again, no, she corrected herself, she had to see him again. But if she wrote to him or sent for him, she would be signaling that she accepted his terms. They would both know that, no matter how witty or subtle her summons. And to accept him on his given terms would be to accept a second-rate life.

But she could not be free of him. Just the thought of him even now in the cold coach, was to make her feel as though she had been sitting beneath a summer sun for hours. As she burned in the cold from the memory of him, she mused sadly that so it always was when one gazed too long at any bright, unobtainable shining object. For just as the sun will sear its image into one's aftervision long beyond the time that one has looked upon it, so doubtless she would always bear his imprint upon her consciousness. But memory was not enough for her.

He was never the pillar of respectability she had thought she would wish to wed. There was no evading the truth that he had been a thorough reprobate, as free with his morals as any from her mama's wild set. But still, she knew as surely as she accepted the rising of tomorrow's dawn that he had caught her life up in his.

She could not send for him, she could not go to him. As she neither wished for nor could wait for some natural disaster or death in the family, she knew she must invent some subterfuge so that she might at least look upon him once again. There was only one last avenue of possibility: If she could discover something to his interest, she could then summon him to hear of it without committing herself to him.

It was in the bleakest hour of the night that she hit upon her mad scheme; indeed, it was then that she could not escape it. For the whispers and random comments she had heard echoed in her head and dismissed sleep. She heard

Gilbert saying that the viscount and his father "were like as two peas in a pod," she heard her mama's sighs over farmwomen's devotion to their offspring, she listened again to the viscount's voice telling the brief tale of his birth. There were too many contradictions in the phantom voices that banished slumber.

She could not believe that his mother had been so low as to sell him for "a crust of bread." No, not when nobility was written into every fine lineament of his person. Nor could she believe that a gentleman such as his adoptive father would have taken in any chance-gotten by-blow and raised him as a son. Not when, as Mama had said, children of all stripes were such easily gotten goods.

The notion had come to her with such force that she had sat straight up in bed, that the late viscount had known the waif's parentage, that he had been well aware of the pedigree of the child he had adopted. Amanda's desire that the idea be true had given it more credence. Though in that one tense interview the woman had said she was the mother, it might not be true. He might have been left to her fostering by some titled lady, through shame. If she had borne him, the woman herself might not have been without honor. It may have been that his father was gently bred. A thousand possibilities sprang to mind, and Christian himself, out of shock, anger, and disappointment, had explored none of them. Due to her own pressing need, Amanda had decided that she would investigate.

It had seemed so possible in the morning, she had found herself buoyed up by courage then. She had packed quickly and told her mother no more than the fact that she must be gone to Ashbourne for a day, to discover something that might aid in her decision as to her fiancé. Mama had asked no further, but had only insisted that she prepare for a possible overnight stay. But she had been adamant above all else that a reliable coachman be taken for protection, as well as a reliable maid for protection against gossip.

Giles had been livid at her departure without his escort and without his knowledge of either her destination or reason for leaving, however briefly. Remembering his fury, Amanda wondered if she would see him when she returned, and felt colder still when she realized that she hardly cared. But worst of all was the realization that her enthusiasm for her scheme had grown cold as the day and her chances for success with it as dim as the light that was now fading from the sky.

When the coach pulled into the courtyard of the only inn at Ashbourne, the Gilded Plum, Amanda found herself very glad that it was too late in the day for her to try her luck with her wild scheme. She put it out of her mind, and instead occupied herself with the delicate matter of booking accommodations. Though the landlord's eyebrows went up as she insisted on separate rooms for herself and her maid, she remained calm as she insisted on the extraordinary arrangements. Beth was Mama's personal maid, and though the countess had sworn that she had picked her for the journey because the girl was known to never let a word of tattle escape her lips to reach another servant's ear, Amanda had the shrewd idea that no word of gossip Beth heard ever failed to reach her mama's ear either. But no matter what the landlord's reactions, the undertaking Amanda was embarked upon was private. If even she was unsure she had the right to pursue her inquiries, she was determined that Mama should never know of it.

After a meal eaten more from necessity than from desire, Amanda took to her room. Though she wanted to sit up and plan and consider her ambitions, she soon found sleep. Thus, she awakened early in a strange bed, in an unfamiliar room. Her first coherent thought was that she had made a dreadful mistake and was on the verge of making another.

She had no right, she thought as she took two sips of chocolate, to pry into the viscount's secret affairs. She had not a shred of a claim to unearth facts about hs past, she told herself as she broke her toast into interesting fragments. But so long as she had come so far, she decided as she sent for her coachman, she might as well just have a look around her.

Amanda left her mama's maid behind to carry on a lively flirtation with an ostler. She told the girl that she was only going for a little ride about the town and did not require escort. But for all of her supposed interest in the bold looks and wicked suggestions of the hearty ostler, the girl did not miss hearing her mistress's daughter tell the coachman to find the direction of a farm holding known as Land's End. Now what, the girl wondered as she fended off a bluff familiarity from her new suitor, was Lady Amanda doing decked out for a visit with the queen if she was only going to a farmyard? For the lady was wearing a smashing pink frock, with a deep rose woolen cape with ermine trim that all the maidservants coveted, and her hair had been brushed until it shone.

Still, the countess's maid thought as she called the ostler a "naughty fellow" even as she batted her lashes to encourage him further, she could not be expected to hike up her skirts and dash after the carriage. She had told the countess that she would keep her eyes and ears open, and that she would. For the moment, she was content to keep them opened very wide indeed, as the ostler embarked upon relating a string of compliments whose recollection would keep her as warm as Lady Amanda's dashing cloak might through the rest of the long winter.

It was, Amanda thought, just as he had said it had been. It took just a little imagination to flesh out the details of the winter-stark surroundings so that she could envision them as he had seen them in the full bloom of summer. There where the lane ended the cottage stood neat and contained within a copse of trees. There were the skeletons of rose bushes trailing about the front wall of the house and standing rigid about the doorways. There was no young man with extraordinary eyes working about the place to be seen, but Amanda could scent and see the curls of wood smoke rising from the chimneys. The coach paused in the lane in front of the cottage for so long that Amanda thought that if she waited much longer, the bushes might indeed begin to put forth flowers.

At last, she opened the door and stepped down from the vehicle. She stood in the cold, one foot poised in front of the other, preparing to go down the winding gravel walk to the front door, and then she stopped. She had come all this way to the very doorstep of her future, and found she could go no further. What could she say? "I am the Lady

Amanda Amberly, here to discuss your bastard child that you gave away decades ago"? Or perhaps, "How do you do. I am engaged to the Viscount North and as he is a well-known by-blow, I thought I might have a word with you about why you sold him when he was an infant"? Or would it be more suitable if she simply said, "I am one of the notorious Amberly Assortment, and as I am to wed a bastard as well, I felt I ought to find out something more about him"?

Amanda's shoulders slumped and she gave the little cottage one last, longing look before she turned to enter the coach again. The past was done; she could not enter it again any more than any other being could. And as it was the past that had brought her together with the viscount, it would be the past that remained to keep them apart. She had placed one hand upon the coach, preparing to enter it again, when she was halted by an earnest young voice.

"Excuse me, m'am . . . miss," it said, "but my mum asks if you would care to step in for a cup of tea."

Amanda turned and looked down to see a pair of worried eyes considering her. The boy was fourteen or so, and for a second Amanda blinked, wondering if some fancy had caused her to actually see the same youth the viscount had seen all those years ago. But as the eyes that looked beseechingly at her were both blue, she was relieved to find that, however odd, at least this encounter was real.

"Please, miss," he said earnestly, "she said as to how I should bring you in for a visit."

Amanda could only nod. She cast a glance at the coachman, but he had heard as well and only touched his hat before he leaped down to cover the horses while they waited for her. She followed the youth up to the door of the cottage as though in a daze.

The front door was drawn open by a woman of her own mama's years. Though she wore country homespun and her fair hair was pulled back neatly rather than artfully arranged, she, in her own fashion, was easily as lovely and youthful as the countess.

Amanda paused at the doorstep, seeing a neat parlor behind the woman, a fire crackling on the hearth, and a lazy old dog rising stiffly to its feet to greet her as well. She suddenly found herself an interloper and could not think of a word to say. Her training came to her rescue and she licked her dry lips, put out her hand, and said nervously,

"Good morning. I am Lady Amanda Amberly."

"How do you do," the woman said very hesitantly in a soft voice. "I am Annie Holcroft. I was Annie Withers. I've been expecting you, my lady."

XV

Amanda sat at the edge of her chair and bit the end of her pen as she tried to think of the words she must use in her brief message. She had rushed back to her room at the inn, flung her cape over a chair, and poised herself at the desk to compose a compelling summons. But she had been unable to phrase it in suitably oblique but meaningful terms, and now the afternoon sun illuminated the best guest bedroom at the Gilded Plum and she had only set down three lines.

When the first sharp knock came to her door, she rose. But she had no time to answer before the door flew inward with such force that it trembled on its hinges. The gentleman had not bothered to knock twice. He burst into the room even as the door had, but he did not venture far into the chamber. Rather, he took only a few steps forward and then stood, arms akimbo, and glowered at Amanda.

She gazed at him as though she had run mad. For it was as though her very concentration upon him had produced him in a vision for her. But she had never imagined him as he now appeared. The viscount's usually immaculate clothes were travel-stained. His cravat was slightly askew, his boots badly mud-covered. His bright hair was in disarray, there were hollows beneath his eyes, and a faint tracing of golden beard showed on his lean cheeks. His eyes glittered dangerously and his whole being seemed taut with scarcely concealed anger.

"Writing again?" the viscount asked. "My dear, your wrists must ache with your interminable scribblings. Penelope stitched, Arachne spun, but Lady Amanda, she is endlessly writing. Ah, but you must have something worthy to put to paper. What is it? Not another letter filled with entreaty for Giles? Or just some delicious bits of gossip you have discovered about the sensational history of a blackguard sprung from the fields to take on the name and airs of a gentleman? Or perhaps you are dangling for an invitation so that you may acquire some more? Come, Amanda, you have not undertaken a journey like this and procured pen and paper just so that you might dash off a bread and butter note. Do tell me about it, I might find it amusing as well."

"I was writing to you," Amanda said dazedly, as she held the note up for him to see, though she never took her eyes from him for a moment as she did so.

He strode into the room and snatched the letter from her fingers. He quickly scanned the lines.

"Yes," he muttered, and then "Yes" he spoke wearily as he dropped the paper. Then he looked at her again with sorrow and puzzlement.

"Why?" he asked softly, all anger gone and only deep disappointment in his voice, "why have you come here?"

Before she could answer, he went on, "I rode the best part of two days to Kettering Manor to surprise you, to . . . it makes no matter now. But I rode down one horse and hired another so that I might reach you more quickly. Imagine then, how delighted I was to discover you had gone. Not to your father, nor even with Giles. Rather, your mother informed me, with a merry twinkle in her eye, to Ashbourne. Ashbourne, of all places! It was not difficult to get your direction as this is the only inn at Ashbourne. For there are no spas here, no gay assemblies, no touring points of interest for you, save one. And that only the existence of a wretched slut who bartered her infant for pennies. I told you of her, Amanda, so that you might understand me better, not so that you might dredge up muck that is best left undisturbed. Whey did you come here?" he asked again.

"Because you ought to have," Amanda answered quickly. "Oh Christian, you should have come back long since.

Nothing is as you had thought. I was writing to tell you to come at once, for there is somethng you must hear with your own ears."

"So you have already spoken with her," he said with resignation. "What did you do? Offer her a goodly sum for the tale, and a bonus for a happy ending to it? Amanda, my meddling fool, a drab who would peddle her own babe will tell any sort of tale you would wish for a handsome enough price. I can understand why you came," he said, gazing at her ruefully, "for I always liked that tale about the frog prince myself when I was a child. But I am precisely what I am, my dear. And if you thought to make the best of my offer by offering up a fiction to embellish my name, it won't do. Neither your kiss nor your hand will transform me, princess, nor will some expensively gotten fairy tale."

"It isn't like that," Amanda insisted. "I came to Land's End because there was so much you had not told me, indeed, so much that you could not have done and more that I guessed at. But when I came to the cottage, my courage deserted me and I was about to turn and go. But she had seen me from the window. And she was expecting me, she said, and had been for years. Oh, not me, but someone like me, some fine lady, she said, as she knew that someday you would wed and that your lady, at least, would want to know certain facts."

Amanda reached down for her cloak and flung it about her shoulders as she said eagerly, "Only come with me now. That is what I was writing to ask of you, and now we can do it at once. Come back with me now and hear it all from her own lips. It is not a fairy tale. There are documented proofs, only I doubt you will need to see them once you have heard the facts yourself."

The viscount stood fixed where he had paused and fingered the edge of the writing desk Amanda had been seated at.

"I think not," he said slowly. "Or at any rate, not at this moment. Tell me the tale, and I shall decide whether it is worthy of facing that woman again. At any rate," he said more lightly, "I am in all my dirt. I rode to Kettering

Manor without pause, and when I heard of your destination, I rode on again as though demented. I believe I need some rest, perhaps time to change my attire, time to———"

"No," Amanda cried so vehemently that she surprised both herself and Lord North. "No, that won't do. For then you'll find another reason not to go. It's best done at once, before you can change your mind. How can you bear not knowing a thing that I know?" she asked then, with such a poor attempt at cunning that he laughed.

He shrugged his shoulders, as though he had just lost some inner debate, and then straightened.

"Very well," he smiled, as he ran his hand against his jaw. "Although I do believe that I ought to have shaved first. Yet, perhaps this is best. It may comfort the lady to see that she has spawned true, and that I suit a barnyard better than a ballroom."

Amanda grimaced at his light words. But she went unhesitatingly with him to the door, and then to her coach for the short ride to Land's End. Lord North sat back in the carriage, his bright head resting against the cushions, his facile tongue stilled for once.

Amanda tried to break him from his reverie by saying conversationally, as they drove off,

"She has married again, and her husband knows all. Indeed, he welcomes your visit, for he knows that will ease her mind as well."

But the viscount wore an abstracted air and she could not tell if he attended to her words at all. He might be weary with his travels, she thought as she fell silent, but no amount of riding could have diminished him so, or could account for the drawn look upon his pale face. She knew she was forcing him to journey toward the last place on earth that he wished to go, and wished that she could spare him this pain even as she inflicted it.

When the carriage stopped at last, she glanced at him fearfully. But he only took in one deep breath and then turned to her as though to admit her existence at last.

"Come, my dear," he said coolly, "this promises to be an interesting performance."

This time it was Annie Holcroft herself, still wiping her

hands on a dishcloth, who came to their summons to admit them to her little house.

Amanda caught in her breath as the slender, fair nobleman encountered the small fair woman on the doorstep. She thought, on a wild interior giggle, that their mutual moment of hesitation might be caused by their inability to put such a bizarre meeting into proper social terms. But Lord North was equal to any occasion, and after a pause, he bowed and said calmly, "Good morning. I am Christian Jarrow. I believe we met before. I understand that my fiancée, Lady Amanda Amberly, has been speaking with you and that you wish to have further discussion with me."

"I called after you that day," Annie Holcroft said immediately, her eyes searching his for some human reaction to her, "but you were gone so quickly. I wrote once, too, or at least, had someone write for me, as I cannot. But you never answered my letter."

"I was off at school," Lord North said. "And no letter was ever forwarded to me."

"I could not write again," the fair woman said quietly, "for I promised not to."

Amanda stood looking at the pair, one whose eyes showed nothing but concern and anxiety, and the other whose eyes seemed glazed over as if by the frost. It was Amanda's shifting from foot to foot that recalled the older woman to her senses and she stepped aside and said hurriedly, "Come in, please. Please be seated. My boys are out helping their father with chores, so we can speak privately."

When they were seated in the snug parlor, with the old dog settled back on the hearth rug, Annie Holcroft began to speak.

"I thought you knew," she said at once, without preamble, as soon as the viscount had seated himself. "But when Lady Amanda told me you did not, I knew that I must explain. Your parents should have. I'm not the person to cast stones, but I would not have done as I did if I thought you were never to be told the truth some day. It may be no honor to be my son, but there was no dishonor in the begetting of you."

She spoke softly and Amanda, having heard it all before, could sit and watch Lord North's face as he listened. His mother's words were well chosen, for she had once, in her youth, been a lady's maid and still bore the markings of gentility in her voice even as she yet bore the traces of the beauty she had once possessed.

"I was married when I was very young," she said at once, "to a farmer on your father's estates. But he was killed in an accident, when our baby was only a few months old. It was not easy for me then, for I had no family and I feared that I would be thrown out of our house. I could never have found work with a babe at the breast. It was your father who saw to it that I could stay on at Windham, and keep our cottage. He was a good, kind, generous landlord.

"I was very grateful to him," she said carefully. "He would come to see if I were in need, he would visit to see how the baby was growing. All of his tenants knew what sort of a man he was and we all thought it a great shame that he had no children of his own, for he would make such a fuss over our little ones. He would bring my little fellow trinkets and toys and sometimes he would stay and let the baby play with his fobs, or when he grew older, give him rides in front of him on his great horse. As time went by, he would spend hours sometimes with me and my boy. For my baby was a stout little toddler, with no end of daring, and your father said he was the most taking little chap he had ever seen."

The viscount stirred. An expression of distaste was clear upon his fine features.

"Please spare yourself further effort, madam," he drawled. "I quite understand now. You are telling me that my father came to love dear little Billy or Tim so much that he straightaway offered to adopt him. And you were so over-joyed at the tyke's good fortune that you accepted. It was only that evil gossip erupted when I appeared at Windham House. I quite understand. A delightful, heartwarming tale to be sure. So then, I am to infer that I am legitimate and legitimately gotten?"

"Oh no," the fair-haired woman demurred at once, quite

missing the sarcasm as she said earnestly, "for Georgie is my oldest son. You saw him when you were last here. He's grown now with babes of his own. I should never have given him up, not even to a fine gentleman like your father, for he was the last I had of my own husband. You are your father's son," she said seriously.

The viscount sat back abruptly, all evidence of the sneer he had worn quite vanished, as she went on more slowly, "Your father kept paying me longer visits, and I could see in time, that he had something on his mind. At last, one snowy morning I remember, he came when he knew that Georgie was having his nap. He said that he wished to speak with me upon a grave matter. He came into the parlor and paced for a long time before he spoke. Then he said that he had an offer to put to me, and that if it did not meet with my approval, I should speak my mind straightaway and that he would never hold it against me, no, nor never even mention it again. He said that I should have no fear of refusing him.

"He and the viscountess could have no children, they had waited for nine years without issue. So he asked if I would have a child with him, so that he could have an heir to carry on his name that was of his own blood, at least. The problem lay with his dear lady wife, the doctors said. He made it clear that it was a business matter," she said hurriedly, as the viscount stared at her, "and he promised me that he would see to it that I never suffered shame nor want. But as he admired me and my Georgie, he thought I might give him a fine child. The viscountess had agreed to the scheme," she added quickly, "for neither of them wanted to see Windham House go to his brother, who was a wastrel. And they both wanted a baby.

"I thought about it for a week," she said, now with her eyes to the carpet, "and I thought on what a good, kind man the viscount was. Then it came to me that I could do no better in this life than to oblige him. I liked him very well," she said softly, "and I knew that there would be nothing between a tenant's widow and a great gentleman, so much as I liked him. But this, I could do for him. And it was clearly a business matter, so I did not feel like a . . ." Her words trailed off.

Amanda, seeing the far-off look upon the woman's face, again took leave to wonder just how much of a business arrangement the young widow had thought it, and how much of it had been more, at least upon her own part.

"I agreed," Annie Holcroft said, holding her head high. "And your father visited me often. But then, once I was sure you were on the way, there was no more . . . He only visited me then to see how I was faring," she said sadly. "Although I often wondered if he should like to . . . but he was an honorable man," she concluded proudly.

"When you were born, you were given over to him immediately, Georgie and I came to Land's End, and we were well off for I was given an independence. He sent me notice of how you were growing, how very happy they were with you. And I was never sorry for what I did until that day you came to see me and I knew somehow it had all gone wrong."

The viscount was quiet after his mother had done speaking. Both women watched him carefully as he sat in deep thought. Then he laughed abruptly. It was a chilling sound. He rose and looked down at his mother, a sort of exultant despair upon his face.

"So I am my father's son. Since you cannot make me legitimate, I expect that's the next best thing. I congratulate you. It is an excellent story. I am to believe that I am not some random object acquired after a few fevered moments in a haystack, a chance-gotten brat of a chance encounter, but rather the carefully conceived son of a gentleman and a good woman paid to bear me. You are, then, I take it, only a little more than a wet nurse, or some sort of surrogate for my own poor barren adoptive mama. What a clever invention! I should be very happy with that tale if it were not for one thing."

He looked down at her scornfully and then said with bitter triumph, "How comes it, then, my dear clever mama, that neither you nor my papa have these strange varicolored eyes you see before you? The very same ones I recall my half-brother Georgie appears to have had? I have searched this land and over again to find one male gentleman, or vagrant, of the right age who possesses such odd eyes, and have not yet found him. Come, be plain with me. It no longer matters. I need no bedtime stories, I am a grown man. Who was my father?"

His mother stood so that she faced him squarely. She smiled and said, "Those eyes are common in my family, your lordship. And have been for generations. They crop up where they will. But you could not have looked too closely that time you were here, and you have never looked me in the eye since you have set foot over my doorstep. Do so now," she said proudly, turning her head to the light, "for your papa was used to say that my eyes reminded him of a warm August afternoon when there was thunder in the air. For my left eye, he said, was as bright and blue as a summer's sky, while the right clearly showed that dark storm clouds were brewing."

As the viscount leaned close in amazement to study the small gray motes which obscured the purity of blue in his mother's eye, Amanda wondered how businesslike his father had found that odd arrangement all those years ago, if he could quote such tender poetry to a woman who would merely bear his son for convenience's sake.

Although the dinner served at the Gilded Plum was the same for each of its patrons, one would not have guessed it from observing the couple in the small inn's private dining room. For one of the guests, a handsome blond gentleman, laughed frequently and poured wine as generously as he poured out his thoughts. His companion sat and ate sparingly, and only listened to the gentleman quietly.

They had declined his mother's invitation to dine. They had left her after they had spoken a while longer, and after they had shaken hands with the tall, soft-voiced man who was now master of the little farm. It had been a subdued farewell, for though there were no longer any recriminations, each of them had known that the relationship established that afternoon could and would never go further. The son had learned details of his birth and family history. The mother had learned that he bore her no ill will and respected her decision. That had been enough, and more, for a lifetime for the two of them.

Lord North had stayed silent, as though stunned, all the way back to the inn. But after washing and changing his garb, he had lived with his history long enough to emerge at dinner as a relaxed, merry companion. Now, as he filled Amanda's glass again, he shook his head in wonder and said, as he had just done moments before, as though he needed to reassure himself,

"Just imagine. The crafty old fox. Two sets of papers. One for the baptismal record for all the village to see, saying that I was the viscount's legitimate son, before God. And the other, for less supreme and forgiving beings, locked in his man-at-law's safe against the day that his brother should challenge my inheritance, saying that I was his son by Annie Withers, legally adopted. A superior ruse, but," he said ruefully, "he could not know that both he and his brother would be gone before I came of age. And he could not guess that his dear wife would withhold knowledge from me, out of spite. Nor could she have foreseen," he sighed, "that bearing her own child at last would engender such regret and hatred for her earlier bargain and its result."

He downed his wine and his face cleared again.

"But it makes no matter," he said. "For I do know now. And I thank you, my little meddler. You can have no idea of how pleasant it is to know who you are at last. It's not only a wise child that knows his own father, it is a very lucky one. You are quiet tonight," he said, gazing at her curiously before he laughed again and said, "but what else can I expect, poor lady? When I have spent the night babbling on about my good fortune. Now it's your turn. Tell me about Giles and your mama."

Amanda told him listlessly of her decision to come to Land's End, and of Giles's annoyance at her journey. She seemed so distracted that the viscount's own expression lost some of its vivacity and he bent himself to entertaining her so completely that soon she found herself smiling despite her lowered spirits.

But the hour grew late and Amanda knew that the

evening which she wished would spin out forever, was done. The fire in the hearth had burned down until it only spat fitfully, and the landlord had appeared several times to clear his throat in the doorway, but still she had delayed the hour of parting from the viscount. Because, she thought somberly, as the viscount related an amusing story about Gilbert, this time it would be a final parting.

She had brought about his present happiness. She had lifted the burden of his unknown ancestry from his spirit, but by that very act, she now knew that she had brought about the end to their relationship and ended any air dreams she might have had about a future with him. For as his father had truly been the viscount, now he must know that both his title and his beloved Windham House were his by rights older than any society might impose. Now he could, without guilt, stroll the bright gallery at Windham House and see his heritage and his past clearly affirmed.

With the mystery of his dark origins erased, he could change his life. He no longer needed to racket about with the careless persons of her mother's set. He no longer needed to punish himself by an alliance with a lady of infamous name, a wife whose very presence would be a constant reminder to himself of his unjustly ignoble state.

And as he had not brought up the subject of his previous offer since he had made his discovery, although they had passed many hours together in privacy since, she realized with sinking heart that he must no longer wish to remember it. So be it, she thought, but for her own pride's sake, she must be the one to end it, not he.

Although doubtless he was relieved that she had not accepted his spontaneous offer, yet even so, she could not regret what she had brought about for him. He need not stoop so low now, Amanda thought, to get himself a suitable wife. He could, she sighed, gazing with longing at the vivid face which had become so necessary to her, he should do better. She had wanted to linger so that she might have her fill of looking at him and listening to his voice. But now she saw that the shadows beneath his eyes were pronounced, and that no matter how ebullient his spirits, his changeable eyes were heavy with fatigue.

Amanda had not wanted the night to end, for she saw the course of tomorrow, but she rose and said, "If we don't leave now, Christian, the servants will fall asleep stacked in the doorway. And I have a long journey that begins at dawn."

He arose at once, berating himself for his thoughtlessness. As they mounted the stairs, he told her that he ought to have noticed the hour, for he was sure he would fade away as soon as his head touched the pillow, having been kept awake so long only through sheer excitement, like a boy in the night before his birthday morning.

When they reached the door to her room, he smiled down at her tenderly and said with a hint of a wicked leer,

"Now then, Lady Amanda, is this the blue or the gray room?"

"It is my room, Lord North," she said carelessly as she opened her door and stepped in, "as you can plainly see."

He paused at the door and then wandered in after her. He looked about him with a frown.

"But where is your maid?" he demanded. "I did not see her before and thought she was off on some errand, but surely she should be here at this hour?"

"She is in her own room down the hall," Amanda replied as she closed the door, surprised at his annoyance. "Pray do not wake her with your shouting. I did not want her to note my comings and goings," she explained, "for I did not know what I might discover at Land's End and felt it was not her business in any event."

"There's wisdom in that," he conceded. "But nonetheless, 'Manda, you ought not to be here with me unattended."

She stared at him in amazement and then began to laugh.

"Good heavens, Christian," she said when she was able, "never say that you are concerned with the proprieties?"

She still wore a smile, but he replied without a trace of mirth, "You think me such a complete rakeshame that I don't care if my betrothed acts with propriety then?"

Amanda turned quickly so that she would not have to

look into that still, stern face, and answered lightly as she flung down her shawl upon the bed, "Lud, Christian, I swear you know better than that. I am not precisely your 'betrothed,' you know."

He placed two hands upon her shoulders and swung her around toward himself, but still she would not meet his eyes.

"What the devil is going on here, 'Manda?" he asked. Her behavior puzzled him, it was uncharacteristic, at once artificial and coquettish. He had thought to declare himself to her once he had recovered from his surprise at the discovery of his origins, but now her attitude discomforted him.

"Whatever do you mean?" she answered, knowing precisely what he meant but being evasive since she did not know how to go on. For she had lost her courage and could not end it all between them here and now, this night.

" 'Manda," he said dangerously, "do not play with me. If you would not let me within yards of your room when you were beneath your mama's roof, nor within leagues of it at my house, how comes it that you stroll into an empty bedroom with me at midnight now?"

Amanda found anger simpler than explanation.

"I cannot help it if you think of only one thing," she snapped, unfairly even to her own ears. "I only wished to say good night."

"And what might that one thing be?" he asked as he stared down at her with his odd, glittering eyes. "Might it be this do you think?"

He bent his head and kissed her very lightly. He had come to reason with her, but forgot all else now but the challenge he heard in her words, and the promise he tasted upon her lips. When she did not pull away, his hands tightened on her shoulders and he drew her toward himself for a long, sweet embrace. When he lifted his head, he could see that she stood waiting, only breathing lightly, her eyes half closed. He studied her face for a moment and then, wrapping one arm about her shoulders he walked her the few paces to the huge bed and sat with her at the edge of it. Then he pulled her back into his arms again.

After a few moments, his caresses, which had been light and gentle, began to change with the rapidity that his conversations always had. His lips left hers and strayed to the side of her neck. One of his clever hands traced the outlines of her breast, while the other surely and swiftly undid the tiny buttons at the back of her frock.

She had not wished to begin this, Amanda thought, she had not known that she could begin this. She knew that she should stop him or herself, and had known that from the moment he had begun. But she had kept promising herself only one more moment of intimacy. Even now, as she experienced both delight and a muddled sense of panic, she could not bring herself to form the phrase to begin her final good-bye.

She kept her eyes tightly closed as though by that means she would deny all that was happening. She felt her woolen frock slip slowly down and away from her shoulders and her breasts. The chill of the night air made her gasp, but it was swiftly replaced by the warmth of his hands and his lips, which made her gasp again. She seemed to be ablaze in the cold room beneath his skillful touch as he murmured her name over and over.

No word of denial came to her command as he presented her with new sensations. But helpless tears sprang to her eyes and coursed down her cheeks at her foolish inability to frame the words she knew she must, the words that would return her world to normalcy. Then she felt suddenly chilled again, as all the splendid heat was withdrawn from her abruptly. She sat cold and confused and she heard his breath go out in an explosive sigh and then heard a loudly muttered curse that made her open her eyes wide. He sat next to her and ran a hand through his bright hair distractedly.

He glowered at her with such force that she shrank back. His gaze dropped to her breasts, which she was shamed to see startlingly naked and white in the dim light. As she attempted to hide herself with her hands, he reached out and dragged her bodice up.

"Cover yourself," he said harshly.

She fumbled at the back of her dress with numbed fingers, and he sighed again.

"Here," he said gruffly, turning her, "let me do it. Bother," he muttered in a more natural tone, "I can't do these things up it seems, although they are little enough trouble to undo. You're always presenting me with new experiences, 'Manda," he said now as conversationally as if he were in a drawing room with her, "for I have never had to button up a female before. Hold still, please.

"No doubt I could get these things done up more quickly if I worked from the front as I am accustomed to usually undoing them. But then we'd be in the same predicament again straightaway. There, that will have to do. Now," he continued, as he stood quickly and looked down at her, "wipe your eyes and kindly tell me what the purpose of that little episode was."

She dashed a hand across her cheek and said unhappily, "I was just saying good night."

"And how much longer would you have continued to permit me to bid you good night in my thorough fashion?" he demanded.

"I was going to stop you soon," she protested.

"Oh, soon," he said knowledgeably, as he paced before her. "And had it never occurred to you that soon it might become too late for soon? I pride myself on remarkable control, 'Manda, but there is a point, and we might have speedily reached it, where even a flood of tears would have been to little avail. And why?" he asked angrily as he wheeled to confront her. Seeing her downcast eyes, he asked more softly, "Was it because it was 'good-bye' rather than 'good night'?"

"Yes," she said very quietly. "How did you know?"

"Oh," he said savagely, "I must be remarkably acute. For all my lovers usually sit stock-still as statues and commonly drop scalding tears upon my face as I make love to them. I rather like spice, and salt adds a little something to my performance."

As Amanda hung her head in guilty silence, he paced a few more steps. Then he commented bitterly, "Your sudden warmth was charity, then. But did you not know that such benevolence extended to a libertine like me might have resulted in your presenting Giles with just the sort of squalling wedding present you vowed never to give to any man? Damn you, 'Manda," he said coldly, "I do not accept charity."

"It was not charity," she cried. "I am not going to Giles. I'm not marrying anyone." Amanda wept now. "It was only that it was hard to say good-bye to you."

"Then why the devil should you?" he asked, bewildered.

"Because," she said on a sniff as she drew herself up, "I won't marry you, Christian. I could not when you said you wished to because we would suit due to our backgrounds. And now that you know who your father was, even that poor reason is forfeit. Now that you know you have moral entitlement to your name, you can court some lady who is of better repute than one of the Amberly Assortment could ever be. Can't you see?" she asked fervently, "that now, with clear conscience, you may seek a wife from whatever rank you please?"

He stood arrested. Then he drew her to a stand and held both her hands tightly in his own.

"I can only see that there could be no one of higher rank than you, 'Manda," he said gently. "I am well served for my cowardly offer to you before. Yes, cowardly, 'Manda, for I didn't dare admit to you how much I wanted you for my wife. I made a joke of it, I made a game of it, for it is easier to take a blow in jest than in earnest. But now I earnestly tell you that I love you. I would have told you so when I first discovered you here, but the tale you greeted me with scattered my wits.

"Why do you think I chased you halfway around the kingdom these last days? For all my jests at being a seducer, I have never really exerted myself so before. It was always enough to merely offer. But I have never offered wedlock until I met you, and if you refuse me, I never shall again.

" 'Manda," the viscount said, taking care to hold only her hands though his eyes signaled all his desire to do more, "I promise to be a very constant husband to you, and I shall never doubt you, either, for I think we both have seen enough of the results of inconstancy to last us forever. I love you entirely, and will always hold your happiness above all else. But that's only selfishness, for your happiness will always ensure mine. Marry me, 'Manda," he said as he held her close again at last. "You must."

As she could not answer, he whispered, "One other little thing. I don't know exactly what you've been thinking of, but I assure you that I am still quite illegitimate, my sweet. Knowing my father's name is delightful, but I was nevertheless born out of wedlock. Yet even if I were conceived with a vicar at each bedpost and a bishop on the pillow, I would want no other wife but you."

She raised a radiant face to his, but he put a finger across her lips and said, "Say 'yes' first."

"Yes," she whispered happily. "Oh, yes," she sighed.

After a moment, he stepped away from her.

"Oh no," he said, dropping his hands as though she had singed them. "I won't go through all that buttoning and unbuttoning again tonight. I won't tarry one second longer here with you. For 'Manda," he said as he backed to the door, "we shall be married soon, and if I stay, we won't be able to confound all the famed mathematicians your mama and mine will invite for the occasion."

As Amanda gazed after him with puzzlement, he laughed and added, "Though some of them cannot decipher a grocer's bill, and others may not be able to calculate above a hundred, still all the dear lady guests, I assure you, are experts at adding up to nine. And when we are at the altar, they shall all nod and commence to count to themselves."

He gave her a longing look, and then said, "Our heir, my love, oh most especially *our* heir, should not make his appearance in this world one second before a full nine moons have safely risen past the moment that the vicar unites us. 'Manda, only here from the safety of the doorway can I tell you that I cannot allow you to seduce me, if only for our son's sake."

He gave her one last regretful smile. "But bolt your door, please," he sighed before he left, "for the combination of my morals and your face as it looks to me now, may yet cause a miscount."

XVI

Fanny Juliana Octavia Amberly, Countess of Clovelly, sighed happily to herself. Her cup ran over at last. The wedding had been a smashing social success and the ball following it would be talked about for ages. Those guests that were staying elsewhere had departed and those remaining beneath her roof had toddled off to their own beds or discreetly tiptoed into others. Now the great house was quiet at last.

Dawn would come within the hour and the countess looked at her own bed longingly, for as soon as she had completed just one more task she could enjoy her own well deserved rest. She sat at her delicate inlaid writing table to set down a few lines upon paper, so that she would not forget them when she awoke.

When Robert, Duke of Laxey, came through the connecting door between their rooms a few moments later, he looked unhappily at the great empty bed. He maintained his own bedroom, as it was considered very unfashionable to share one's own chamber, but he never actually slept in any bed but the countess's. It was no longer done solely for the sake of carnal pleasure but rather, as he always told his lady, because he couldn't get a wink of sleep without her soft, plushy form cuddled up to him.

Now as he absently scratched at the deep grooves the whalebone of his corset had left upon his stomach beneath his nightshirt, he said with only a trace of petulance, "Dash it all, Fanny, I thought you'd be abed by now."

"I would be, Bobby," the countess answered absently as

219

she wrote, "but I had just one more thing to take care of."

"Can't think of what it could be," the duke grumbled as he shambled to the bed. "Thought everything was done. And done very well, too," he conceded handsomely, as he climbed beneath the coverlet. "It was a bang-up affair. Ought to be proud of yourself. Everything went smooth as silk. Thought we'd have a spot of trouble between our little family and his lot, but everyone could not have been merrier."

The countess paused as she thought of the groom's mama's doleful face throughout the wedding service, but then she said reasonably, "Quite so, Bobby, but then I expect it was because they were all on their best behavior. Even my husband minded his manners. Our friends exerted themselves to be as stiffly correct as possible, and North's family attempted to unbend so that they wouldn't appear priggish, and somehow everyone seemed to meet in the middle and have a fine time."

"Just so," the duke grunted happily as he arranged his hands over his stomach and found just the right position on his back. "Why by evening, everyone had unbent so much that you couldn't tell the two groups apart. None of this bride's side, groom's side nonsense."

The countess smiled to herself as she thought of the results of that intermingling, some of whom were even now continuing their new associations in her house and at inns nearby.

"Lovely fellow, that Gilbert Jarrow," the duke continued, now giving up the idea of sleep for the equal comforts of a nice gossipy rehash of the events of the day. "Danced his feet off all night with your Mary. Think they'll be a match from this day's work, Fanny?"

"I doubt it," she answered calmly. "He's very young yet, as is our Mary. And I'm not sure I'd encourage it either. Now that North is setting up a household, his brother's gone to live at their estate in the Cotswolds as he said he's always wanted to, but the viscountess is going with him. I'm not sure our Mary is equal to putting up with a dragon like that."

"Brrr, quite right," the duke agreed. "Face like a Monday morning. I wish young Gilbert joy of her. But," he said brightening, "she and that Sir Boothe were the only wet fish. Surprised at him, I really am. Fellow oughtn't to drink if he can't hold it. Took three footmen to pour him into bed, don't you know."

"Ah well," the countess smiled, "he had his reasons, I'm sure."

"Can't see them," the duke commented drowsily. "Splendid affair, everyone merry as grigs. And why shouldn't they be? Beautiful bride, charming groom."

The countess thought of the couple, and felt a lovely prickling of tears in her eyes. She had wept at the ceremony, of course, it was expected of her, after all. But the real moment of joy had been when she had come upon the pair unaware, as they were preparing to leave on their wedding trip. She had stolen into the corridor to bid them goodbye, for they had told her they wanted no great fuss made over their leaving the festivities. She had surprised them alone, as they were preparing to steal away.

The elegant Lord North had been standing locked in an embrace with his graceful new wife. The countess had sighed at the completeness of their embrace, much impressed by what she could see of the groom's expertise, and the bride's response. She had been about to make her presence known, when the viscount had lifted his head and said tenderly to his lady, "One. My love, at last we can start counting."

"Oh, you'll have to do better than that," Amanda had whispered tenderly, as her hand caressed his shining golden hair, "for three is the number I had in mind."

"Three?" he asked quizzically.

"Yes," she had replied, ducking her head a little, "for I had this frock made especially for our wedding trip."

At his amused look of incomprehension, she had gone on, "I'm surprised you haven't noticed, Christian, since I put it on most especially with you in mind. It only has three buttons," she said shyly.

He had thrown his head back in a shout of laughter, and before the countess could reveal herself, he had swept

Amanda up into his arms and carried her out to their waiting coach.

Now the countess nodded in satisfaction as she bent to her note again.

"Aren't you coming to bed?" the duke asked piteously.

"In just one moment," the countess answered.

"What are you writing, anyway?" he complained.

"Only a note to the housekeeper, about some redecorating that North suggested to me today."

"What?" the duke asked, sitting up in bed, "suggested redecorating on his wedding day? If that don't beat all. I knew the fellow was up to all the rigs, but I didn't know he gave a hang for furnishings. What's amiss with Kettering Manor anyway?" he asked suspiciously, for the house was his pride and he complimented himself that it lacked nothing.

"It was only that he noticed something amiss with one of the rooms and took me aside to ask that I see to it," the countess said calmly. "He said that Amanda had not noticed as yet, as she had been too excited each time she stayed with us, but that he had been aware of it from the first day he rested here. He suggested I have it taken care of before she visited again, and he is quite right."

"Which room?" the duke demanded, so upset that there was a failing discovered in his beloved manor that he knocked his nightcap askew in his distress.

"The gray bedroom," the countess replied as she finished up the note.

The duke thought for a moment and then a sly smile spread over his face. There were a great many things he did not know, and he was the first to admit it, but he was an expert on the subject of his home.

"North's got windmills in his head. Ain't no gray bedroom," he said triumphantly.

"Precisely," his lady said as she rose and blew out the candles, "but there shall be."

"Very good," the duke said with relief as he lay back in the darkened bed. "Wouldn't like the manor to lack anything. Excellent idea. Should have had one long ago if we lacked one," he mumbled sleepily.

"No, my dear," the countess said gently as she got into bed beside him, "as it turns out, it was very fortunate that we did not. At least," she mused as she curled up against him to sleep, "North said it was."

About the Author

Edith Layton has been writing since she was ten years old. She has worked as a freelance writer for newspapers and magazines, but has always been fascinated by English history, most particularly by the Regency period. She lives on Long Island with her physician husband and three children, and collects antiques and large dogs. Her previous titles—THE DUKE'S WAGER, THE DISDAINFUL MARQUIS, THE MYSTERIOUS HEIR, and RED JACK'S DAUGHTER—are available in Signet editions.